PLAYING FOR TIME

LEESA BOW

Playing for Time

LEESA BOW

This book is a work of fiction. Any references to real events, real people, and real places are used fictitiously. Other names, characters, places and incidents are products of the Author's imagination and any resemblance to persons, living or dead, actual events, organisations or places is entirely coincidental.

All rights are reserved. This book is intended for the purchaser of this book ONLY. No part of this book may be reproduced or transmitted in any form or by any means, graphic, electronic, or mechanical, including photocopying, recording, taping, or by any information storage retrieval system, without the express written permission of the Author. All songs, song titles and lyrics contained in this book are the property of the respective songwriters and copyright holders.

DEDICATION

To my dear friend, Mark Daniel, whom I shared many fond memories.

I miss going to the footy with you.

Thank you for chatting football while I researched my story.

You taught me many lessons in life.

Most of all,

'It is what it is'.

PLAYING FOR TIME

LEESA BOW

PROLOGUE

Unknown: *Your number is still in my phone.*

I've attempted to delete your name and don't have the balls.

Even though you'll never read this message, it helps in some messed-up way to keep you real.

It's been three years since you left. Two since my last text. Yeah, it took two years to work up the courage to send you another text. Hell knows why I don't want to let go, and yet, I struggle to hold on.

Pretty sure I'm losing my shit because when I can't sleep, I hear you whispering it wasn't my fault. Like you did when we were seventeen again, and I could do no wrong.

What I'd do to rewind time.

Have you talk to me one last time and fill in the blanks to lessen the burden of blame.

I'm not sure when I'll text again, so I want you to know I'm achieving what I set out to do.

I can hear you asking, am I happy?

Hell, you know I compartmentalise the shit out of emotion, so let's say I'm happy when I smell freshly cut grass beneath my feet, the leather between my hands, and feel the chilly air inside my lungs.
You probably think I've learned nothing. Still selfish and fucked-up.
When I'm doing my thing—that thing you hated the most and when I'm near exhaustion, struggling to breathe—is when I feel closest to you.
Because it's how I felt when you left me.

CHAPTER 1

ALLI

The same musky aroma fills the room, a combination of sweat and sexual desire.

In the warm air, it clings like tentacles to skin, initiating each patron when the heavy black door closes. For some, confidence blooms under the dim lights that obscure identity, enhancing mystery to availability. Until neon lights flash and spotlights sweep the crowd to reveal grinding hips, tricking the unaccustomed into believing they took a wrong turn into the club's VIP room.

Weaving to a safe spot, I've learned to ignore the judgement in painted eyes and the sideways glance. When I reach the back of the room, the fluttering in my gut eases. "It's just another club," I murmur to myself. And yet, every time I come here, my heart speeds up to the point the thud-thud-thud in my ears is louder than the damn bass pounding off the walls.

"The Thunder footballers are over there." Carli nods in their direction and hands me a stemmed glass. She stretches her neck even though she's wearing chrome heels. "I can see Darcy Rayne."

I follow her line of gaze to the other side of the club. My senses were alerted to him the moment we walked in. The moment I tasted the sexuality in the room. Like a dirty word lingering on my tongue, disdaining my thoughts, as though I've inhaled the arrogant vapour surrounding him like a smoke machine.

One sideways glance from him intensifies body heat of every girl standing within a twenty-foot radius. I'm also vulnerable, and it is what annoys me most. For months I've received glances, telling me he is *aware*. But it's not enough for him to walk over and start up a conversation, even if he could break through the ring of fire of female bodies surrounding him.

He alters his stance so his tall, muscular frame pushes away from the brick wall. Head and shoulders above the crowd, he has an unobstructed view of the room. His gaze moves left to right, slowly calculating.

In the darkened room, it takes more concentration for my eyes to focus and my brain to catch up. Especially here where carnal desire drips in the air, and fleeting glances potentially lead to a hookup. For many, the decision to pair up is instinctive. Who fuels the fire in your gut? For me, on the rare occasion, it depends on alcohol consumption. Not Darcy. His bright eyes are attentive. I'd bet not a single drop has passed his lips.

His constraint equally fascinates and scares me.

Our eyes lock, and my heart misses a beat. Something passes between us like a shutter opening to reveal sensitivity behind those intense eyes.

It's a small connection sparking intrigue.

Just as quick, he shuts me out as though he detects the probing. His gaze continues to sweep the room, and I'm back to watching virtual chess, only *every* girl is awaiting his next move.

Seconds later, his eyes land on me. I meet his gaze once more. Only this time the shutters are closed, guarded, and he looks away.

Not just another club.

A club where Darcy Rayne frequents.

Carli mumbles something provocative. She lusts over athletes, especially those with a *reputation*. Our attraction to the same guy, an athlete with a reputation, differs dramatically.

"And the last time he was on my flight he was super friendly." Carli's voice imposes. "Do you think he'll remember me now?" For Carli, one of the perks working as a flight attendant is meeting famous people, including football players.

He embraces two brunettes under each arm, and it confirms my suspicion of what he defines as friendly. "We are more acquainted to remember him than he, us. Did you bat your eyes at him and go all mush?"

Carli shoots me a disconcerted look. "We need to be approachable and welcoming when the team travels on our flight."

"Approachable, not allusive."

Carli cocks one perfectly shaped tattooed brow. "Tell me how it's a bad thing when it comes to footballers?" She nods toward the bar where a dozen football players stand. "If he doesn't remember me, he might you."

I have a bad feeling, and yet I follow because ever since we met on our first day of training, we've had each other's back. She stops a few feet away from his clique and adjusts her flowing dark hair. Hell, her hair would be the last point of attraction to the likes of him.

In the crowded space a guy bumps Carli, and in her extreme heels, she stumbles bumping into a blonde in Darcy Rayne's circle of lust. Blonde girl moans causing Darcy's attention to switch to Carli. He frowns, and I assume his mind is ticking over as though he's remembering her. Carli adjusts her little black dress. His eyes survey her, literally. I consider the criteria to be part of his orbit. Carli starts toward him. His eyes shift from Carli to me. Something crosses his face, and I freeze when his brow furrows.

Carli steps into his line of gaze and… flirts.

Admittedly, it usually works.

"Darcy," she drawls and bats her long lashes. "The next time I'm working when you fly interstate for a game—"

"Another time." His gruff voice interrupts her. He looks beyond the circle to the other side of the room. *Hell, did he dismiss her?*

Carli retreats red-faced.

I lead her away. "Forget about him." Tonight was supposed to be about forgetting our problems. A fun night out after a hectic week of overnight stays in different cities. "Where are all the nice guys?" I can't let on to Carli that underneath my frustration he actually gets to me in a way I prefer not to think about.

Carli sighs. "With their girlfriends."

"We're fishing in the wrong ocean."

His ocean.

More than anything I want to remove the hook that pierced me on the first glance, allowed irritation to dominate my opinion of Darcy, and remind myself he's a player on and off the field.

Lust. It's a damned thing. Especially when I'm doing my utmost not to feel it.

Sunday afternoon I arrive at a city bar to meet my friend Paige.

Terracotta floor tiles, marble pillars, and coastal images hang on the walls. It's our summer mirage while suffering through the coldest months of winter. The bar is not the most popular, yet it has a steady flow of customers, and the noise is at a level where we can talk. I order a drink and locate two barstools.

The barman places a wine glass in front of me.

"Make it two," a familiar voice says from behind.

I spin on the stool and stand to hug Paige. "I missed you. How was Europe?"

"Sunny. Wonderful. Perfect." She smiles as she edges her rear up on the stool.

"Forget the weather. I want to hear about those hot guys in your Snapchats. You were cuddling a guy in a different country almost every week."

Paige waves her hand at me. "You make it sound like I was on a dick hunt." Her blue eyes sparkle. "Talking of hot guys, I caught up with your brother in London."

"Yeah, I saw your Insta."

Paige places a hand over mine. "You know he's doing really well. You'd be proud of him. He even has a girlfriend who's into the same things as him."

Her tone raises my guard. "What do you mean?"

"You know... she likes things like art galleries, museums, rock concerts, like Nate."

I swallow a few more mouthfuls of wine. "Are they serious?"

Paige stares at me.

How long has it been since my brother and I talked on the phone? We chatted a few months back and yet there was no mention of a girl. Or the phone call a few months before that.

"Hey. I thought you'd be happy he's found someone nice. She's sensible and beautiful."

"I am. It's just one day I thought he'd come home, or we'd be living in the same city, or even the same country again."

"And leave me?"

I smile at Paige. "No. I thought you'd be with me since we always planned to work in London and tour Europe."

"Which is why you were supposed to come with me instead of me telling you all about it."

"You know I couldn't get the time off. Trust me, I'm over this weather, and I promise this time next year, I'm heading north with you."

Her expression falters. "He's still clean, Alli. Thought you should know. He's really got his shit together. You'd be proud."

I nod. "I was always proud of him, even when…"

"Time heals most wounds," she says, not as a statement but more in understanding. "He showed me around London. Well, the big sights at least. You saw my pics on Insta, right?"

"Yeah, they were great."

"He took those shots. He didn't want to be in them because you know Nate, prefers to be on the other side of the lens."

My brother, with blond hair and deep-set brown eyes, could easily be mistaken for a model, not the guy behind the camera. "That's Nate. All about the perfect shot."

Hell, I wish things had turned out differently, and he hadn't moved away when I was in my early teens. Our grandparents had raised us both with love. It wasn't enough for Nate. He was older than me and soon turned to drugs. Eventually, my grandparents kicked him out, and he moved away. I remember the fights and how aggressive my brother became while using.

Paige gives a nudge. "Hey," she whispers. Her eyes showing empathy as though she knows what I'm thinking.

"How's his photography business doing?" I say, keeping the conversation light. "Did he take you to his gallery?"

Paige nods. "He's so busy, he talked about expanding it to the upstairs room."

Part of me is happy, the other part is sad I'm not there to share it all with him. When Nate first told me he was leaving, I begged him to stay or at least take me with him. *"You have a future here, Alli,"* Nate had said. *"I'll get more work as a freelance photographer in London than I do here in Adelaide. I have to go. There's nothing here for me anymore."*

Yet *I* was here.

Nausea grows knowing my brother might not come home now he has met someone.

"So, where did you travel after London?" I need to direct my thoughts away from Nate.

"France."

I already knew... because Instagram.

"I have to tell you a story about the gypsies." She raises her hand to get the barman's attention. "First, we need more wine."

Two hours later, after hearing all about Paige's escapades, we step out into the rain to head home. We remain standing under a dripping roof waiting for the shower to ease. "So anything exciting happen to you while I was away?" Paige looks up at me with a hopeful expression.

"Nope. I've been working more shifts than usual while staff from my department are on leave."

Paige nods. "How is Gran and Pops?"

"The same."

"Let me know when she's having a good day, and I'll come visit."

"Sure. What do you have planned for next weekend?" I ask, choosing to talk about her social life rather than mine.

"Going to the footy, of course."

I'm not going to suggest I go with her. When we reach the bus stop, I still have my phone in hand and swipe it when I receive a text message from an unknown number. Paige is talking about the upcoming game only I don't hear her words as my mind is trying to comprehend the message.

Three years ago I changed my phone number.

Months later, I received a similar text from the same random number. The previous message date confirms it. The initial message scared me believing the sender was troubled and needing help. I wasn't the ideal person to give it.

I forgot about it until now.

The new message is just as alarming.

Unknown: *Happy birthday.*
I want to say it even though you'll never hear it.
What would you be doing today if you were here with me?
Guess we'll never know.
I don't want to remember everything, but I do.
Dates. Anniversaries. First times.
Tell me how to erase those memories so I can move on.
I've tried everything. Now I'm trying something new, and it's worse.
It sucks.
You won't hear from me on our anniversary because it's not an anniversary if we're not together, right?
There's no guarantee I won't think about you. It's okay. It's not all good.
I'm still mad as hell at you.
We mightn't be together now, though, time could have been the decider.
You took on fate by yourself.
It infuriates me and yet, I still take the blame.

Yet, you knew I would. And times like this I struggle to deal with it.

"What is it?" Paige asks when I fail to answer her question.

I hesitate. "Oh, it's a text from Carli about our rosters for the week."

I drop my phone into my bag and calm my thoughts from worrying about the person who sent it. Whether or not to respond. I'm not comfortable in divulging something as big as this to anyone. Not even my best friend.

It's not mine to share.

CHAPTER 2

DARCY

Before zipping my suitcase, I check the contents for my black jocks and the horseshoe key ring making sure they are packed. I head down the stairs, my phone in hand, and wait for the taxi. I check the time and simultaneously it vibrates. My mother's name is on the screen, and it's not even six in the morning.

"This is unexpected," I say.

"I wanted to catch you before you board the plane." It's impressive she knows I have an early flight. Presumed would be more accurate since my parents pay no attention to my schedule.

"I haven't even left the house yet. What's wrong?"

"I wanted to check the time of the game."

For ten years I have played in the Australian Football competition, and my mother still doesn't check the papers or the Internet. Football is everywhere. This country lives and breathes it like it's a way of life and yet, my parents refuse to embrace it preferring to live in a bubble sans football. Not sports. Australian rules football to be precise.

"It hasn't changed since my last text," I tell her.

"Your father may have to attend a business—"

"What? On a day I asked you to keep free months ago."

"He's trying." She whispers it, and I'm not sure she even believes it herself.

I can tally their game attendance on my fingers.

The same foul taste comes remembering their reaction ten years ago when I announced I wanted to play football—professionally—my childhood dream. My parents *expected* me to study engineering and work in the family business. At eighteen, I surprised everyone when I was picked in the first round football draft and transferred to Adelaide. Frustrated more than surprised my father, since I defied him. He didn't consider football to be a serious career path and is still waiting for me to 'grow up' and come to my senses.

"Tell him to try harder. This is my life, and it's about time he accepts it."

"I'll talk to him if it means that much to you."

Her words stun me. It's short-lived as the taxi pulls up.

"Don't bother. The taxi is here, I have to go."

On the drive to the airport, I consider my choices.

There's no denying football gave me everything I needed for a guy in his twenties.

Years of indulgence.

And yet, I wanted *more*.

Not the women or luxurious commodities. Only improvement. Be a bigger presence on the field. Be results driven. Focused.

Before boarding the plane, I check my phone for a text from my parents.

Nothing. Then I open the email Coach sent pushing intrusive thoughts aside. Thoughts about being close to proving my father wrong.

ALLI

Walking alongside Carli, we make our way to the departure gate. I don't miss the spring in her step.

"The Thunder are on our flight this morning."

There it is.

More surprising is her upbeat tone knowing she'll see Darcy Rayne, and after the last time, I assumed she would steer clear.

Carli brushes the navy material of her skirt. "Maybe they like a girl in uniform? Damn pity it does nothing for my rack."

"I'm sure *they're* not fussy."

"Neither am I when it comes to athletes. Being fit helps them to stay in the game."

Her comment deserves an eye roll. "Truth or myth?"

"I rank them highly."

"Over who?"

This time she rolls her eyes at me. "It's Friday, and all I can think about is the weekend."

"The weekend or getting laid?"

"Both. Do *you* have plans?"

"Paige is back from her holiday, so I'm meeting her out for a quiet drink."

She grabs my arm. "There they are," she says, ignoring my reply.

"Awesome." I avoid her line of gaze. I don't want to think about *him*. Not while I'm working. We head down the jetbridge toward the plane, greet the captain, and then open the overhead storage compartment to lock away our bags.

The first passenger to board is a small dark-haired boy, around five years of age, and unaccompanied by an adult. My stomach plummets when I notice his red eyes. After checking his boarding pass, I nod at the captain and lead him to his seat near the front, placing his bag in the overhead locker.

"You're going to be fine," I say gently. "I'm Alli, and I'll take care of you. As soon as everyone is seated, I promise I'll come back." He nods, although he looks unconvinced. His anguished expression takes me back years. My stomach tightens remembering my own personal pain, the reason I once hated flying.

"Welcome," I repeat to travellers before glancing at their boarding pass and greeting by name, before pointing out their allocated seat. I glance over the queue. I can pinpoint the impatient ones, those who dislike waiting in line with ordinary folk.

The first player of the team steps up. I note his black polo shirt, a cloud and thunderbolt logo on the left side. Most of the players who follow smile politely, some nod curtly, and a few ignore me. More players board, and I'm among giants. Like I'm on the set of *Avatar* greeting the Na'vi.

I hold out my hand for the boarding pass before greeting the next player, taking the ticket from large, strong hands. I glance up tilting my head back more than usual. My chest flutters, and I hesitate. My brain catches up, and I straighten my shoulders. Those hazel eyes are greener today reminding me of a pine forest. This close I'm inhaling the woody scent of his aftershave, and it messes with my train of thought.

Focus.

"Good morning, Mr Rayne. Your seat is in row five by the window."

"I need an emergency exit."

Why do passengers expect me to make things right if they haven't bothered when checking in? Even though his height declares there is a need for extra leg space.

"If you could take a seat, we will rectify the problem as soon as all passengers are seated."

He takes the ticket from my hand before meeting my gaze with his own steely one. "I can't sit in a normal seat…" he glances at my name badge,"… Alli."

"I apologise, sir. Carli will be more than happy to attend to you when everyone is seated."

He turns away and mutters something under his breath before following his teammates. I force a smile and greet the next traveller while trying not to allow his behaviour to fluster me. Same black polo. Same frown. Although, he appears older, so maybe he's the coach, or trainer, whatever.

"I'd appreciate you sorting out Darcy," he says, as though his next pay cheque depended on it. "We don't want him cramping before the game tomorrow."

Oh please, it's a two-hour flight.

"Certainly. As I mentioned, one of our flight attendants will take care of it."

I glance along the aisle to Carli talking with Darcy. "I believe it's being taken care of as we speak."

When the last of the passengers are seated and overhead lockers closed, I ready myself for the safety demonstration. I stand near the young boy and wink at him. "How are you doing?"

"Okay," he croaks.

"You'll be fine." I pat his hand.

The recorded voice sounds through the speakers, and I return to my position in the aisle holding up the emergency exit card located in the back pocket of each seat. Out of habit, I scan passenger faces noting who's listening. Most of the footballer players have their head lowered. They've heard it before. And the fewer eyes on me, the better. One of the players is mouthing the safety announcement word for word. His teammate seated beside him chuckles at his antics.

The man dressed in a business suit is already asleep with his head on the window. A ping of jealousy hits me at people who can power nap at any time. My gaze lifts scanning deadpan expressions in the aisles, stopping at Darcy Rayne.

His eyes lock with mine, and momentarily I'm intrigued. Remembering our earlier greeting, I look away and reach down to the seat to pick up the life jacket and demonstrate, cued by the voice over the speaker. I focus on the back wall while trying to ignore him.

"Cabin crew prepare for take off."

On hearing the captain's instructions, I snare the safety gear from the seat and stash it away before sitting in the seat beside the boy. The other attendants disappear behind curtains.

The plane stills, the engines roar. I glance sideways. His bottom lip trembles. "Hey, this is the fun part." I cover his hand with mine. "It's like a ride at Movie World." His glassy eyes tug at my heartstrings. "We'll pretend this is a fun ride." I pat his hand. "And I'll be here with you to keep you safe." My heart hollows a fraction. If the plane went down, I knew I couldn't promise his safety. I'd do everything in my power to protect him even if it meant giving my life. Because the thought of cabin crew not protecting passengers on board has turned my stomach since I was ten years old.

His eyes close when the plane soars along the runway, gripping the armrest as the force pushes us back in our seats. The nose points to the sky, levels, and a few sigh in relief. I squeeze his hand, and his eyes open. "Just like a ride," I gently reinforce.

He offers a nervous smile.

"Can I tell you a secret? I was once afraid of flying, too. I love it, now."

Afraid an understatement.

He blinks. His little hand remains clutching the armrest.

"I have to get refreshments for everyone. I'll come back and check on you." I lean close and whisper, "There are football players onboard, and they might get angry if I don't get them something to eat." His little face lights up. I fold out his table and from the pocket pull out a colouring-in pad and pencils. "I'll bring you something special to eat."

I meet Carli in the galley, and we set the ordered refreshments on the trolley before pushing it along the aisle. Midway, I reach the row where Darcy is seated. I repeat the menu of sandwiches or pasta on offer, careful not to give him eye contact and yet, I notice he makes a face. "Would you prefer a cold beverage, sir?"

"Sandwiches and a water. Please."

He takes the cup, and our fingers brush. Warm fingers. I jerk my hand away and move to the next row. I make the mistake of glancing back before serving the next passenger. His gaze lifts as though he senses it.

A mistake because I enjoy watching those lips turn into a sultry smile. Turning away, I give him nothing and curse under my breath.

DARCY

Every time I get on a damn plane my mind wanders. The cabin becomes a portal connecting to my most inner thoughts, a personal bubble where it's acceptable to ignore the person rubbing shoulders with mine. In my case, it's a rookie player from the country, and the music blares from the pods jammed in his ear. I'd say something, but he's the brother of Rhett Williams from our archrival team in Adelaide, the Blackbirds. And I promised him I'd look out for his kid brother, Dustin.

Even the in-flight entertainment isn't enough to diminish the thoughts threatening to undo me. I'm visualising the future playing out on an invisible screen before me.

Playing in front of my parents tomorrow is not about impression. It's respect. Respect to the decision I made. How hard I've worked, and how far I've come on my own.

I curse under my breath for allowing myself to become distracted and not switch my booking for an emergency exit seat. When I asked the flight attendant to fix the problem, I was caught in the most amazing brown eyes. I know her, seen her working on my flights before. Not as close when I stepped into her personal space to ask for help. Those eyes stole my next breath, and then familiarity hit me. It wasn't until she pushed the trolley past my seat that I remembered. Remembered her long legs in that tight little dress. Remembered the way she looked at me at the club. So, when she read the menu in a tone she'd rather not be near me, I smiled at her good intention.

I lift my gaze. She's scowling again. Her body tenses like she's nervous, and I can't help feeling a touch victorious. And thankful for shifting my thoughts away from my parents so I can focus on tomorrow's game.

Swiping the screen of my phone, I minimise the playlist and open the notes Coach sent in an email. It includes personal training times for the next two weeks and one-on-one with a specialist ruck coach.

Coach is always looking ahead, beyond each game leading up to the finals. In red capitals, he highlights the league ladder. The Sydney football team is a game ahead of us in points. We're both fighting to remain in the top four. I expect to have a good game considering Sydney's ruckman is older, smaller, and slower than me, but their rovers are quick and can read my tap outs. Coach has four new plays to outsmart Sydney. And winning comes from tactical plays, not brawn on the field.

There's nothing sweeter than winning, and my focus is on the Grand Final in two months, something my team hasn't achieved in ten years. After taking out a list of individual trophies, the big prize is within reach. Nothing will stand in my way of helping my team become champions. I have my father to thank for my competitive spirit. Yet, not even *he* will deter me.

Unwillingly, my eyes find the blonde. Alli. She walks the aisle checking on passengers after the pilot announces our descent. She turns, and I give a subtle nod. She stares back, yet there's no hint of a smile.

I can't help the smile tickling my lips because I admire her effort. My gut tightens with a challenge because *attitude* is everything.

It's enough.

She disappears when the plane is set to land. I turn my focus to the window to the city below that was once my home.

It looks the same.

The same expectation to return 'home'.

I switch on my phone as the plane slows along the runway.

A new message lights up the screen.

> **Mum:** *Darcy, call when you land. Your father failed to change his meeting and can no longer attend the game. I'm sorry. I'll try to watch your game on the television. Tonight he has arranged a dinner and would like me to accompany him. You are welcome to stay at our home instead of the hotel although you already know that. Clare is home. She misses you. Call me x*

CHAPTER 3

ALLI

I'm in the kitchen cutting up fruit when my phone lights up on the bench.

Carli: *I'm keen to go out tonight! Want to meet me at the Shore's club?*

By working opposite shifts we haven't spoken in a week.

Me: *I've been up since five and planned on an early night...*

I doubt she'd take it as a legit excuse.

Carli: *Whatevs. Be at mine at six.*

Ignoring her text, I find the number to call the nursing home before I go about my weekend chores. The weekend is when I find time to visit Gran to maintain the continuity that's important for her. If she is having a bad day, the logical side of me knows there's no point in visiting. Then guilt overrides logic.

"Blue Skies Nursing Home. Aubree Taylor speaking."

On hearing Aubree's voice, my shoulders relax. Aubree has worked at the nursing home for years, and even though she works part-time, she knows Gran well.

"It's Alli. I'm checking how Gran is today?"

"Hi, Alli. You should come. Thomas is with Evelyn now, and they're sitting outside enjoying the sunshine."

It doesn't surprise me Pop is already there. He spends most hours of the day sitting with Gran. "Thanks. I'll be there soon."

I hang up with the usual thought of how Pop should be living with me, especially with him spending so much time at the nursing home. Although I work long hours, we would at least get more time together. And my home—my parents' home—is familiar to him. Only he's against the idea of moving out of his house.

The one he shared with Gran.

I understand he has built wonderful memories in their home, and if forced to move out, his mental health might deteriorate. Lord knows my mental health swings to an unhealthy state at times, yet I can't keep allowing the past to dictate my future. It's something Gran felt strongly about before she fell ill. Sometimes I wonder if my home—my parents' home—kick-starts more of the sadness inside of Pop. Another reason he's opposed to moving in with me.

Pushing the vacuum back and forth with force, I ignore the crazy thoughts running through my mind. Thoughts of Nate and his newfound happiness. *Will he want to sell the house we inherited from our parents?* We both agreed never to sell, but real estate is expensive in London, and he might require his half of the house for a down payment on a loan.

My chest tightens, my breathing constricts the more I believe it's a possibility.

I can't sell the house.

It's filled with memories of my childhood... and *my* family.

My grandparents.

My parents.

Nate.

Pressing my hand against my chest, I switch off the vacuum and flop onto the lounge. Dark thoughts creep in clouding my mind until I close my eyes and concentrate on breathing slow and deep like Gran had taught me so early in my teens.

I repeat the word *strong* in a mantra, until my breathing slows, imagining myself on a tropical island swinging in a hammock. The ocean lapping the shore.

I stay here until the suffocating sensation eases, and despite feeling a little shaky, I stumble to my feet.

When I was twelve, Gran explained how to use visualisation to ease anxiety after I reacted to meds. It's been enough to keep me off the medication.

If only Nate was as lucky.

By the time I arrive at the nursing home, it's mid-afternoon, and Gran is on her bed having an afternoon nap. Lately, she tires easily and has to lie down for at least an hour between meals.

Sitting beside Gran, I take her hand in mine and rub it gently so as to not wake her. "I love you," I whisper. Keeping hold of her hand, I sit back and look over at Pop on the other side of the bed. "Did she have a good morning?"

"Depends on what you call good?"

I smooth my thumb over Gran's knuckles. "Did she have an episode?"

"No." Pop slouches in the chair. He stares at Gran as though she's the stranger.

Gran's ivory skin is barely lined. She looks peaceful. Not afraid, at least when her mind is resting. Pop, on the other hand, has aged. His tanned face is wrinkled after years of working in the outdoors and worrying about his family. He certainly has had his fair share of stress.

"Aubree said we have to appreciate the good days," I say softly. He doesn't respond, and his withdrawn expression is concerning. "Are you okay?"

He shrugs one shoulder. "Yeah."

I know he's not being truthful, yet the more I push, the less he talks, so for the next half hour we sit in silence waiting for Gran to wake.

"I found her this morning wearing her dress back to front again. She changes her clothes several times a day."

I nod. "Some days she has no concept of time."

"Some days?" His expression holds fear more than he's willing to admit.

"I have tomorrow off so I'll see you in the morning," I say when Gran remains sleeping. Pop nods. After kissing Gran's cheek, I walk around the bed and kiss Pop in the same way. He doesn't say anything.

The moment I'm in my car, my eyes clamp shut. I allow myself a few minutes before clicking my seat belt in place. Pop is hurting, like me, but there's nothing we can do for Gran only show her our love.

Gran used to speak frankly and was a little bossy. She would tell Pop and me what to do whenever we were faced with a problem. It's obvious Pop misses her guidance, and now he's lost when faced with decisions. Before Gran lost her memory, she had pushed for me to become a flight attendant, to deal with my fear of flying. She was with me to celebrate my first day on the job.

Having already been diagnosed with the early stages of Alzheimer's, we had measures in place that helped her cope. It's the small things we need to focus on, and I need to remind him of those.

Looking back, I'm happy I made her proud, but I would never have survived my first day if it weren't for Carli taking me under her wing and talking me through a near panic attack. As though Carli knows I'm thinking of her, my phone lights up with a message.

Carli: *Pre-drinks at mine.*

I'm not in the mood, although I could do with Carli's support, and a couple of drinks to numb my feelings. I start the engine and in a vague state of mind drive directly to hers.

Carli opens the door smiling until her gaze dips to my ripped jeans. "You can't go to the Shores dressed in those."

"I know," I say quickly before stepping around her. "Because I'm not going. I'll be in bed by nine."

"Oh, come on, we have days off together."

I follow Carli into her living room to a bar in the corner with coloured bottles in a line that could rival a small pub. I collapse onto the red modular in front of a ridiculously oversized television screen. I notice she's watching the football. "Can I switch it to a music channel?"

"Nope. I'm listening to the footy scores. The Thunder won a home game today, so they're guaranteed a finals berth. Anyways, what can I get you?"

"Nothing strong. Seriously. I ran ten k's this morning, and I'll be asleep soon."

Carli grins at me. "I have the perfect remedy."

I watch while she pours and shakes up an espresso martini.

"Down this. You'll feel great."

So great, by ten o'clock I'm standing in line with Carli waiting to enter the Shores nightclub. Carli's little red dress replaces my jeans and sweater. She dismisses my qualms emphasizing the dress is meant to be a tight fit, except it's like wearing a cut-off glove, and I prefer my clothes to be more like mittens.

The nightclub is a full house with patrons standing shoulder to shoulder around the bar. I head straight to the bar and order another drink. And in that short space of time, I lose Carli.

When a guy standing near me gives me the eye, I move away, interlacing my way through the crowd, endeavouring not to swagger.

I stare at the iron balustrade staircase feeling challenged to take two steps at a time.

When I reach the top, I'm thankful Carli is at the bar nearest to the steps. She waves me over to a vacant stool, although she looks engaged in controlling some guy's hands.

"You don't look good, Al. I'll order you a water."

"Actually, I have loads of energy. I want to dance."

"Why don't you sit for a while. And you should stick with water for the rest of the night. You'll thank me in the morning." She pats the stool beside her.

After ordering a bottle of water, I'm forced to entertain myself while Carli cements her lips to the random guy. Swivelling on the stool, I scan the room, distinguishing the nice guys who don't have their hands all over the closest girl's assets from said creeps. Drawn to a looming shadow, I turn to the staircase. Four guys hover by the railing, and it takes a few extra seconds to recognise the tallest guy is Darcy Rayne. Holy shit! He looks friggin' hot dressed in a white button-up shirt with sleeves rolled to the elbows. The shadowy light emphasises his chiselled jawline even more.

I swivel on the chair. With Carli still preoccupied, I succumb to peering from a safe distance. Darcy straightens. His height an advantage to an unobstructed view. His head turns and our eyes meet. I look away, but it's too late because I saw his expression change.

Busying myself when Carli is breaking some kind of smooching record is all too hard. Being in the same room as him makes me uneasy, excited and uneasy. I lightly tap Carli's shoulder. "I'm going to take an Uber home."

Carli disconnects her lips and turns to me. "I thought you had loads of energy?"

"Did. I want to go. I'll get my car tomorrow."

"Wait. I'll come with you."

"No," I say with emphasis and somewhat embarrassed when random guy frowns at me. "I'm fine, really. You stay, have fun." I smile at him so he knows I'm not stealing his hook-up. As I go to turn, a large hand snakes around my waist and twirls me in the opposite direction. And somehow I land between warm, muscled thighs.

Darcy grins, and here in this club, where anticipation fills the air, his smile does all sorts of things to my sensibility. Even with the influence of alcohol, I'm not numb to the heat from his hand around my waist.

"I was hoping to see you again. Didn't figure it would be this soon."

Did I miss the memo where we went from sneaky glances to him handling me?

I take hold of his hands trailing over my hips and still them. "I was hoping it *wouldn't* be this soon." In truth, I *wasn't* expecting to run into him tonight when he had played a game, let alone have his hands on my body. I'm lost in sea green eyes, those pools of lust, and tightness travels from my throat all the way down.

"A pretender." His smile grows regardless of my intent to stall his advances. It's as though he knows I have no defensive plan.

I'm drunk and struggling to deal right now. Carli is gaping, which halts my panic, and then I remember the last time we were here when Darcy had upset her.

"Well, if it's not my favourite flight attendants," Darcy drawls over my shoulder looking at Carli. "I'm sorry if I seemed on edge the other day. With an upcoming game… you know how it is?"

Carli nods and waves her hand at Darcy. "Oh, I understand. You'd never be intentionally rude." She smiles at him and bats her lashes.

"She's being nice. I thought you *were* rude."

His hands slide over my hip, down my back to my rear.

"I'm sorry if I upset you. I'm sure I can find a way to make it up."

"Really?" My hands grip his hard in a direct warning.

"We could start over."

"So you won't have to apologise?"

His ridiculously long lashes lower as his gaze falls to my lips. "You know I first saw you months ago on a flight," he says, leaning close to my ear. "So last week wasn't our first meeting."

I look away to gather my thoughts and notice a group of girls edging closer. Waiting. The stares over rims are plain stalkerish. Like I'm prey, and when Darcy is done, they're ready to pounce. No. He is the prey. And for a second I feel sorry for him. Until my thoughts move to an awareness of people watching us. It's a cue to remove myself from the cause.

"Actually, I apologise…" I wiggle free, "… because I was leaving. It was nice chatting. Perhaps another time."

I turn to Carli, and at the same moment my clutch vibrates. My attention is invested searching for my phone. *A missed call from my brother.* I hold up my phone. "It was Nate. I'll go outside and take it." Before I get a chance to move, my phone buzzes in my hand with an incoming text.

Nate: *I'm engaged to the most beautiful girl in the world, and I can't wait for you to meet her!*

I glance up at Carli. She frowns and reaches out to touch my arm. "What's wrong?"

My eyes lower to the phone. "My brother is engaged."

"That's a good thing, right?" She smiles, reassuring.

I nod, despite feeling otherwise and throw my phone back in my bag. The lump in my throat expands. I need water. No, I need something stronger.

Two jeaned knees nudge my hips. "You're still here."

I'm frozen to the spot staring at Carli, and she at me. I suck in a breath and turn. "Yeah, I am. I had a change of heart. I've decided to have another drink."

"So, what will it be?"

"Since I should be celebrating make it a champagne."

Darcy pushes up from the stool, his warm body brushing mine as he stands. He leans over and signals the barman, who ignores other patrons to serve Darcy.

His eyes remain fixed on my mouth as I raise the glass to my lips. "What are you celebrating?"

I sip the bubbles, watching him watching me. "It's a long story," I say between mouthfuls, forcing the cool liquid down.

My head spins in a mixture of disappointment, and the desired effect of the alcohol. Talking to Darcy, being this close to him, has me feeling something else. Excitement and anticipation, a Band-Aid to the hurt.

His hands tighten on my hips. "I have all night."

I take another sip peering at him over the rim of the glass. "My brother announced his engagement."

"This is a surprise to you?" His eyes look deep into mine, and I feel the probing to understand the question.

"It is, unfortunately." I tilt my head then raise my glass before taking another sip.

Something shifts between us. He looks at me as though he's seeing me for the first time. "Do you want to get out of here?"

One finger touches my cheek and guides my face closer to his. The other hand settles on my back. The finger on my cheek is now a hand. His face lowers, eyes not wavering from mine.

Lips brush over mine and linger, giving me a chance to oppose his advancement. When I do nothing, those lips press to mine. A kiss, surprisingly gentle, and not at all what I expected.

His gentle caress sparks something deep. I'm *slightly* aware I'm still standing, bag in one hand, glass of champagne in the other. I'm *fully* aware I'm kissing Darcy Rayne and need to drop everything, so I can cup his face and lose myself in the moment.

I'm doing my best to shut out the warnings in my head. When Darcy pulls away, I stumble.

"Do you want to get out of here?"

For the slightest millisecond, I want to say *yes*, so I nod, ignoring all warning. His eyes flash open. Without stopping to say goodbye to his friends, he takes my hand and leads me to the staircase.

Outside the nightclub, the cold air hits like a slap on the face.

"Hungry?" Darcy eyes the yiros shop across the street.

I'm breaking all my rules, so I answer, "Sure, why not?"

Even from this side of the road, I can tell the shop is filled with hungry, inebriated customers. He takes my hand and walks with me, heads turning, his name whispered as we pass. "It'll be easier to wait out here. I'll only be a few minutes."

I agree, and through the window I watch the shop assistant wave at him. A full shop, so I assume the wait to be around fifteen minutes until Darcy holds up two fingers. The guy behind the counter nods, and as was the case in the club, Darcy's served ahead of others with no money passing hands.

Alone, and out in the cold night air, practicality takes hold. Between Nate's news and the white rum topped with champagne pumping through my body, my thoughts whirl. Especially at the notion of going back to Darcy's house. Or was he going to suggest mine? My chest constricts as though someone has tightened the strings on a corset.

Breathe, I remind myself.

A taxi pulls into the kerb only metres away. I stare at it for a moment and realise it's not taken, and my fight or flight response activates. Glancing over my shoulder to the shop window, I find Darcy leaning on the back wall, head down scrolling on his phone. I turn away before changing my mind, open the back door of the taxi and slide in.

CHAPTER 4

ALLI

Last night I didn't have trouble falling asleep.

The thump-thump in my head a reminder of the stupidity.

I've managed to keep an apple and a couple of analgesic capsules down. As much as my body demands I remain in bed, I can't stay here and allow my mind to drift and think about last night. Not about Darcy and Nate. Blaming all the above for the nausea, I bring up the Uber app on my phone and type in Carli's address.

After a short car ride, she opens the door with a smile from ear to ear. And eyes brighter than mine despite the outline of kohl.

I groan. "Were we drinking the same shit?"

She waves a hand for me to follow her into the kitchen. "I feel fine even though I've barely slept."

"So, last night went well?"

"Better than *well*. Why aren't you smiling? I thought you'd be bouncing through the door?"

"If you're referring to Darcy, we didn't end up together. I changed my mind and caught a cab home. End of story. Except for the pounding in my head."

"What? Why?"

I exhale loudly, not in the mood to defend my decision.

"Well, you're crazy not to sleep with Darcy."

"Because I didn't want to?" I shake my head. "I'm not getting into it now. I'm meeting Paige before visiting Gran so I'll see you next week. We can talk then and you can tell me about your guy."

That makes Carli smile. I have no doubt she has much to tell.

An hour later, I'm sitting with Paige in a café in the city feeling a little better because I'm laughing at her jokes. Woes are temporarily forgotten until I mention the text from Nate.

"What did you say as a reply?"

I sip my latte. "I haven't responded."

"Your brother is over the moon and sends you a text with happy news, and you ignore it. Imagine how he's feeling?"

Paige is right. I'm not overjoyed, and yet I should be. "I'll do it now." I quickly punch in a reply apologising for my late response and tell him how happy I am for the both of them and hit send.

"It's not that I'm unhappy because I truly want the best for Nate. I was sidetracked when I read it."

"Sidetracked?" By the way Paige is staring into space, I know she's estimating the time difference. "What time did you get the text?"

I lean back in the chair and pull my coat around my chest. "I was with someone. Kind of."

"Who?"

I shake my head. "Doesn't matter. I didn't end up going home with him."

Paige rests her elbows on the table and leans forward. "You *thought* about going home with someone?"

"I only thought about going home with him after I received the text. It was a reaction. It spooked me that Nate had found a permanent someone, and I have no one special."

Paige shakes her head. "Your brother hasn't been your security blanket for years. I get that the future scares you, but you have to give yourself credit. You're stronger now."

Even with Nate living on the opposite side of the world I'm comforted knowing he would come if I needed him. If he's committed to someone else... and with my grandparents aging, the thought of being alone scares me.

I glance across the road to the parklands. The grass is at its greenest this time of year, and the trees are coated with yellow and orange leaves, glistening when the sun hits the dew. People in thick coats scurry along the pavement. The city feels alive. Yet, above the beautiful autumn colours greyness fills the skies. And I'm staring at the sky.

"Anyways back to last night. So, how did you let the poor guy down?" she asks like a dog with a bone.

"He went to get us a yiros, and I jumped in a taxi. He'll get over it."

"You knew him?"

I glance at her sideways knowing my confession will spark a reaction. "It was Darcy Rayne."

Paige's mouth falls open. "What. The. Hell? You left the Shores club with *Darcy Rayne* to get a yiros with the intention of going back to his? And what were you doing before this? Because I've seen him when he's out—"

"We kissed, that's all." I swallow a mouthful of coffee.

"You kissed?" Her voice rises a notch.

Her excitement seems overly dramatic. "I considered going back to his only I doubt I'd forgive myself the following day for sleeping with someone like him. He's a one-night guy."

Paige sits back in her chair and assesses me. "It's Darcy bloody Rayne. Do you follow him on social media?"

I shake my head.

She starts to say something and changes her mind. "Probably a good thing."

Paige pulls out her phone and takes a selfie of us both. She places her phone on the table and swipes through filters on Instagram.

I like Instagram for the photos and being less wordy. And many of my snapshots are reposts of Nate's photography. Wordless, beautiful images. When I see her post, I admit it's not shabby and repost it to my own profile.

Allibradley
Over the moon to have this girl home #BFF

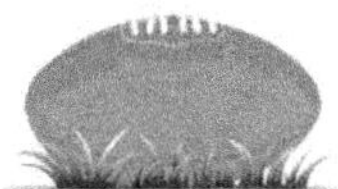

One night of partying and then four days of extended shifts including sleepovers in three different cities cause my immune system to weaken. It's Friday night, and I'm sitting in front of the television wearing one of Nate's old sweaters he left behind. It wraps around me like a warm blanket, armour comforting me as much as it keeps me warm. After dosing myself up on flu tablets, I scroll through social media apps until I find photos of Darcy.

An hour later, I toss my phone aside and switch from lying on the bed to the lounge to watch reruns of *I Love Lucy*. The show was my Gran's favourite. By laughing at the same things I did with her helps me to feel connected. And I need to believe she is close, watching over my shoulder always even though she doesn't always remember who I am.

A text from Carli interrupts my reminiscing.

Carli: *Darcy's team was on my flight yesterday :)*

Me: *Did he speak to you?*

Carli: *Only a little. He was polite.*

I'm back to thinking about him and the other night and imagine his reaction. If I'm being realistic, he's more likely to consider I was being immature. If Darcy didn't mention anything to Carli, then I assume it didn't bother him.

So why am I allowing it to bother me?

The esplanade is heavy with the scent of seaweed from overnight rain. The ocean garden lines the shore in bundles this time of year. The turbulent water grey, and yet I still have a need to be close, smell it, breathe it in. After being sick for the past week, a thicker layer of perspiration covers my body. It's enough for me not to finish my run and set me on a path directly to my home.

I'm stretching on the floor of the living room, and my phone lights up with a message.

Paige: *Are you keen to go to the farmer's market?*

Farmer's markets were a Sunday tradition going back years to when Paige and I were at senior school. There was something about the fresh scent of bread, the visual delight of an array of colour of freshly picked fruit and vegetables, and the aroma of espresso coffee.

Me: *Yes! Just been for a run. Will meet you in 45.*

Paige: *You are insane to run after the flu, and in this weather! See you at Frisky Bean.*

The thought of organic coffee has me showering in record time.

And in thirty minutes I'm standing in warm, casual, active wear at the pop-up booth waiting for Paige.

She waltzes toward me, her long blonde ponytail swaying behind her. She's wearing jeans, a long red coat, and black knee-high boots. Another foot taller and Paige could be a model. A black gloved hand waves at me.

"My gurl," she says. "You're looking better."

"Feeling better. A little lethargic."

"And yet you ran." She gives me a sideways glance before holding up two fingers at the barista.

"Not far. I feel better for it," I say. "No sugar in mine," I add.

"There's a new Greek food pop-up," she says. "A friend at work mentioned it. Some treats are made from almond meal and not too sweet, so I thought some would appeal to you."

"Sure. As long as we hit our usual stops first. I don't want my favourite rye sourdough to sell out."

We chat about her work and then wander from stall to stall inspecting organic foods and sampling new ones. Paige has a weakness for homemade chutney—on toast or with cheese on crackers with her favourite wine. I'm not completely sold on it until a lady offers a taste of her orange and cranberry chutney.

I groan after eating it. "This is good," I say, nodding.

"Welcome to a whole new world of pleasure." Paige pops another cracker from the sampler plate into her mouth.

I laugh. "Is it too early to drink wine because wine has it's own set of nutritional rules, right?"

"You should spread some on your fresh bread." The lady nods at the bread in a paper bag, the tip poking out. "It's great with chicken or pork on a sandwich."

"Sold." Paige hands over her credit card.

"Make it two." I dig into my pocket for cash.

A long, muscled arm reaches past me to try the chutney on a cracker presented on the sampler plate in front of me.

"Excuse me." The deep voice comes from behind.

"Of course." I freeze, recognising *his* voice, only to force myself to step aside without looking over my shoulder.

The warmth of his body radiates heat with him being this close. I glance sideways to Paige, her mouth gaping. Then I angle my body away, so there's no chance he'll see my face. Paige's expression tells me everything I need to know, and my heart reacts, speeding up, preparing to flee.

"Thank you," I say quickly when our jars are handed over. I turn in the opposite direction to him and walk away calmly as possible.

"Did you know—?"

"Yes," I say quickly. "Did he see me?"

"I'm not sure. I mean he didn't look at you, but he stood awfully close."

"Trust me I was aware." I let out a deep breath and continue toward our favourite strawberry stall.

Half-hour later we head toward the exit gate. I hug Paige and look over her shoulder and notice Darcy in the distance. I assume he's with his teammates since the people surrounding them appear to be from hobbit land. The space between us is no barrier to his gaze locking with mine, and although its only seconds, its long enough to measure understanding. His expression doesn't change, yet his eyes tell me more. One look, and my heart races like I'm an animal caught in a beam of light, unable to move despite the gap between us.

He *did* recognise me.

DARCY

Walking down the aisle of the plane, I scan ahead to see if *she* is on board. Two flight attendants greet us with no sign of Alli. I keep mulling over *that* night and what I did to spook her. At first, I thought she wandered toward the beach. Girls tend to like nights by the sea, and she was into me as much as I was into her. Before I reached the jetty, I realised she'd taken off leaving me with two damn yiros. When my teammates saw me standing alone, the smart-arse comments rolled in and haven't stopped.

Switching to aeroplane mode, I drop my phone into my trouser pocket and sneak a glance toward the kitchen. A flash of dark hair. So her friend is on the flight.

I ignore the damn safety presentation pre-take off.

My teammates' eyes are closed, world blocked, listening to whatever music pumps them up for tomorrow's game in Brisbane.

The warmer weather will be better than what Adelaide has produced lately. When the seat belt sign switches off, I stand, peel off my jacket, stuff it on the overhead compartment, and glance toward the kitchen.

I spy her in the galley.

Taking my seat, I contemplate what to say to her.

Half-hour later, I pull out one earphone. Wheels of the trolley squeak not far behind. The trolley goes by, and her friend is facing me. I give her a nod. Then Alli walks up behind the trolley carrying a pot of coffee, her back to me when I realise it's her.

Both girls serve the passengers in front, and I spend the minutes watching Alli bend to grab trays from the trolley. Christ every little thing she does turns me on until Carli leans in and blocks my view.

"Would you like a snack, Mr Rayne?"

"Thank you." I take the sandwiches and a juice while answering Carli politely and in a casual tone. "Anything planned for the weekend?"

"Yeah, Alli and I are staying—" Alli coughs, and Carli cowers. I assume Alli is giving her a dark look since she almost revealed their weekend plans. "Enjoy your meal."

I'm to assume both girls will be in Brisbane this weekend.

And so will I.

The trays are collected, and I ask for a coffee refill. Alli avoids me again. I tell myself to deal with it and the unfamiliar sensation in my gut. When I saw her at the market, I approached with the intention of asking her why the fuck she'd taken off? What I did? Instead, I froze and ordered a jar of chutney I'll never eat. I'm not sure what it is about her that makes me act like an inexperienced boy crushing on a girl who is out of his league. An awakening to the unfamiliar. A sensation I'm not entirely thrilled about. An unwelcome distraction. I stick my pods in my ears and listen to my favourite hard-rock music focusing all thought on tomorrow's game.

Although Brisbane is struggling to make the top eight, it won't be an easy match. Brisbane's players tolerate the warmer weather better than other teams, and tomorrow they will be looking for a win to gain a finals berth. Their ruckman, Phil Jordan, is smaller and faster than me. Jordan may wear me down around the ground, but he won't beat me at contesting tap-outs to the players. I control the centre. If my boys give me a shit kick, then he'll be on those loose balls. My hands clench thinking about him getting the better of me. Then I knock my knee on the damn table.

Hell.

I press the call buzzer and wait.

Minutes pass, my call ignored. One attendant hovers in business class, and Carli attends to an elderly man. I'm about to lean forward and get Carli's attention when a warm body brushes my arm. Alli leans over and turns off the call light.

"May I help you?" Her brown eyes show no expression.

"Can you please take the cups and rubbish so I can fold away the table?"

"Certainly." She reaches to grab the cup. Simultaneously, I grip it to pass it to her. Our hands overlap in a momentary tug of war on the cup. She shoots me a confused look. "I'm sorry I thought—"

"Apology accepted." I hold her gaze a second longer.

She looks to Cooper sitting next to me. He's grinning even though he's not looking our way. Her gaze flicks back to mine. Her eyes round then she saunters toward the back of the plane.

"You suck at being discreet," I tell him.

"Coulda warned me it was yiros girl."

CHAPTER 5

ALLI

I find Carli in the galley. "He's pissed at me."

Ian's eyes dart between Carli and me before he turns to the fridge with sudden disinterest.

Carli gapes. "You thought he wouldn't be?"

"I hoped he wouldn't be. He never said anything to you?"

Carli shakes her head. "What did he say?"

"It's more the way he looked at me."

The captain announces, "Cabin crew prepare for landing."

My shoulders relax, grateful for the flight to end, so I can escape the small confines of the plane and breathe easy again.

My mood brightens as soon as I step out of the terminal because Brisbane in August reminds me of London in summer. I've only visited London once in June, and the mild days and breezy nights had a romantic feel about them. Brisbane gives me the same tingly sensation knowing I won't be freezing my butt off during the day.

Carli booked two nights at a hotel in the heart of the city. After swapping my wool blend coat for a sleeved dress and a light cotton jacket, we head to her favourite Italian restaurant.

She pushes open the door, and the aroma of garlic and basil waft out into the night.

Passing reserved tables, we follow the waitress to the far back corner. My stomach gurgles, the delicious smell reminding me I haven't eaten since breakfast.

Carli orders a bottle of sav blanc from one of our favourite wineries south of Adelaide. I like trying wine from different regions, though, sometimes it's comforting to stay with the familiar. I take the last mouthful in the glass while still perusing the menu. Her phone vibrates on the table. She reads the text and punches in a reply. "I've been seeing Michael," she confesses. I give her a puzzled look. "You know, the blond I met at the Shores?"

I'm surprised because I imagined him to be another one-nighter. "You like him?"

Carli shrugs. "He calls me during the day to check how I am. Even cooked me dinner and did all the cleaning up. What guy does that?"

"You have a point."

"He's already sent flowers on two occasions for absolutely no reason." Her brow arches as though she's looking for my approval.

"And… you're not sure you like him?"

"I do like him. I usually fall for the wealthy bad guy. You know, the one who treats me like shit, which makes me want him all the more."

"You fall for the wrong guy, and I won't even allow myself to fall. No safety net in love, so I'm not going there." I laugh and yet, deep down, my obsessive nature scares me.

The conversation halts when the waitress arrives to take our order. I ask for the steamed barramundi.

"You shouldn't be so fussy. When a guy breaks your heart, it only makes you stronger, makes you realise what you don't want in the next guy." She shrugs.

It makes sense to anyone other than me. "I'm finally getting my life together, and I can't let my heart break all over again, even if it's over a guy. I want to be sure a guy will do the right thing by me, treat me with respect. Be loyal."

"When you find the shop where boyfriends are tailor-made, let me know." We clink wine glasses.

"Well, this Michael sounds like a keeper." I smile. "What are you unsure about?"

Carli's chin dips. "He works in a men's clothing store and doesn't care about a career."

I wait a moment before commenting, "It shouldn't influence whether you like him."

Carli squirms in her seat, adjusts her long, dark tresses to fall perfectly over her shoulders. "I know I sound like a bitch, but I've always wanted a guy to surprise me with gifts and fuss. He's only just getting by."

"I've always taken you to be strong and independent. Not once did I believe you *needed* a guy to take care of you." Carli's gaze shoots to the tablecloth. "Besides, he did surprise you with flowers. He spoils you by doing the dishes. Not expensive gifts but a kind gesture counts for more in my opinion."

"I'm not as resilient as you." Her eyes meet mine. "You have control over your life and know what you want and what direction you're heading."

I laugh cynically. "Yeah, right. Me with all my hang-ups. Weren't you listening when I admitted to being afraid of falling in love?"

"You're so called hang-ups help you stay on track and keep control of your life." Carli smiles her beautiful smile that usually reels in the guys. "And I don't believe you're afraid to fall in love. I think you're waiting for the right guy to come along."

"I walk a fine line and struggle with it daily."

Our conversation ends when the meals are delivered. After one mouthful of the herbal sauce on my fish, I groan in delight. "This is good." Carli nods rather than answer me with a mouth full of pasta.

Across the room, a baby cries, and the mother is rocking it in her arms. She glances up, anguish in her expression. The lady next to her stands, takes the baby and walks while gently rocking her arms, a sway in her step. I'm watching her because frankly, it warms my heart. In a few minutes, the crying stops, and the older lady smiles before taking the baby back and giving it to the mother. The lady leans and kisses, I assume her daughter, on the head.

It dawns on me I'll never have that. No mother or grandmother to help when I'm struggling. None to share in the joy of grandchildren. Gran struggles to remember *me*. And when I remember how close we were, my heart cracks a little more. There are moments when my armour weakens, and I feel insecure, a little anxious. Now is one of those times. The feeling comes over me quickly, and I have to focus. Respond by slowing my breathing. I don't have time to ponder over it because a dozen men dressed in teal polo shirts file in through the front door. I freeze, a fork halfway to my mouth. One by one they sit at a long table. And then I see him. Carli takes one look at my face before spinning in her chair to what has spooked me. "Oh."

I place my fork beside my plate. "Are you finished?"

Carli's ravioli meal is only half-eaten. She arches her brow. "Don't let him ruin our plans."

"I don't want to be here." My body tenses with the surprise of seeing him.

"Let me finish my meal, and we can leave."

For the next few minutes I try not to squirm. In the end, curiosity defeats me, and I glance over at his table. I don't have to search as my eyes find his easily. I'm acutely aware of his teammate talking beside him. He turns to take up the conversation.

"Alli, relax," Carli says between mouthfuls of food. "Why are you so nervous around him?"

"I feel... it's hard to describe."

"It's okay. I get it." She takes a few more mouthfuls. "I'm done." She pushes her chair out from the table. "We'll pay at the counter and not wait for the bill."

While handing over my credit card to the waitress, I sense him behind me. I know he's there by the change in the air. "What are you girls planning to do in Brisbane?" I note how he includes me in the question. I don't turn but instead become highly interested in the EFTPOS machine, telling the waitress I'll cover the bill.

"We have the weekend off," Carli says. "We're staying at the Hilton down the road.

"What a coincidence," Darcy remarks.

"Your game is tomorrow, right?"

Of course, Carli would know when the Thunder play, and the two sound like they're now best friends.

"We play in the afternoon."

His voice flows like honey, the sweetness attracting me like a bee to a flower. I remind myself attraction is the cause to my uneasiness. I've never felt so strongly about a guy.

Avoid the temptation to taste the nectar.

To stay safe, I avoid the sweetness.

Yet, the more I see him, the more I'm tempted to have one taste. I had thought about it, and right now when I'm feeling weak, it's what happens after that scares me most. Caring about someone and then have no control when they slip away.

After receiving my card, I place it back in my clutch resisting the urge to turn. "We should meet up in the hotel bar for a drink," Carli offers.

Before Darcy answers, I spin around.

His gaze fixes on me. "We have a curfew, and water is all I drink the night before a game. I don't consume anything that will hinder my decision-making," he says as though he's only talking to me. A dig at when I took off?

"Well, good luck for tomorrow although I'm sure you don't need it." Carli beams up at him.

"Yes, good luck," I say without looking at him. I lean toward Carli. "We're set. Ready?" I head toward the front door.

As soon as I step outside, Carli falls into step alongside me. "That was a little rude."

"That I paid for your dinner? So, why did you start talking to him?" I swear under my breath and continue toward the hotel. "And why would you tell him where we're staying and then ask to meet back at the hotel bar?"

"Whoa, wait one minute. Firstly, thank you. Secondly, *I* was being polite." Carli grabs my arm pulling me to a stop. "Acting natural means you're not hiding anything and not embarrassed. You pretend you don't like him, yet I saw the way you were looking at him. You're scared. I get it. I'm trying to help you out. Drop your guard this once and see where it takes you because you might be surprised."

"He's a player. Pun intended. Do you know the last time he was in a relationship? Because Paige and I had talked about his sans relationship history on the phone. That factor bothers me."

Carli remains silent as we continue toward the hotel.

"I've bounced around the idea of being with him. Who wouldn't? Then I thought about why there is a string of girls in line. Can you name the last girl to break *his* heart?"

"None comes to mind," she murmurs.

"Exactly. I'm *trying* to avoid him because I could be the next girl with the broken heart. Scared of what will happen if I crumble."

"I'm sorry," Carli says in a soft voice.

"It's fine."

"You know he could say the same about you because you don't have a relationship history, and you don't date. Maybe you have something in common?"

She has a point, and it makes me consider what's holding me back. The hotel doors slide open leading us to the foyer.

"So why do you like him? For most girls it's the football factor. Clearly, it's not the case for you."

"It's what appeals least to me."

"Then what?"

I shrug. "There's something there, I'm not denying it. And in rare moments, I see a different person behind the façade. A rawness about him that makes me want to get to know the real Darcy because I think there's a lot more to him than just a player."

Carli hits the elevator button. "And it would require more than one night. And you believe he's only interested in a hook-up?"

I nod.

"And it's what spooks you because you think you'll fall hard after the one time with him?"

"I'm sure of it."

It's not until the elevator stops on the fifth floor do I speak again. "You want to hang out and watch a movie?"

Carli hugs me. "I love you, but you need to relax a little. You know one time might be all you need to decide whether or not he's worth it." She pats my back twice. "I'll see you in the morning. I'm going to take a shower and then call Michael."

"Let me know if you change your mind."

"Sure. Actually, I'll pop down and grab some chocolate from the vending machine. Can I get you anything?"

I shake my head. "Catch you tomorrow."

DARCY

"Hey what's with you, man? You've been quiet since dinner." Cooper punches my arm as we walk through the foyer to the elevator.

"Focusing on tomorrow's game."

"We match them on every position. Coach has it covered. Get the ball to me, and we'll own the centre."

"Don't get cocky." For a short guy he has a big ego.

"You know what I'm saying."

I don't go into a game confident we have it in the bag because I don't appreciate looking like a fool. I fight for every damn win whether it's a sure thing or not. The harder the fight, the better the joy of winning.

Then I think of Alli. "Yeah, I just worked out my problem. I'm going to try something different."

"Stick to Coach's plan, mate," Cooper emphasises. "Don't risk breaking the rules."

We stop talking when I spot Carli standing at the vending machine. "She's a friend," I tell Cooper. "Catch you later."

"Still hungry?" I'm smirking at Carli as she retrieves three chocolate bars from the machine.

She rolls her eyes. "I can't make up my mind."

"Don't you have a minibar?"

"It costs a fortune."

"Right." We stand in silence a moment, and Carli smiles knowingly.

"Her room is 507 in case you were wondering and wanted to call her."

I nod. "Not sure she wants to speak to me."

"Try a different angle." She smiles then turns leaving me with that thought.

Next thing I know, I'm standing outside her door taking a breath before I knock, twice. I grab hold of the doorframe as though I need assistance to stand because now I'm questioning what the hell I'm doing. Instinct guides me, yet I'm second-guessing why I'm here. There's an undeniable attraction, only the timing is wrong. The fact I'm here on the night before a game instead of focusing on our game plan, and my opponent is a distraction I can't afford. Not when it's my team's year to shine. I'm about to leave when the door opens, and Alli is standing there smiling wearing tiny pyjama shorts and a tank top. A new energy overcomes my thoughts, and I'm invigorated with a different plan. Her fresh scent wafts over me. And now I'm imagining her in the shower. Naked. I tap my fingers on the doorframe. "Alli."

She blushes. "Oh, I thought you were…" I arch a brow, "…Carli, and she changed her mind. Is something wrong?"

"I thought we could talk." My gaze drops to her long legs.

"Now's not a good time."

I raise a brow. "No?" I look past the door. "Do you have company?"

Alli folds her arms. "No."

Hell, I can't tear my gaze from her nipples pushing against the thin material of her pyjamas.

She angles her body away from mine as though she's about to close the door. "I'm watching something, and I doubt it would interest you."

"Try me."

Her gorgeous lips part, and she blushes.

"What *are* you watching?" I can't keep the teasing out of my voice.

Alli groans, and I decide I love that sound coming from her. "Do you have a point in being here?"

"I do. I want to talk to you." She tilts her head so I add, "Not out here."

She yanks the door open, and I have no option but to take a seat on the single couch beside the bed. Her room is tiny. The television is opposite her bed.

"Don't get too comfortable," she warns as she walks to the other side of the bed putting as much space as possible between us. "You're not staying." I can tell she doesn't know where to sit. She glances at the bed then at me. She sits crossed legged on the edge.

"Fine." I sit forward and look right at her. "Why are you angry at me?"

"I'm not angry." She pauses the television image.

"Really? So, why are you afraid?"

Her eyes widen a little before she composes herself. "What makes you think I'm afraid of you?" Her voice holds a slight quiver. I don't point it out. "We've met on several flights. Did I seem afraid on those occasions?"

I drum my fingers on the armrest considering my next response. "No, you were polite. It's different to when we're out and the way you look at me..." I hold her gaze and watch as she stiffens enough for me to notice, "... it's as though you would like to…" she stands, and I backpedal, "… be friends." We both know it's not true because I remember the look in her eyes. She wanted me as much as I wanted her. Only it wasn't lust, a quick fuck lingering behind her eyes. It was more. For weeks I've wanted to know more, but my gut keeps telling me not now. *Wait.* Because I can't allow myself to get caught up with a girl in the one year that could mean everything to my career. In a matter of weeks the football season will finish. Yet, I have this feeling telling me to act now before I lose her. It's the only stupid justification as to why I'm sitting here having an awkward conversation.

She leans one arm back on the bed, eases her body into it. "In a way, yes. Probably more an acquaintance."

"So, you'd consider us being friends?"

She gives me a wary look. "I don't understand why you needed to come to my room to ask me that?"

"Because friends don't run. I did something to scare you. I'd like to know what it was."

Her lips part, and those honey eyes widen. "It wasn't you. Well, it was, and it wasn't. You were over friendly."

There's a first time for everything. I smile. I'm usually accused of being the opposite. "You gave me a vibe that it's what you wanted. I don't go around forcing myself on girls. I want you to know that."

She gives a sarcastic laugh. "Oh, I know. I did notice the line of girls in waiting. Can you go anywhere without your harem following?"

I give her a long look. Instead of reiterating my disapproval in those girls, I take pleasure in knowing she has stalked me in a way. "I can. Although it's not the issue, is it?"

She stares at the television as though searching for answers. I follow her gaze to the paused image. She's clamming up, and it's not what I want. "You never did say what you're watching."

"It wouldn't interest you."

"Press play."

She whips her head my way, mouth open. "You want to watch *I Love Lucy* with me?"

"I know you're probably thinking weird shit, only I do want to be friends with you."

"So, you won't pull a move on me?"

My smile is back. "I already did. We both know how it ended." I stand and flop onto her bed, my boots dangling over the edge. I grab an extra pillow from the carpet and stuff it behind my head. I don't care what we watch because lying beside Alli beats being in the room with Cooper and listening to him fart.

Something changes in her expression as though her walls have lowered a little.

"So, I didn't hurt your ego?" She's smiling, and moves her long legs up and onto the bed while keeping a decent space between us.

"I don't have an ego, but I do have feelings." I give her a sideways glance. She's avoiding my gaze, keeping hers pinned to the television. She points the remote, and the black and white show plays.

After a few minutes, she looks my way. "I guess we both gave mixed messages."

It isn't an apology, yet it's enough. She slides back and leans against the pillows with her legs stretching out in front. Damn the view is hard to ignore.

When she giggles, I look up to the screen.

"This is my favourite part."

"You've seen it before?"

"Many times. It was one of my favourite shows to watch with my grandmother."

Her voice holds more emotion than she realises. Enough for me not to say anything for the remainder of the show and lay here and enjoy being with her. It's the most relaxed I've been before a game in weeks.

"I better get going," I say when the credits roll even though I don't want to leave. I stand and make my way to the door. "Will you be watching the game tomorrow?"

She shakes her head. "Carli and I have a few things planned."

"Do you ever attend games?" She rubs her fingers together. When I glance up, her expression is uncertain.

"I don't although my friends have asked me to go with them."

I nod slowly.

This *is* my life and it hurts that my parents don't support me. With Alli, it's a challenge. "I don't usually watch old black and white television shows, and you don't usually watch football. So—"

"You didn't watch the whole show."

"Is that an invitation?"

A tiny dent appears between her brows. "If I watch a game?"

I nod. "I'll message you next week."

"You don't have my phone number."

"Do you have Instagram?"

"Yeah. Alli Bradley."

I lean closer. Her eyes change to a knowing look that I'm going to kiss her. I do, only her cheek. Like a friend. "Good night, Alli Bradley."

"Good luck for tomorrow," she says quickly.

I turn and smile. "I won't need it if I know you're watching." I hit the doorway twice waiting for her to say she will.

Nothing.

"See you next week," I say and close the door behind me.

CHAPTER 6

ALLI

Four days post-Brisbane, and I'm standing in the kitchen and not at all expecting his message—on Instagram.

Darcy: *Hey, what are you doing? Just finished training and considering what to have for dinner. Thought maybe we should do it together, some time...*

I watched the highlights of his game because I was too stubborn to watch it live. Too cautious to allow Carli to notice my sudden interest in football. Every night since, I wait for the evening sports news hoping I'll catch a glimpse of him. Something in Brisbane changed my opinion. Whether it's what Carli had said resonated, or the fact Darcy made the effort to come to my room and talk about what happened between us, but my guard has lessened.

Me: *I heard your team is doing well.*

Darcy: *Did you watch the game?*

Me: *Only the highlights. Have you watched any Lucy reruns?*

Darcy: *Desi Junior's band is cool.*

Now I know he's messing with me. Anyone can Google it.

Me: *Impressive. My friend is organising tickets. I'm a quick learner so don't get ahead of yourself.*

Darcy: *Are you talking about football?*

Me: *Just stating a fact.*

Darcy: *A dirty fact?*

My breath catches.

Me: *No. Friends don't talk dirty.*

It takes a few seconds for his next message to come through.

Darcy: *This weekend is the last home game before the finals series, and our game is already sold out. If you haven't purchased tickets, the only way you'll get any is through someone like me. But there's a price.*

Nice try.

Me: *My friend, Paige, has tickets. If not, I'm sure she's willing to pay.*

Darcy: *Not what I'm thinking.*

Me: *This is getting confusing.*

Darcy: Dinner. You and me.

Me: *A date?*

Darcy: *A guy can only take so much waiting to be asked.*

Me: *You were waiting for me to ask you out?*

I pause before sending it because he has me stumped. Stumped since I readily lowered my guard and allowed him to permeate my walls to giving him a chance. A chance not to break my heart.

Me: *Just dinner. Talk soon.*

Friday night I finish work and renege on cooking dinner. Instead, I head out to a noodle bar for take-out with a need to curl up on the lounge with a woollen blanket in front of the television and eat dinner.

I curse for not using the bathroom at home because I can longer ignore the urge to cross my legs, so I don't pee myself. I order my favourite dish then dart around the tables toward the back of the restaurant. Feeling somewhat relieved, I head back to the waiting area. Out the corner of my eye, I recognise

Darcy's rustled brown hair and his solid frame beneath a blue shirt. His back is to me, yet there's no doubt in my mind it's him, and not sure how I missed him before. My breath catches, now a normal response when I see him, in person or on the screen. I slow up, so I can assess his dinner guest.

A guy, smaller in stature, olive-skinned, and dark hair. He looks much younger than Darcy. It's not my intention to interrupt, then my legs take me to his table on their own accord.

"Hey."

Darcy turns, his hand clutching the knife on the table. His frown tells me I have interrupted something. "Alli."

"I ordered take-out and saw you." I smile, and yet he's scowling. I look to his friend whose eyes are bloodshot.

"Not a good time, Alli."

"I'm sorry. I didn't mean to intrude." He nods and says nothing more. I step away giving them space, wishing to disappear. I spy my meal in a plastic bag with my name scribed on paper stuck to it on the counter. Thanking the waiter, I grab it and head for the door. A fool to believe Darcy would be excited to see me. Whatever was going on between them looked important, yet they were in a public place, so how bad could it be? And friends don't act that way toward each other.

It would never have gone this far if I didn't read the text from Nate.

Shit. Nate.

I glance at the clock on the dash, and with a quick calculation, note it's late morning in London. So, after eating my Thai noodles, I pick up the phone and wait for the dial tone to make the distant noise connecting overseas.

"Alli," he says warmly. "How are you?"

"Great." I focus on the ocean landscape canvas on the living room wall, one of Nate's works. "Congratulations. I'm sorry I've taken so long to call."

"I got your message and knew you'd call soon, and I didn't want to wake you not knowing your roster."

"Paige tells me Rebecca's perfect for you."

"Yeah, I really want you to meet her. I think you'll love her."

"I'm disappointed I couldn't take time off to go with Paige. I'm not sure when I'll get holidays. Maybe February?"

"That's only five months away. Start saving."

I laugh. "I'm weighing up whether to have a week in Thailand around then since I get cheap flights. I could spend a week there and a couple with you?" The line falls silent. "Nate?"

"Rebecca mentioned something about going to Thailand as well. It gave me an idea."

"What sort of an idea?"

"Let me run it past Rebecca first."

Hell, she's already running his life. "Sure. Have you called Pop?"

"How are they?"

"The same." I hate there's a wall between Nate and Pop. "He would love to hear from you."

"Okay… I have to go. Stay in touch, Alli."

I imagine I'm looking straight into Nate's understanding brown eyes like I did as a little girl when I needed reassurance. "Sure."

"Love you, Al-girl."

My eyes close momentarily feeling the love of a family member who offers security. "Love you, Nate-bear."

Nate's photography lines my living room walls, and even by staring at the prints, it reminds me of him, but it does nothing to absolve my loneliness. The house creaks the eerie quiet of being on your own. Times like this I dislike living by myself.

My first flight in the morning is scheduled at seven, and the last thing I want is to sleep. I physically can't run after a meal, though I can walk and push weights. So, I change, grab my keys, and head to the gym, to a place where I feel safe.

Saturday morning I make an espresso and open Instagram on my phone. I scroll through images of health food, selfies of girls revealing weight loss, and snaps of the previous night parties. I swipe to the photos I took this morning while jogging along the beach. I choose an image of the ocean with the jetty in the background, and in perfect timing, the sun had peeked through cloud cover to reflect light on the sea.

Allibradley
Spring is here #sunshine #beachrun
#perfectdayforfootball

Before I close the app, I check my notifications.

Darcy_rayne23 is now following you.

I'm still staring at the screen when another notification pops up.

Darcy_rayne23 liked your photo.

A small thing, and yet a part of me hopes it's a step to being more than friends, since out of his one million followers, he only follows three-hundred people.

DARCY

I'm smiling after reading:

Allibradley is now following you.

Temptation is there, yet I force myself to close my phone because distraction is the last thing I need before a game. My first instinct was to message Alli and apologise for the other night, but I can't deal now. I'll see her tonight. A voice in the back of my head reminds me she won't be happy. How was Alli to know my goddamn teammate virtually fucked up his career, and I was the first person he confided in? He was bloody crying—in public—and I was about to suggest we leave when Alli walked up at the worst possible timing.

Focus on the game.

I slip my phone in my back pocket when it vibrates.

Heather Nelson calling...

Talking to Heather is not something I care for before a match, yet her fundraiser is important to me since my cousin lost his kid at six months of age and only two years ago.

"Heather."

"Hi, Darcy, hope I haven't caught you at a bad time?"

"Nope."

"Great," she says in a high voice. "I wanted to let you know everything is set for the fundraiser in two weeks. I know you could be playing finals, and as much as I pray the Thunder make it, I also hope you can still attend the ball as our ambassador.

"You know SIDS is something I feel strongly about, and I'll be there if I don't have a game interstate. If we win today, and next week, then a home game will be likely. So..."

"Okay. Well, good luck for today."

"Thank you."

"I'll email you the agenda of the night. I'll send the details."

"Do that."

"Thanks again, Darcy."

Before I switch my notifications to the *Do Not Disturb* setting, there's a message from my sister, Clare.

> **Clare:** *Good luck, bro. Will be watching your game. xoxo*

She has been at boarding school in Melbourne the past year, and leaving home at only fourteen, she had to grow up fast.

> **Me:** *Thanks, kiddo. Catch up next time I'm in your stomping ground.*

This time I switch my phone to silent before repositioning my headphones to listen to my pregame playlist and lose my thoughts to the music.

CHAPTER 7

ALLI

"They're actual supporters?"

Paige nods. "He kicked it out on the full." She eyes me like I should understand the player wearing number six deserves to be yelled at. "Fans are passionate, and they want the Thunder to win. So, when Bailey does something good, then they'll cheer him on like a hero."

"Right." Not really. "And you know all their names that correspond to their numbers."

She grins at me.

The way fans scream, I'll memorise the players that mess up the quickest. The ball is thrown in from the boundary line, and Darcy taps it to a guy who barely reaches his waist. He takes off like the wind and kicks it toward the goal posts. Another player, number sixteen, marks it, and the noise level of cheering turns deafening. When number sixteen kicks the goal, the sound effects of a storm fill the entire oval. The crowd erupts, and I'm filled with excitement. I check the score, and the Thunder is only two points behind.

My heart skips a beat every damn time Darcy goes near the ball. I'm afraid he'll get hurt, which is unlikely given he's the biggest player on the field. He handles the ball sharp, and fast, which surprises me given his height. Naively, I assumed tall people to be clumsy as though their centre of gravity struggles to find an axis. Then again, I'm not acquainted with many athletes, and these elite footballers proved to be the opposite with more balance and grace than someone half their size. Darcy's height doesn't impede his skill and agility. In fact, his height attributes to him being a greater force out there. He wins the tap, and I cheer my heart out along with the crowd. Even clap enthusiastically because it honestly helps the blood flow to my fingers. It's a winter sport. I'm colder from nerves.

My eyes find the tattoos on his shoulders and upper arms which are hidden beneath his T-shirt. A need grows inside me to trace the outline, study the art and the beauty of the ink. Unlock the secrets to why Darcy wanted these particular images and what they mean to him. He stops and stands like a warrior amongst the men in a protective stance, a leader overseeing his squadron.

When the umpire makes the next boundary throw in, Darcy leaps into the air and simultaneously his opponent jumps from behind, digging knees into Darcy's back. Darcy goes down.

I gasp. "He's hurt."

"He's fine, it happens all the time," Paige says without looking at me.

The trainers run out to help him. Three of them discuss something before Darcy turns and heads toward the bench.

"He's having a rest," Paige says quickly as though its obvious to her, yet she needed to inform me before I panic further. "They'll check him out, and he'll be back on in a minute."

As Paige predicts, Darcy returns to the field and heads toward the goal. "What the hell, he's not rucking?"

"Because he's hurt?" I'm studying him for any signs.

"Doubt it. The coach has swapped him to full forward."

The game clock has reached the final minute, and neither team has scored after several attempts. Number six—Bailey—kicks the ball, and the crowd cheers. *Now* they like him. The ball spins in the air. Before anyone shouts blame at Bailey for the bad kick, Darcy leaps from behind a pack of players and marks the ball. Supporters fly out of their seats waving teal-coloured flags. Along with everyone else, I'm clapping as hard as my palms can bear and cheering loud.

Then silence falls across the stands. Darcy holds his lower back briefly before walking back with the ball. He pulls up both his socks before lining himself up at an angle in front of the goals.

I swallow a nervous lump in my throat and grab hold of Paige's arm. "Can he do it?"

Paige stalls a minute. "He can. Though, at this point of the game, there's more pressure riding on it."

"How does he handle pressure?" By the way I'm trembling I have no idea how to manage the adrenaline pumping through my veins.

Paige turns and smiles. "Usually, well." I nod, and then we both turn our focus back to Darcy.

"Come on, Doc," a supporter calls out.

Darcy holds the ball in front of his thighs and runs several paces before dropping the ball onto his boot and kicking it high into the air. My knees tap together. My fists squeeze tight. I watch the ball sail toward the white posts. The crowd behind the goals erupts first, waving flags high. Supporters leap from their seat. Paige screams. She grabs hold of my arm with both her hands and jumps up and down, and then I'm bouncing with her, realisation setting in.

"They won," I yell at her.

"Yes," she screams.

I glance across the ground and spot a flag.

CALL THE DOCTOR.

"What's with the doctor references?"

She smiles. "Darcy Rayne? His initials…. DR."

I shake my head understanding the expectation put on him a little more.

The city is alive with fans spilling out onto the streets, too excited to go home after their team has won. By ten o'clock I'm ready to call it a night and head home. Fatigued from the emotional day and now overtired to wait any longer for Darcy to message and meet up. Paige had explained the post-game commitments when a team wins. It didn't ease the disappointment, and any later would classify as a booty call. I remind myself of what I have planned for tomorrow. A morning run, then I'm visiting Gran, and to Pop's later to help with cleaning—if he allows me. Paige understands my commitments, so I leave to catch an Uber home.

I arrive home, change for bed, and almost done with removing makeup when my phone pings with an Instagram message.

Darcy: *You hungry?*

Me: *Why?*

Darcy: *I have two yiros and thought you'd like one.*

Quite the joker.

Me: *Pass. I'm going to bed. Catch you later.*

Darcy: *Text me your address.*

Me: *Another time...*

Darcy: *Text me your address. I have something to tell you.*

My fingers hover. I'm arguing with myself it's a booty call. The hopeful side of me is being positive reminding me we're friends and to send my details. Forget the other night, forget everything and talk to him because the fact is I *want* to see him, and it's overriding every other thought. Desire is already taking over. And now, I'm fast forward to thinking of having sex with him even if it's not his intention.

My thoughts spiral to it's what he wants, what he's coming for. The real test will be in the days to come.

I type out my address and hit send.

Only a few minutes pass before there's a knock. There's no way he could get here that fast.

At least I managed to clean my teeth.

With my foot behind the door, I open it a crack. "Happen to be in the neighbourhood?"

"Actually, yes." His smile grows. "Only two streets away." He places a hand on the door and pushes it wider. "I left the clubroom with the intention of going home. You crept into my thoughts and next minute I was in the car driving toward Glengowrie."

I shoot him a quizzical look.

"Another detail Carli shared. She didn't say anything else."

"Right." I'm undecided whether to be happy or mad with Carli.

His body heat shrouds me, and I'm vaguely aware of the cold night air seeping inside. "Come in before I freeze."

"I needed to apologise in person," he continues, following me inside.

I lock the door and walk toward the lounge. "I'm not going to pretend the other night was nothing."

"I can't explain everything. You'll hear about it in the papers soon enough. I wanted to reach over and smack him in the head. He has literally messed up his football career. I'm his captain. I was the first point of call."

I nod. "I knew the moment I saw your face something was wrong. The way you spoke to me—"

"I'm sorry."

"Thank you." We're close, and I need to put some space between us. "Can I get you a drink or something?"

"A water would be great, thanks."

I head to the kitchen while Darcy stands in the lounge. Looking over my shoulder, I notice him gazing at the walls, taking in my home. God, he looks too big for the small room.

"I like that you've left some of the original seventies décor. It suits."

"I have ideas for renovations but keep changing my mind." Not a complete lie. Renovations are not top of my priorities, especially if it means destroying happy memories.

He picks up a small white vase from the lamp table, and after a quick assessment, replaces it. The pottery vase is the first piece my grandmother helped me to make. Anyone else would consider it junk. To me it holds years of memories. He repositions it beside a glass frame. It catches his eye and lifts it closer for inspection. It's an old photo of my parents, Nate, and me. Taken the Christmas before my life changed forever. To a stranger, it's a normal family photo. I'm a little giddy with thoughts spinning about the fact he's in my private space, touching my private things, and I've allowed him to be here.

"Did you go to the game?" he asks while studying the image.

"I did." I reach and take a glass from the cupboard. Then I turn to observe his expression while he studies the photo.

"Did you enjoy it?" There's nervousness in his voice I don't understand.

I turn and simultaneously he looks away and repositions the photo on the table. "It was my first time and surprisingly, yes."

His eyes meet mine, and he smiles. "Where'd you sit?"

"Western grandstand. Near the front and out in the open so I'm glad it didn't rain."

He nods and looks away to the window as though he's in thought.

"You fell down not far from our seats. I was worried."

His brow pinches. "Worried?"

"Yeah."

He smiles, and it looks like he's genuinely amused.

"You must be sore after games."

"I'm used to it."

"So, why do you do it?" I whisper. "I mean why put your body through pain, and for years?"

"It's what I do. The aches are never as bad after a win. You should see me when I lose." There's slight humour to his tone. "Certain things soothe all aches."

"Like water?" I roll my eyes and hand him the glass.

He chuckles. "Not the first thing that comes to mind."

"Oh, you mean anti-inflammatory tablets and water." I grin at him then sit and flick on the television.

"I've been watching *I love Lucy* on *YouTube*." He sits beside me.

"Are you serious?"

"She's quite the comedian even though some lines are corny." His expression lights up as though he genuinely means it.

"Yeah. How can you not laugh?"

Reaching into his pocket, he pulls out his phone. A recently watched episode loading. "It reminded me of you?" Darcy is grinning, and for the life of me, I have no idea what he's talking about.

I scramble closer and mute the television before tossing the remote onto the coffee table in front. Darcy holds his phone so we both can see the screen.

I don't remember this episode.

The characters are training to be flight attendants, and Darcy laughs, winking at me. My gut rolls over in instinct I might not find humour in the same light as him. I can't help but smile at how Lucy helps a co-worker overcome her fear of heights. In the back of my mind it hits too close to home reminding me how Carli helped me get through the training and my first flight.

Lucy is excited at becoming a flight attendant because of the prospect of meeting famous people like sports stars. "Boom," Darcy says and chuckles.

Downing the remains of my glass, I push up from the couch and head to the kitchen to refill. "Obviously not why I decided to become one."

"Hey. I didn't play it to mock you. Thought you'd see the funny side."

"I do," I say unconvincingly and march into the formal lounge room.

Darcy follows. I turn and note how his gaze is fixed on my brother's photography. "Who took these?" he whispers, taking a step closer to inspect the signature.

"My brother. He lives in London."

Darcy straightens. He turns and cocks a brow. "Your brother is Nate Bradley?"

"Yeah, why?"

"I know him, know of him. A mate of mine knew Nate before he went to London. He went to school with him. When I moved to Adelaide, we got talking, and his name came up, so I checked out his website and bought some of his work."

"Really? What images, and who is your friend?"

"Mason Slater. He played footy for a while then quit. It was a Glenelg beach shot and the other a London skyline."

I vaguely remember Mason. Nate's friends are five years older than me, and he didn't bring them home to our grandparents' house. I never saw much of his friends after he moved out of our grandparents' home into this one. Then again, I didn't see much of Nate either when he partied at night and slept during the day.

I glance back at Darcy. His brow pinches, eyes searching.

"What's wrong?" I'm staring into his eyes only they're guarded, hiding his whirling thoughts. His Adam's apple bobs.

Something has changed in him.

"I've just realised," he whispers.

"What?"

"Your parents were killed in a plane crash." His voice is guarded, and his tight expression throws me off kilter.

"It was a long time ago." I manage to keep my voice level. I return to the other room, to the couch and sit, grateful to turn my back and hide my expression. It's my turn to be guarded and not at the memory. More the fact he's waiting for me to react as though I'm being judged.

Even when the grief subsided, I never really came out of the anger stage. Anger for my parents getting on that plane when I cried for them not to go without me. Hell, it sounds selfish, but I was only ten. I didn't know how to handle the anger, so I shut it down with the overwhelming sadness. And now, frustration because people act like there's something wrong with *me* when they find out. Study my reaction with curiosity waiting for my emotions to crack. For Darcy to act cautious causes that damn ball of emotion to grow in my throat.

He walks over and sits beside me.

"I don't remember a lot about the accident, only how it affected everyone. Especially my grandparents. My Gran helped me through some tough days."

He retrieves his phone from the couch between us. The image paused on the screen.

"We used to watch the shows together. She helped me to overcome my fear of flying and insisted I become a flight attendant. So, this episode," I shake my head. "Anyway, I'm surprised you even watched any of the shows."

"Where is she now?"

I clear my throat. "In a nursing home."

"She sounds like an amazing lady."

"She is." We sit a moment in silence.

Springing to my feet, I grab the remote and point it to the television. I'm standing only feet from Darcy. "Any requests?"

He slides forward on the sofa. "I should go," he says sounding torn. "I have an early morning beach session."

He's not looking at me. His gaze is fixed dead centre at my navel. My hand lifts and rests to where his gaze burns the skin peeking out between my top and PJ shorts.

He lifts his hands and places them on my hips with enough pressure for me to take a step closer.

I want to guide his face so he's looking up at me. Only he leans closer before I do. He places a soft kiss on my stomach. My skin tingles, and the muscles beneath tighten. I gasp when he repeats the kiss, slower this time. I can't help the sigh that slips out. Large hands tighten and pull me close enough to give my lower abs more attention. More caressing with his tongue and his mouth. My hands grip his hair. I should tell him to stop...

Seconds pass.

His forehead rests on my stomach like he's apologetic. Until the tie of my PJ's loosens as he tugs. Darcy tilts his head and his heated gaze meets mine. We still for a moment, both held captive by the other's gaze. The moment he sees desire in my eyes, his fingers slip under the band and guide my shorts to my mid-thigh. I squeeze his shoulders, and he pauses. Anticipation fills the air. He's waiting for a signal. He's looking so deep I feel his eyes searching mine, and it takes my breath away. Hell, my vagina is throbbing with need. I want this. *Tonight* I want this, and I'm letting go of any inclination there'll be regret tomorrow.

I give a signal, a quick nod and wiggle to step out of my shorts. Instantly, his mouth is on my clit, sucking, licking, kissing. My knees threaten to give way as pleasure courses through my body, stronger tingles shooting up through my abdomen. "Oh," I moan, my knees weakening with every touch.

Darcy nudges my legs wider, his fingers teasing my entrance. He tilts his head, finds my gaze, and watches my expression while his fingers slide all the way in. "Je-sus, Alli."

I inhale sharply and murmur his name. Those long fingers are strong enough to take the impact of a football as it powers through the air. Strong hands that block an opposing tackle. Hands holding so much power tear at the flimsy seam binding me together. My breath sharpens, and I'm about to come when he lifts my leg and places it over his shoulder.

I'm vulnerable and yet, I'm floating in the most exquisite pleasure I've ever known. My hands fist his hair to keep myself from collapsing as colours burst in front of my eyes. He pulls me onto his lap as my legs give way.

I'm straddling him with my head buried into his shoulder, panting and trying gather a coherent thought. I go to move and feel the length of him between my legs.

"Do you want to take this to the bedroom?" he whispers in my ear.

"No." I don't want to think beyond tonight. The bed would make it *more.* "Here. Now."

He pushes up easily even with my weight on him, and he balances me beside him, letting go to retrieve a condom from his pocket.

"Really?" I say, still out of breath.

"I suck at being friends," he says with no remorse.

He unzips his fly, and his large erection springs free. It's relative to his height, but I've never been with a guy as tall as Darcy, and the sheer size of his cock is a little frightening. I knew he had a reputation, and now it all makes sense. I yank off my top while he rolls the condom along the length of him.

He pauses a moment, and before he removes any clothing, I jump into his arms and straddle him.

"You're so fucking sexy," he rasps.

His words surprise me. I kiss him hard, a primal need. He carries me a few steps to the wall and pushes my back against it for support.

"Lower your self a little," he says against my lips.

"What?" I whisper.

"Use your abs and tilt your pelvis down."

I let go, and with one hand, press between us to feel for his cock. Holy hell, it's near my anus. Right now I'm grateful to my gym routine. I hoist a little and change my angle and slowly lower myself until I feel him. I gasp when the head of his cock touches me. Darcy takes his hands from my waist to under each thigh. My legs spread further, and then he pushes all the way inside.

I scream out, a combination of pleasure and pain. I tighten my hands not allowing myself to lower further.

"Are you okay," he asks.

I open my eyes and see genuine concern.

"Yes," I gasp. "Don't let me slip lower than this."

His brow lifts a little, and his concerned expression is replaced with a serious sexual glare. Large hands tighten around my thighs. He presses his lips to mine and kisses me, and nothing like the night at the club. I pant with every thrust, moan with all the sensations filling my entire body right down to my toes. I climax quickly and feel every orgasm blend with the next because he doesn't slow, only pumps harder and faster until my body becomes soft as jelly.

"Alli."

I open my eyes.

He smacks my butt.

"Alli, lift."

My hands grip his shoulders to stop myself from slipping further. "Do you want me to keep going?"

"Yes," I croak.

Never has my vagina ached and desired more. More of the ecstasy is shooting to my core in spasms. He switches his movement, pinning me against the wall. His hips are relentless, pounding into me again and again. Wet lips find mine, and his tongue caresses deeper. He's claiming my body, fucking me in a way I'll remember for days.

He stops then curses before shuddering to a still, forcing his cock deeper inside. Resting his head on my shoulder, his chest expands with every breath.

"I'm slipping," I warn and grip his T-shirt harder. "And why are you still dressed?"

He chuckles and plants a quick kiss on my lips. "Because you never gave me a chance."

His cock is inside of me, still hard. He carries me to the sofa and allows my legs to touch the cushions before I slide off him. I cringe a little at the pain. He walks into the kitchen and disposes of the condom. Only now I realise his jeans sit mid-thigh. He was clothed. And I naked. I sit and reach for my PJ bottoms.

"Don't even think about it," he warns.

He rips his T-shirt over his head, and I'm mesmerised by his exceptional physique—bulging pectoral muscles that angle his nipples slightly south, chiselled abs you want to caress with your tongue, and biceps that ripple with every movement.

"Lie down."

I tilt my head in question, and yet I do what he asks. He kneels beside the sofa and lifts my leg before lowering his face to the part throbbing like a bitch.

"I don't think I can—"

"I know." Like the night at the club, his kiss is gentle alternating between blowing gently and soft kisses to soothe my labia and clit. My hand goes to my throat because even the slightest touch is arousing me beyond the pain. My breaths turn heavy again. His tongue runs along the length of my sex.

"Relax." After a few minutes I do, and he settles beside me, kissing my inner thigh, making a trail to my navel where he had started.

"What do your tattoos signify?" I croak, needing to distract my thoughts. Flames circle one bicep. The other arm has my interest as the ink work is unique.

"It's a Celtic symbol." He says it quickly before his lips are back to kissing.

"For what?" I whimper.

He reaches for the throw rug and places it over me. "Are you cold."

"I blame you for the goosebumps. And don't avoid the question."

He smiles, pats my feet, and I lift them to rest on his lap. "Inner strength, something like that."

The question burns, he who is the ultimate symbol of power, who or what made him weaker?

I let it go only because I'm insanely sated, still floating in a cloud of sexual delirium. He snares the remote from the armrest and switches the channel to sports. The humdrum voice of the commentator enticing sleep. I close my eyes, unable to physically move, unable to recall if I had ever felt this way. Of course not. I'd remember it. Hold onto it like a bottled memory. In this moment, I don't care what will happen from here.

I wake with a jump when Darcy attempts to move beneath me.

"I need to lie down or go home," he whispers. "My legs are numb, and my back's aching where I was hit today."

"Of course," I murmur.

"It's okay." He smiles at me. "I can name worse things than you naked and asleep beside me."

All desire now tamed, I'm overcome with shyness. I tighten the throw around me and stand. "You can sleep here if you want..." I hesitate a little.

"It's fine. I need to be up early, so I'll head home."

He stands, pulls on his tee, and I follow him to the door. He leans in to kiss my lips, soft, and gentle. "I'll call you."

I nod and close the door behind him. It's what guys say. A standard goodbye line. It leaves you with hope after giving yourself to them. Calling is a step up from messaging. And yet, my hope fades because he can't call if he doesn't have my number.

And he didn't ask for it.

CHAPTER 8

ALLI

My grandfather lives between the Bay and the city, and fortunately, Gran's nursing home is only a few kilometres from his home.

Pulling into Pop's driveway, a figure catches my eye in the garden. My heart melts a little seeing him bending to pick daffodils and daisies. He glances up when he hears the car.

"G'day, love."

"Are you picking those for Gran?"

"Yeah, I am." He straightens, and I notice how his trousers hang loose over his hips and pucker around his waist, pulled tight with a belt.

"How are you?" I plant a kiss on his cheek and give him a quick hug.

"Not bad for an old fella. Come inside. I'll make a cuppa before we go."

Pop sounds oddly chirpy. I follow him inside to the kitchen, the benches stacked with dirty dishes. "You get the tea, and I'll make a start on these," I offer, knowing how Pop hates washing dishes. I take the opportunity to take a quick look around. Everything else appears tidy and clean, a good sign.

I finish the dishes before Pop pours cups of tea, and then I sit with him at the dining table.

"Are you cooking meals?" There were plenty of dishes, yet none were pots and most had crumbs. Crumbs more evident around the toaster. "You know I can make double and freeze them for you."

He raises an eyebrow. "You eat salad, and I like my meat and mashed veg. And none of the stir-fry or raw vegetable stuff."

"Raw stuff is good for you, and it happens to also taste good. It beats toast."

We sip tea quietly. "How is Gran?"

He looks at me with the cup pressed to his lips. His grey eyes glisten before he looks away. My grandfather is a tough man. I've never seen him cry. As days and weeks pass, I'm not blind to his demeanour wearing thin.

"Evelyn didn't remember me again yesterday."

I reach across the table and touch his hand. Sometimes Gran forgets our names, although she knows we're family. "She recognises our faces, just can't remember our names." Not completely true, but I can't allow him to lose all hope.

Pop shakes his head, keeping his gaze on the table. "She looked at me like I was a stranger. I showed her our wedding photos and a photo of Nate and you," he pauses. "She looked afraid."

My stomach turns. I take another sip of tea and hope today is a better day. Two years ago, Gran suffered vertigo after contracting a nasty virus and fell. She fractured her hip and didn't recover. She walked with a limp and needed assistance to get around. Her Alzheimer's became more noticeable and Pop was advised to place her in care. At her age, Alzheimer patients deteriorate not improve, so all we can do is pray each day is not that day.

Fifteen minutes later, we pull into the car park of the Blue Skies Nursing Home. It's a beautiful cream brick building of three levels, built around a central courtyard. The nurse leads us into the courtyard lined with roses at the back, lavender bushes through the centre, and flowering annuals bordering the grass. This time of year, the scent of sweet peas and the lavender waft into the air helping to calm the patients.

Dressed in a floral dress and a lilac cardigan, Gran sits under the shade of a tree. A white hat and glasses protect her face from the sun. A nurse is seated beside her observes the folding of dishtowels.

"Hello, Gran," I say, bending to kiss her on the cheek. "May I take these off for a minute?" I remove the sunglasses to get a glimpse of her eyes. If she's afraid, I'll see it. "Are you helping the nurse?"

"Yes. We've had a busy morning." She glances up and smiles. She keeps her gaze on me and rubs the side of her face. I know she needs a minute to remember.

"Did Gran eat breakfast this morning?" I ask the nurse in a softer voice.

"Yes. Most of her scrambled egg."

I nod. Gran needs supervision as she forgets to eat. Her plate of food may be in front of her, but it doesn't necessarily mean she will feed herself. Pop endeavours to be at the nursing home for most meals so he can encourage Gran to eat.

The nurse stands and picks up the pile of towels. "I'll return later, Mrs Bradley."

I pull another chair closer to Gran and sit beside her. "It's okay, Gran, it's me, Aaliyah." I pick up her hand and rub it gently. "I've been working. I'm a flight attendant."

Her eyes flicker across my face. "My son was killed in a plane crash in North Carolina. He and his wife died. So tragic." Her blunt voice takes my breath away. I study her expression for grief or distress and find nothing, only emptiness behind her eyes.

Pop's mouth gapes, and the flowers fall forward in his grasp. He remains tight-lipped, and I wonder if Gran has said other things to him the past few days. We never talk about that fatal flight as Pop believes it causes unnecessary stress on the family only to relive the nightmare over.

"Yes. My mother and father."

Gran makes a tsk sound. Then her expression changes like a window shutter. "He was my son."

I exhale and nod.

She turns to Pop. "Our son."

Pop kneels beside her. "Yes, love. We took care of his children, Aaliyah and Nathaniel." Pop pats my hand.

Gran nods, and her gaze switches to mine. In it is the warmth I remember. "Alli."

My eyes burn holding back tears. "Yes, Gran, I'm Alli. You have been taking care of me since I was ten, and now I'm helping Pop take care of you."

It's after six when I arrive home.

Instead of preparing dinner, I slip into my training gear and run out of the house. I don't stop running until I can barely breathe. I slow to a walk, shaking like it was my first time running and my body isn't use to it. Emotion can do that. Zap your energy. Today was a good day compared to others, but

Gran had an episode right before I left. A reminder of how quickly she can deteriorate. I was lost on how to help her. It was heart-wrenching to witness her fear. The staff insisted we leave because her meds would help her to sleep. We called into the shops on the way home, and I bought lamb chops. I cooked enough meat and vegetable dishes to last Pop three days.

I want to cry thinking about it, so I place my hands behind my head to open my chest and ease the tightness. Walking home, I consider ways to help Pop and dedicate my free days to supporting him.

In the shower I'm careful not rub my tender bits. Today Darcy sprang to mind every time I sat, though, but I had too much going on to give him more thought than that.

The more I thought, the more I acknowledged he wouldn't give out his number without consideration to his sexual partners because I'm sure he would be harassed by some. In hope of not being inconsequential, I checked my phone several times for confirmation he tried to contact me.

This time when I check there's an Instagram message.

Darcy: *How are you feeling today?*

It's the validation I need.

Me: *Sore*

I'm not going to say fine because I'm not fine. And I assume he's not asking about my day.

My cheeks warm thinking about the night.

Last night…

A smile eases onto my face remembering I slept the entire night.

Darcy: *Are you up for a second round tonight?*

No, I reply quickly.
I don't hit send.
I delete it.

Me: *Yes. But not tonight.*

He didn't call. He asked for more sex.
And I don't care because there is still hope.
Hope.
Not regret.

CHAPTER 9

ALLI

First flight of the day and a passenger has already managed to get me riled.

From the moment the seat-belt sign switched off, he pressed the call bell like room service in a hotel. Every five minutes he demanded something, even alcohol—even though it was only seven in the morning—and extra food. Now he wants a blanket as the air-conditioning is too cold. Not once did he utter a single please or thank you.

My final leg ends in Melbourne, and I have ten hours before tomorrow's shift. Considering the hotel is across from the airport, fair to say I won't be enjoying the city. At least Carli also worked the same flight. It's time I fill her in on Darcy.

"You want to meet in the hotel's restaurant for dinner?" Carli asks as we tidy the kitchen area.

"Sure. Then I'm relaxing in the spa." Anything to soothe my aching feet.

After completing an aisle and seat check, we grab our overnight case and head out of the terminal to the transport bus waiting to take us and other cabin crew to the hotel.

As soon as I reach my room, I shower and dress in navy trousers and a white bell-sleeve top before meeting Carli downstairs. Within minutes of being seated, Carli's conversation is all Michael.

"He's already planning for us to go to Bali together," she exclaims.

My eyes widen. "You've only known each other—"

"Over a month," she finishes. "I know…" she shrugs, "… he's the one. He's right for me." She sips her glass of sav blanc slowly. "What about you? Anything with Mr Darcy?"

"I slept with him on Saturday night."

Her mouth falls open. Before she has a chance to respond, Emma, our senior, strolls up to our table. "Sunday night is the gala fundraiser for the Banking Corporation section of our airline. We're a major sponsor and have tickets to the event to support the fundraiser. Every year we support a different cause and book out a dozen tables. Considering both you girls are rostered off on Sunday, I thought I'd offer you an invitation to attend as we have two seats available after recent cancellations…" she pauses. "It's a formal evening meaning formal attire. You will be representing the airline," she adds with emphasis.

"Yes," Carli almost squeals. "It would be an honour."

Emma turns her gaze on me. "Yes," I say feeling obligated to sound upbeat.

"Good. I'll email the information." Then she turns on her heels not wanting further conversation.

Carli's grin reaches her ears. "I've always wanted to attend these galas. And it will be my first formal event with Michael."

Emma did not mention partners. "He can have my ticket."

Carli tilts her head. "I thought it included a plus one?"

"I doubt it." Carli shoots me a look. "What?"

"I thought you'd be glowing after one night with Darcy, but you seem upset. You've been in a mood all day and that poor passenger—"

"Are you serious? And, I thought you'd want to know more about what happened."

She shrugs. "I've heard the rumours. Know he's well endowed." She winks. "The problem now is will anyone else live up to him?"

"You're talking like it's one night."

"Was it?"

"He came to my house. He..." I rub my forehead. "Maybe it's why I'm on edge."

"*You* should go to the ball. It will be fun and might cheer you up." She raises her wine glass as though she has found the answer to all my problems. "And you should ask Darcy..."

"Formal events are not my thing. Besides, I was hoping to spend the day with my grandparents not waste hours getting spruced up."

Carli nods although her expression tells me she's not convinced. "How are they, really?"

I signal to the waiter for more wine before I answer.

I turn off the iron and start to prepare a salad with chickpeas for dinner.

With the salad bowl in my lap, I position myself on the couch ready to watch *Outlander*. I enjoyed the books and am excited for the series, and redheaded Jamie is the perfect remedy to take my mind off Darcy.

I'm still thinking about the episode as the credits roll when my phone beeps with an Instagram message.

Darcy: *I want to see you tonight*

My breath hitches seeing his name yet I don't have the energy for what Darcy expects, and star fishing isn't my style.

Me: *Been a tough few days. Just got home. Eating dinner then going to bed. Good luck for your game on Saturday. I'm working, though I will try to check the score.*

I turn as *Outlander's* opening song puts a smile on my face.

Darcy: *I'm at your front door.*

A quiet knock confirms it. "What the..." I glance down at my legs in my oldest yet most comfortable track pants with holes in the knees.

I open the door, and Darcy holds out a bunch of flowers. Before taking them, I watch his gaze travel over me. "Dressed for a night in. Perfect."

I take a whiff. "Thank you. I have to ask, why the flowers?"

"Something tells me you were impulsive the other night. I wanted to show you I could also be impulsive."

"It hardly equates." I close the door behind him. "I give you my body, and you give me flowers."

He chuckles and takes a seat on the couch while I find a vase. "The flowers are also a thank you."

"Meaning?"

"For trusting me. I know it must have been hard for you to open up to me."

Oh. "So these are not about giving you the best sex of your life?" I shoot him a questionable look.

Darcy laughs quietly. "Maybe it's why I'm wanting more."

"Like I said not—"

"I know."

"So, I take it you're keen to watch more Lucy?" He pulls back a little, and I want to laugh but don't. I place the remote on the table. "Your choice."

His gaze lowers, and it sends a shiver down my spine. One finger runs along the length of my arm. "Are you proposing something?"

"I'm open for suggestions as long as it entails leaving my clothes on." Darcy's lips curl. "And yours."

His brow rises taking on its own personality. "Like a board game?" Darcy's tone is challenging. I can sense the confidence, a touch of humour, yet there's something else.

"Are you afraid to lose?"

He holds my gaze. "I don't take favour to any kind of losing."

"You play a game where every week there is a winner and a loser. You haven't spent your life winning at everything."

He leans back, his gaze still holding mine captive. "No. But I have spent my life doing everything in my power not to lose."

"Sounds like an addiction." I look away. "Is that why you're afraid to fall in love?"

"Why would you ask that?"

His tone demanded my attention. "I've never heard of you being with anyone more than a night. And you're practically saying you hate failing at anything. I assumed it includes relationships. No chance of failing at love if you're not committed to someone." I lower my gaze. "My friends can't recall you having a girlfriend either."

"Sounds like it's a topic of conversation." I don't miss the frustration in his voice. "I'm a private person when it comes to my personal life, so you won't see it on social media. I don't go into a relationship with a fear of failing. It's about trust and knowing who's right for you. Who can go the distance, share and enjoy the same things as you. It's two way, so the responsibility isn't all mine."

I nod.

"And since we're being blunt, I have been in love before."

I remain silent.

"A long time ago. And it's something I chose not to talk about." His shoulders rise and fall. "What about you?"

"Nope," I say nonchalantly.

"Yet, you hook up."

This time I frown. "Not often."

"We both have walls up for different reasons."

He's managed to turn it on me. "I don't have walls up. I can't help it if Mr Right hasn't magically appeared into my busy schedule on planes or in nursing homes or in cemeteries." My voice rises a little. His eyes are surveying me, and I'm doing my best not to give him anything, struggling to keep a deadpan expression. "I'm not a lot of fun to be around."

"And that's why I can't keep away because you're no fun."

I know the humour is supposed to cheer me a little, but I call him out. "Sex is sex. Fun as in defining my personality."

"You have a sense of humour. Your sarcasm makes me laugh. Not always when it's directed at me."

The walls I pretend don't exist melt a little. "You hardly know me."

He takes my hand and interlocks our fingers. A small gesture, and yet it's enough to speed up my heart. "Like you, I'm too busy to meet many people."

I snort. "Except for the female company you keep every week."

"I thought *you* would understand loneliness even when surrounded by people." His eyes appear somewhat bluer tonight, and I'm captivated by a sense of innocence, the dark lashes lowering as though he's shielding part of him from me.

"Loneliness can stem from losing someone you loved. I feel like I'm going through it again with my Gran. It's like my heart is a ticking time bomb. Waiting to be shattered again. Is that what you mean you understand me? Is it how your life is?" He frowns. The words are harsher than I intended. "Do you still have your family?" I ask in a softer voice.

Darcy turns away. "Yeah. I'm not close to my parents…"

He draws away from me. The hand holding mine releases and rubs the back of his neck.

"Why not?" I whisper.

"I moved interstate at eighteen. Ten years of living away and rarely seeing family puts space in a relationship."

"You have an offseason. Surely, you go home?"

He glances up to the ceiling. The hand behind his neck acting as a support brace. "Not for long."

He's pulling away from me, and the last thing I want is to make him uncomfortable because I know how that feels. So, I decide not to ask any more family-related questions.

"I was expecting how-many-girlfriends questions, not family."

"Family is more important to me. I'm not interested in past girlfriends."

"Glad we got that sorted." He leans over and snares the remote. He finds the sports channels and stops on a football replay. "I need to watch a particular player, and I'll concentrate better with you in my arms."

It's a bad line, and we both know it. I don't care, yet I still pull a face at his line before sliding into open arms and leaning against his muscled chest. I close my eyes and allow the commentator's voice to drown out reality because all I can think about is how safe I feel wrapped up in Darcy.

DARCY

Ripping my sweaty socks from my feet, I shove them into my boots and with a déjà vu moment remember...

'You smell like a football locker room. Like old socks, the ones left months under the seat of a hot car growing a musky scent you can't rid.'

It's one of the last things *she* told me on the night we argued about football and the all my time football demanded. Add the aroma of liniment, and ironically locker rooms are the place I feel most at home.

Yet, last night I felt at home. It wasn't so much where I was but who I was with. The balance changing, the pendulum swinging, and I'm thinking less about *her*, even after Alli asked about former loves. My insides fire up, muscles tighten acknowledging I *can't* change shit up. Not so late in a season. Everything needs to stay like it is for the next few weeks.

I need stability in my home. My team's home where dreams are nurtured, and ours so damn close to fruition, I can taste the nectar.

Leaning back against the wall, I watch Sambo and Jenks bump shoulders and chest with the younger blokes. A warrior dance after training when testosterone overcomes men in a confined space with the knowledge we will get a win. Tonight every Thunder player gave it their all out on the training field, and if we take this level of play to the game on Saturday, we will be heading straight to the Grand Final.

Everyone except Hadley.

My gut churns. A rash decision ruined his football career. No matter how much I told him to get his act straight, he thought he knew better, thought he was invincible. Untouchable. Three strikes, and you're suspended. Drugs are not tolerated and yet, so many dickheads play a fine line. Hadley is not a lone ranger, but hell, we are on the road to the Holy Grail. Instead, he will be defending himself to the media. Not to mention the lashing our club will receive. *Fuck*. I slump to the bench and reach for my training bag.

The timing sucks, but I can't linger on the bullshit. Something else much bigger is almost within reach.

So, why am I thinking about the night I listened to his sorry arse tell me how he gave a urine sample only hours after smoking a joint. It was strike two. It was the same night Alli strolled up to me in the restaurant eager to say hi.

Hadley didn't consider he would get tested again for at least a few months. Another misjudgement. A week later, three representatives from the anti-doping authority came to his home to test him a little after midnight. The dickhead was having a party to celebrate our win cementing top eight on the ladder, a finals berth, and cocaine was the preferred cocktail of the night. It angered me that someone must have tipped them off. Caught with a couple of friends and chicks half naked, the sports anti-doping authority had all the evidence they needed, especially photographs of the white powder dotting the tip of his nose.

First point of call was me.

Because fuck, I magically fix things.

No one could help Hadley this time, least of all me. Still, I contacted my lawyer and set him up to make sure he gets the help he needs, like many other fallen athletes. When the rug is pulled beneath you, when all the luxury and attention of being an elite football player vanishes, the loss of glory can send the best of us spiralling to rock bottom. I've seen it many a time over the ten years I've been at the club. It pisses me off our little chat did nothing to prevent it. Maybe I take more blame than I should in the matter. As captain, failing a teammate, I fail myself.

Jenks shouts, "Back yourself and believe," and the players around him repeat the chant. The comradeship brings me back to the room. This could be our first finals appearance in ten years, and Hadley blew his opportunity for a misguided night of fun.

My obligation now is to my teammates. To some of the blokes I'm the closest thing to a damn big brother because the club *is* our family.

My family.

Out of habit, I pull out my phone before heading to the shower and dislodge the horseshoe key ring sitting beside it. I stuff it back in the side pocket so it's safe. A cheap gift from Clare. It's worn shabby because, hell, its years old, only I'm not removing it and risking unnecessary bad luck when we're this close to making finals.

A new message lights up the screen, and surprisingly it's a missed call from my mother. A rare call. She sent me an apologetic text earlier, and I replied with a simple message.

> **Me:** *It's fine, Mum, I don't expect Dad and you to make it to the game.*

I open the new message.

> **Mum:** *Daniel and I will be in Melbourne on business starting the week before the final. I'm so excited to see you play, son. Call later.*

"Daniel," I snort. "Too hard to say, Dad?" I murmur. No interest in my football for years, and now my team is hitting national news, they want to support me. She, of all people, should understand my life after playing at an elite level in netball and basketball. I love my mother, but sometimes I'm sure she pretends not to notice the animosity between dad and me. My father is a stubborn man—the day he told me football was a thug's game, I lost all respect for him.

"My life, and I'll make my own choices," I had told him.

I was eighteen at the time, and, as a rookie, I was already the second tallest player in the national competition. From that day, albeit I was young, yet old enough to release, severing ties with my father may not have been the smartest move. He'll never support something he considers is detrimental to my future, even if I chose the path.

The phone vibrates in my hand, and I curse almost dropping it. Christ, it's my mother. She has no clue of my schedule.

"Mum," I say loud enough for her to hear me over the bustle, yet quiet enough not to attract attention from the guys.

"Darcy," she says affectionately. "Did you get my message?"

"I did."

"Oh, I'm so excited to see you play. It feels like years—"

"It has been, literally," I point out.

"You know how busy your father is." Her tone is sharp. "Well, it's worked out perfectly. He'll be in Melbourne on business, and we'll stay the weekend for the finals. You can get us tickets?"

It sounds more like a demand, like I owe them.

"Yeah. Shouldn't be a problem, after all, you *are* family," I say without holding back the sarcasm.

"Perfect, and the timing couldn't be better with your father flying out to Singapore the following week…" Mum's voice fades to the background when Jenks storms up to me, lurking.

"Is that the hot hostie you're banging?"

"Fuck off," I mouth. "Mum, I have to go. I only finished training moments ago and need to shower."

Jenks makes a strangled noise and laughs at me. "Bad luck, bro. Thought you were getting lucky." I want to fucking tackle him and shove his face into the smelly footy boots beside me.

"Sure, love. Keep me posted, won't you?"

"Yeah. See you soon." As if it has ever been a promise. I end the call and toss my phone onto the seat beside me. "Piss off, Jenks," I say when he comes at me. "I'm not in the mood."

He covers his dick with his hand and thrusts.

I glare at him and say nothing. Jenks shoots a knowing look as though he's hit the nail on the head because now I'm thinking about Alli.

Rubbing the base of my neck, I push out the latter and get my mind back to the present with the help of Coach announcing we have a meeting in half an hour.

For the next few weeks, I need to focus on everything football.

Nothing can get in the way of a premiership.

If I'm being honest, the closer I get to Alli, the more I'm losing focus, so for now, I'll take it slow. It's what I should do for her and my game. The way my dick twitches every time I think of her, it's going to be hard to stay away.

I curse for being weak and no better than Hadley.

Only the difference is I'm not prepared to fail.

CHAPTER 10

ALLI

When the last passenger disembarks, I switch on my phone.

My grandmother didn't raise me to be starry-eyed, yet the Instagram message has me swiping the screen hoping it's from Darcy.

Darcy: *Want pasta for dinner?*

Being a Friday night before the game, I didn't expect to hear from him especially with him mentioning a mandatory team meeting the night before a game.

Another message appears.

Darcy: *I'm leaving training now. Let me know if we're on tonight?*

I quickly type a response.

Me: *Just landed. Pasta sounds perfect.*

I'm alerted to Emma calling my name from the front of the plane. Grabbing my bag, I leave with the other hostesses, everyone chatting about their plans for the weekend. Some talk about football and their husbands. I keep a tight lip regarding Darcy.

"What are your plans, Alli?" Emma asks, walking through the gate and wheeling our suitcases behind.

"I'm scheduled on tomorrow then have two days off."

"Carli said you've given your ticket to her plus one," she says unamused.

"To Michael," I correct. "Because I hope to spend the day with my grandparents."

"We're *hoping* for staff to represent the airline. When you accepted the ticket, I didn't expect you to give it away. Please reconsider." Botox eyebrows make it hard for me to interpret if she's upset.

"Okay," I say, obligated, even though I have little desire to attend the ball.

We part ways, and I head for my car.

Before starting the engine, I send Darcy another message.

> **Me:** *Heading home now. Do you want me to cook? What time should I expect you?*

I start the car, and my phone beeps.

> **Darcy:** *Dinner at mine. I'll pick you up as parking is tricky. Be there in an hour.*

> **Me:** *I assume you'll be having an early night. Are you okay to drop me home?*

Without waiting for a reply, I drop my phone into my bag and pull onto the main road, and in a slight panic since I'll barely have time to change. Stuck behind a bus, I don't curse because I'm staring at a large poster image of Darcy's face and massive shoulders. Thick arms cross his muscled chest in a teal and black Thunder guernsey.

"It's just dinner," I whisper.

I arrive home and check Instagram for his reply.

Nothing.

When I close Instagram, there's a text message from an unknown number.

I start to read it, realising it's another emotional text.

A voice of reason inside my head warns me to stop reading it. I'm caught up in the heartbreak and can't stop my eyes from reading on.

> **Unknown:** *Remember when we told each other everything?*
> *Before...*
> *You used to talk about 'asking' the universe. Ask, and you will receive.*
> *I know you're here because something is guiding me. Hell, I sound crazy but only you of all people know what it is I want. What I have strived my entire adulthood to achieve. And yet, of late, part of me is questioning the sacrifice.*
> *So... have you asked the universe to shake shit up? Well, if it's your plan, you should know it's scaring the fuck out of me.*
> *You always said change is good for the soul.*
> *I disagreed.*
> *I'm learning to listen, and although I don't think of you as often, I still remember your words.*

And that's a good thing, right?
So, if this is you and your universe getting back at me,
then allow me a little time.
One more month.

The scarf around my neck feels tighter, and I pull at the knot to loosen it.

I want to help.

Even if that's by telling the sender they have the wrong number.

Not now because it will require delicate words and thought.

And not when Darcy will be here in a matter of minutes.

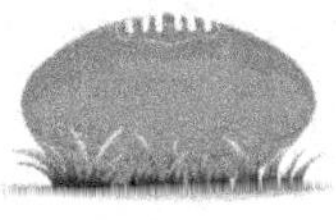

DARCY

From the moment Alli walked into my apartment, I haven't been able to take my eyes off her. My gaze rakes over her in a red, figure-hugging dress. She has blown in like a summer westerly wind. Hot and out of sorts. And yet, all seems calm despite every nerve ending is on high alert, like I'm standing dead centre of her storm.

Our eyes lock, and she looks away before taking a sip of wine. "You're an okay cook." It's only her second glass, and she's less jittery than before dinner.

"I am. Have been doing it for many years."

"Do you always eat pasta the night before a game?" She takes a sip as though she needs to drink for extra courage.

I shrug a shoulder. "Most times. I need carbs before a game. If I play well, then I'll repeat a certain pasta dish."

Her eyes round. "Are you superstitious?"

I swallow a mouthful of water while I ponder a way to explain my behaviour. "I stick to a routine when it works."

She gives me a slow smile. "What else works?"

"You want my secrets?" Her smile fades. I stand and walk to the other side of the table. Eyes reminding me of sands of the earth staring up at me. Wholesome. Seeking. Innocent. "Come with me." I hold my hand out for hers, help her to her feet. Not that she needs it, but I want to be a gentleman, which is why I donned the trousers and white button-front shirt. "Bring your glass."

I guide her to the balcony off the main living room overlooking the ocean. It's dark with only the light of the esplanade lamps reflecting below us. She gasps. The same way she did when I gave her the quick tour of my apartment.

"I've always loved the ocean." Alli breathes in the salt air as she says it.

"So have I. It's why I bought the apartment. I like to sit out here and listen."

"Listen or think?"

"Both."

She nods before taking another sip. I follow her gaze to the line of moonlight dancing over the ocean. The moon is in its waxing phase, merely nights away of being complete. "At least it's not a full moon for the game tomorrow night."

"Do you believe it to be unlucky on game day?"

My hands go to the rail, and I squeeze it tight. "Not as long as I stick to routine."

"My being here is not routine." A statement, yet it questions me at the same time.

"No." I take her wine glass and place it on the table behind her.

"So, dating before a game is uncommon?" she whispers. With nothing in her hands she wraps her arms around her middle.

"No dating."

In the gentle sea breeze strays of white hairs waft around her face. Raising my hand, I watch her reaction as I slide loose strands behind her ear. Her eyes are locked on mine. Portholes at sea. Looking closer, I'm recognising vulnerability. Not a sign of her weakness, more in recognition we are both lowering our defences. "I like you, Alli. Being with you makes me happy. Tonight I want to be happy, and not think about anything else other than how happy I am when I'm with you."

She nods without shifting her gaze. "For some reason, I thought you'd be studying your opponent and wanting to talk football with me?"

"With you?" My lips stretch to a smile. I slide my hand around the back of her neck and lean close to kiss her. Her lashes lower and shut. Heart-shaped lips part, and then I'm doing what I longed to since I sent the text earlier today.

Soft lips open for me. My arms tighten around her back, and I hold Alli against my body. I taste her while feeling all of her pressing into me.

Fighting the urge to take her now, I keep my touch soft and slow. By the way Alli is kissing me, I want to carry her to my bed. Only it's not what tonight's about. Tonight is about change, and hopefully, the right kind of change will bring better luck tomorrow.

Alli's body presses against my dick. I groan, losing all niceties. Leading her into the kitchen, I place her glass on the bench. Her fingers work the zip of my jeans, and I'm reaching for the hem of her dress only to pause when my phone buzzes on the marble. I curse seeing my father's name. "I should take this."

"Dad," I say more abrupt than I intend.

"Am I interrupting something?" His deep voice booms.

Glancing over my shoulder, I look to Alli. She's watching me. "I was about to head to bed." I focus on Alli, sending signals this *is* my intention.

"I wanted to let you know we're staying at the Park Hyatt in Melbourne in two weeks. Your mother is excited. And good luck for your game tomorrow."

"Thanks." Rubbing the back of my neck, I turn away from Alli.

My father hasn't called in… I can't bloody remember when. And his timing couldn't be more off.

"If you lose, you get a second chance, right?"

"We're not going to lose. I can't talk now. I'll call you tomorrow after the game." I hate promising him time.

"Make it Sunday as I have a dinner commitment with a client."

"Fine."

I end the call and take a deep breath.

"I hope I wasn't the reason you couldn't talk to your father."

Tossing my phone on the marble, I ignore it sliding across the bench. "He's an ass. He can wait."

"Darcy," she rasps.

"Hey, I'm not the jerk here."

She shakes her head lightly as though I am.

"Not getting into it tonight," I repeat and stride to the sink to fill a glass of water and gulp it down.

She follows me to the sink and rests her hands on my back. "It's more about appreciating what you have."

I swallow the water and calm myself before turning around. "Our circumstances are not the same."

"How does one's circumstances matter when we're talking about—"

"Not tonight," I demand.

Her chin dips as she lowers her gaze.

Fuck.

I can't deal with her sad eyes. Not tonight. My head needs to be clear and not filled with guilt. "I'll take you home."

"No."

"Pardon?"

"No. You don't get to do that. Dismiss me because I'm making you think about family. You don't get to be selfish. You want to be my friend? Then you have to talk to me."

"We're not friends." Her lips part. "We're more."

"Talk to me," she whispers. "Don't push me away because if you do—"

"Okay," I mutter. I briefly look up, away from her gaze to clear my head. I need to think without her eyes holding me captive. "What do you want me to say? We're not the happy-family type, so no point lying." Her eyes are wide and silently asking me to continue. "And right now you're not ready to hear the truth, and I'm not getting into it the night before a game. My *father* hasn't bothered with me for years, so I'm not wasting precious time considering what I'm missing out on."

"Okay," she whispers. "It upsets you—"

"No, *he* upsets me." Both arms stretch out to the bench and take my weight. I lower my head. "I can't do this tonight. I asked you here because you make me happy, and right now I'm not feeling the buzz."

Soft hands touch my back, spread around my middle. She places her head between my shoulder blades. "You don't have to say anything else. Take me home if you believe it's best for you."

We both know it's not what I believe is best.

Having her near calms me.

Only, is Alli what I need leading up to the finals when I need the fire in my gut to keep burning?

ALLI

After a spot clean of the aisle, Carli finds me tidying the galley. She's smiling as though her lips will split. "They won!"

I check my phone. No message.

"That's great news," I say. "So, a Grand Final. Darcy will be ecstatic."

"Do you think he'll ask you to attend the game in Melbourne? What's your roster a fortnight from now?"

"No idea to both," I say firmly. Grabbing my case from the overhead storage, I follow her out the exit door to the terminal.

"Are you meeting him later tonight?"

"We didn't make plans. He needs to be with his team," I say like an understanding *friend*. My stomach fills with an odd sickness. Is this how I want to feel when he's out celebrating. I've seen how girls throw themselves at football players in nightclubs. As though she reads my mind, Carli touches my arm.

"Hey. He won't do anything stupid."

I nod, wanting to believe it. And yet, I'm all too aware we're not *together*. He could if he wanted to.

"He's going to be focused solely on football for two more weeks," she says as though I need to know. "If you're a distraction, he'll stay clear of you," she warns. "It doesn't mean he doesn't want to be with you. This game is a big deal. A decade since they have made it to a Grand Final, and they're the favourites to win."

I get it, although I don't understand why he wouldn't message me.

"So, tomorrow night. You want to get dressed at mine?" Carli asks.

"I can't," I say as we head out the doors into the cool night air.

Carli tightens the scarf around her neck. "I'm so annoyed Michael isn't coming. I mean I know it's his sister's birthday, but this is a big event, and I was looking forward to having him by my side."

"At least he understands the value of family. I respect that," I say firmly.

We reach the car park, and Carli is already texting Michael.

"See you tomorrow night."

"Call me if you change your mind about coming in the limo with me."

I smile at Carli. "Fine. I'll call you when I leave the nursing home."

After stopping to buy take-out noodles, I arrive home to a dark, quiet house. I switch on the lights and fire up the heater. It's mid-September, but the beginning of springtime doesn't always mean warmer weather in southern Australia. While I eat noodles, I scroll through Instagram admiring pictures of beach landscapes and fine art.

Darcy's post appears in my feed.

darcy_rayne23
Grinners

There's a photo of him and some teammates, mouths open with a fierce expression as though they are yelling at the camera. Some are pulling at their guernseys.

I can't help wonder what he's doing at this moment.

So, I send an Instagram message.

> **Me:** *Congratulations! Great news. Have fun celebrating :)*

I continue scrolling through Instagram and then receive a message from him.

> **Darcy:** *Thanks. I'm at the club for presentations. There are so many fans here they have to stand outside because the rooms are packed. It's a bloody awesome feeling knowing you're playing in a Grand Final!*

I smile because he's happy.

> **Me:** *Have a great night! I'm eating dinner then going to bed.*

> **Darcy:** *Now I'm thinking about you, last night, in my bed.*

My insides coil because I know it's the reason I'm feeling uneasy. Last night... I slept naked beside him with him curled up behind me, his arm heavy around my waist. I've reached the point where it's hard to come back *if* something goes wrong.
I suck in a deep breath.

> **Me:** *I've also been thinking about last night... see you tomorrow?*

Darcy: *Sorry I have recovery at the beach. Then the team is gathering at the club. I also have this thing I have to attend tomorrow night. Call you Monday.*

Two more weeks.
I got this.

Me: *Perfect. I have Monday off.*

Darcy: *Keep it free for me.*

I let out a sigh and smile.

CHAPTER 11

ALLI

Green lawn.

It rarely changes over the years, even in the months of a drought. The cemetery where my parents are buried is more a beautiful garden than a graveyard. Along the fence line, trees dot the edges providing shade for people to sit and rest. Or pray, if it's too hot near the graves.

The headstones are smaller. It doesn't mean the people buried here are of less importance. I understand people with money want to erect huge monuments in honour of their loved ones because they were special. Rich or not, someone means something to somebody, which is why I like the smaller and almost identical headstones here. Everyone has importance.

The downside is finding a particular grave when, wherever you look, it's the same. As an impatient child years ago, I watched visitors come and go from under the shade of a tree while I waited for my grandparents to finish doing whatever they did at my parents' grave. Visitors who came once a year or maybe it was their first time, they would point, walk, twirl, and discuss with their partner all awhile looking dumbfounded.

My grandparents never got lost. Fresh cut flowers from their garden were placed in a vase by the headstone once a week for two years. When things became difficult with Nate, the visits slowed to once or twice a month. When Gran was placed in care, Pop still managed to pay his respect every couple of months. Because Gran would want him to.

My life has changed. I don't visit as often as I did. Coming here no longer fulfils me in a way it does Pop. But when Pop asked me to accompany him this morning, I couldn't say no.

Grass covers every grave, so with every step, I carefully plod leaving as much distance as possible so as not to step on someone's personal space because my grandparents taught me about respect from a young age.

I stop behind Pop when we reach the headstone in the middle of a row. My parents' headstone. I lower to my knees and read the inscription.

In Loving Memory of Genevieve and Alexander Bradley,
tragically taken.
Beloved parents of Nathaniel and Aaliyah.
Daughter of Con and Dianna Warwick.
Cherished Son of Evelyn and Thomas Bradley.
Gone from our homes, not our hearts.

I never knew my other grandparents. They were both deceased before I was born. Some part of me is curious since Mum has a brother, yet Gran had told me not to search for him and to let it be.

I watch Pop empty the contents of the vase and refill it from a water bottle he brought with him from home. One by one he pushes stems of white calla lilies and snapdragons into the plastic vase. I helped him pick the flowers before we came. The lilies are hardy, growing wild in his backyard. He saves the flowers in the front garden for Gran. The garden is her pride and joy.

After positioning the vase by the headstone, Pop bows his head and closes his eyes. I do the same and say a silent prayer. I miss my parents, but I struggle with some memories of the stories Pop tells. I remember the emotion of them passing more than anything else.

After repeating the same verse I rehearsed as a child, I'm aware of the sun warming my cheeks, the cool breeze in my hair, and the smell of damp grass. I open my eyes and sit quietly watching Pop. Today he bows his head longer than usual. My gaze flicks from him to the headstone. I glance down to the grass and pick at a blade while thinking how hard all this has been on him. My recollection of fond moments with my parents is vague except a few. Pop's stories and happy times could fill a library.

I swallow and read aloud the bottom line on the headstone.

"Gone from our homes, not our hearts."

Pop glances up, his eyes moist.

"What's your favourite memory?" I whisper.

He looks at the headstone as though he's talking to my parents. "The day Alex proposed to Gen was the happiest I'd ever seen him. They came bursting through the front door to tell us the news. The one thing he said stuck with me. *'Dad, I'm going to have everything you do. A wife and family I'll love with all of my heart. The best life.'*" Pop's voice cracks a little. "You did, son. And we did the best we could."

My throat turns dry. "They would be proud of Gran, and you."

"Not sure your brother would agree." He bows his head.

"Yes, he would, and so would Mum and Dad. He was out of line on many occasions."

His head remains lowered. "He was family."

"Don't do this. Don't beat yourself up about the past. Nate's happy, and if all the bad things didn't happen, he wouldn't have left. He needed to leave. He wasn't happy here." It hurts to say, and yet out loud helps with acceptance. "When did you last hear from him?"

Pop stands and brushes his knees. "Strangely, last week. There was a message on the answering machine to call him. I haven't had a chance."

"He has news." When pop looks at me, I smile. "Good news. He's matured and getting on with his life. You need to call him."

"International calls cost a fortune."

"We'll use my phone. Tell me a time he can call you." When we reach the path, I link my arm through Pop's. "He's a different man now." He glances at me and I add, "Paige told me a few things."

"Is he coming home?"

"No," I whisper. "Although, he might visit soon." Maybe. When I consider the wedding, I realise how difficult it will be for Pop to attend. And he won't go without Gran. I swallow down the ball of emotion growing in my throat. "Let's go see Gran."

When we walk through the nursing home doors, Aubree greets us in the foyer. Her dark hair is pulled high in a ponytail making her appear even taller than her six-foot height.

"Hi," she says and smiles. "I'm finishing for the day, but Leroy is with Evelyn helping her onto the bed for a nap."

"Enjoy the afternoon. It's actually turned into a nice day."

"Thanks, Alli. Bye, Tom."

Aubrey is married to another high-profile football player. Some days I want to mention I'm seeing Darcy, only I don't know how to bring it up in conversation. Considering it's only been weeks, I doubt anyone will think it serious with his dating history.

Pop and I walk the long hallway, and my stomach tightens not knowing what to expect. If Gran is having a 'bad day', she often reacts to the male nurses as though they are attacking her. When we reach her room, soft wails come from the other side of the door. I sense Pop stiffen alongside me. I allow him to enter first and follow him to her bed.

"Evelyn, I'm trying to help you," Leroy says in a stern voice.

"It's okay, we can take over now," I say stepping to the other side of the bed.

"Let me be. Leave me," Gran calls out, waving her arms.

Pop takes her hand and holds it down on the covers. "Evelyn." His voice is soft yet firm. "You're okay. No one is trying to hurt you."

Gran opens her eyes. Her expression shows no sign of recognition. She looks fearful.

"Gran," I say, stepping forward into her line of sight. "We brought flowers from your garden." I hold up the flowers to show her.

She studies the blooms a moment. "Thank you, dear," she whimpers and waits before saying, "Can you find a vase?"

"Of course. You planted most of these years ago. Do you remember?"

"My garden?" She scratches at the inside of her arm. It takes a moment before she smiles. "Has Thomas been looking after my sweet peas?"

"I have."

Her gaze flicks to Pop, but her expression doesn't falter. "I don't know you?"

"Evelyn." His voice cracks. "I'm Thomas."

Gran glances at the framed photo of their wedding day on the bedside table next to her. Her gaze slides back to Pop. "No," she whispers.

"Evelyn, it's me." Pop touches her hand, and she makes a startled noise. In a gentle voice, he starts to sing *I Got You Babe*. Her eyes soften and like a shutter, her expression relaxes. He's sung the song to her for as long as I can remember.

It's their song.

"Tommy." Gran purses her lips, and he stops mid-chorus. "You never get that part right." She chuckles lightly.

"It's because I need you to sing it with me, love."

With that, Gran sings along with Pop. Her soft voice cracks on some notes, a little shaky on others, and the love in her eyes warms my heart.

"I'll get some water," I say holding up the vase and leave the room to give them some alone time.

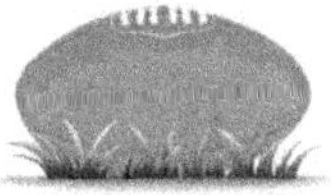

DARCY

"Christ, is that necessary?" I ask and groan. My face pushes into the hole on the massage table, and I fist my hands by my side. "Fuck."

Cleo laughs. "Darcy, you disappoint. A big strong guy like you and—"

"Let's trade places and see who's hurting then."

Cleo laughs again and uses some pointy device to dig deeper into my lower back. "If I don't do this, you're likely to tear a hamstring."

Clenching my teeth, I shut up knowing she's right. Cleo is one of the best sports physiotherapists going around, and she's treating me on her day off. Who am I kidding? Since Cleo signed a contract with my team, she rarely has a day off.

"Got any plans tonight?" I ask trying to distract myself by means of casual conversation.

"Yeah, I'm going to bed early and catching up on sleep."

"Aren't you a barrel of fun."

Cleo doesn't respond. Instead, she shifts and then alters her attack on my hamstring. "This is what I do for kicks," she mocks. "I like to hurt big, tough guys."

"I bet you do," I grunt.

She chuckles low. "Roll over." She holds out the towel to screen me while I shuffle on to my back, then spreads the towel over my groin. She stands at the end of the bed and slowly raises my left leg beyond ninety degrees. "See..." she says as my shin comes close to my face, "... improved flexibility already."

"You're a superstar," I say wincing a little.

The truth.

I'm thankful to her because if there's a chance I'll break down, Cleo will identify the problem early and keep my body supple.

"Yep." She repeats the same action with my other leg and holds it for around thirty seconds. "Okay," she says releasing me. "Up and get dressed, big boy. Catch you at the same time tomorrow."

"You will."

Every day until the finals.

There's no way I'll risk an injury before the game of my life. Cleo blocks the same time on her schedule for the next two weeks. "Enjoy the ball tonight." She pushes one black spiral curl behind her ear. "Don't go crazy on the dance floor."

I shoot her a questioning look. "It's a gala ball, Cleo."

"Wouldn't stop me."

After showering, the last thing I want to do is dress in a suit to go out. My whole body aches as fatigue sets in. Yesterday I played one of the best games of my career, and nobody I cared about sat in the stands to witness it.

It's not the reason I play, yet as the end of my football career approaches, I would love to share the joy of the game with someone special. My parents were never interested, until last week, and maybe now because my name is all over the media.

The screen on my phone brightens. The notifications listed are too many for me to reply to all. Not tonight at least. I scroll the list and note the absence of one.

Before the game, I promised myself not to think about Alli. If I'm going to keep a level head, I have to keep it in my pants. No distractions. From now on, my focus is solely football.

Tonight will be a perfect remedy. I'll be sitting beside wealthy philanthropists, middle-aged women, and politicians. Not my usual night of fun, but the SIDS fundraiser is a big deal. Attending the funeral of a six-month-old will stay with me for a long time and not something I care to repeat in this lifetime. I can only imagine the pain my cousin, Harrison, and his wife, Megan, are going through. She's pregnant again, and I imagine over the moon with joy, and yet fearful. Walking into my robe, I select a pale blue shirt and navy suit because black is not a colour I want to wear tonight.

I don't bother eating before driving to the city. These events are catered, and I'll be there well before appetisers are served.

Valet greets me out front of the five-star hotel. Walking into the lobby, the staff directs me to the elevator. The ballroom is on the first floor. "It's fine," I say and point to the grand staircase and take the steps two at a time. On reaching the foyer, I wind around suited men and ladies in gowns, heads turning as I pass. Many of the men give a simple nod. My height allows me to scan the room, and I spy Heather mingling with the distinguished guests. The club assured me merchandise and two VIP Thunder memberships were signed and sent, although I want Heather to account for what was received. I keep moving until a strong hand tightens around my forearm halting me.

"Darcy."

"Harrison." We hug and pat each other's backs in a manly embrace. Megan, his wife, steps up to me, and I pull her into my arms and kiss her on the cheek. I admire her growing belly in a navy gown. "You look radiant, Megs."

She smiles, and her lashes flutter. "Thank you. I feel wonderful." I note the extra positivity in her tone.

"And you look it."

Harrison pats my back as though my compliment pleases him. "I thought you wouldn't be here considering—"

I interrupt Harrison from saying more. "You know I'd do all I could to come tonight. It means a lot to me."

Harrison nods. "Heather told me you were, but after yesterday's win, I thought footy commitments would take priority." He holds out his hand. "And congratulations on making the Grand Final."

I shake his hand with vigour. "I'm still coming to terms with it. A dream come true, mate." Then I glance at Megan, her hands resting over her belly, and know they understand the anxiety of waiting for bigger dreams to come to fruition.

A waiter walks past with a tray of beer. Harrison nods to me, and I shake my head. "I'll be drinking water with Megan tonight."

"Then I'll celebrate for all of us," he says. A waitress interrupts offering prawns on skewers. I take one and offer Megan another.

She shakes her head. Dark curls caress her shoulders. "I react to seafood when I'm pregnant."

"Add it to the list of other foods she can't eat while pregnant," Harrison quips.

"There's a list?"

Megan sighs. "One day a girl will steal your heart, and you'll have a lot to learn."

I laugh once as though it won't happen.

The master of ceremonies steps onto the stage and announces for everyone to take a seat. It's been many months since I caught up with Harrison and seeing him this happy is a relief compared to our last encounter.

The first of the speeches take place as the entrée is served. The speaker thanks everyone for his or her support and acknowledges gratitude to everyone attending tonight. At the completion, a low hum fills the room. I note every table in the ballroom is at capacity. Guests will dig into their pockets tonight to support the foundation. The sheer number reiterates the night will be a huge success.

After finishing the last mouthful of entrée, I glance up to the usher opening the huge double doors to allow a late attendee to enter the room. At first I frown, and then my entire body stiffens.

A tall blonde wearing a jade green gown catches my eye as she floats across the floor. Not any blonde. One with hair styled straight and cut at the shoulders. I'm baffled as to how she got to be here, and why she didn't mention it. I keep an eye on her and where she's directed to the far side of the room. Thankfully, she is facing me, and I'm able to watch her every move. Then I realise she is seated next to Carli. Words are exchanged, and Alli shakes her head.

My shoulders relax. At least it's Carli and not some guy.

A date.

What would I have done?

"You okay?" Harrison asks.

"Yeah," I say not taking my eyes off Alli. "Someone I know."

"Best you put down that glass, mate, before it smashes in your hands." He's right. My fingertips are white. I place the glass in front of me and pick up the event card on the table and read the list of speeches. One before the main meal, and then a break.

"Good evening, everyone."

At the sound of the voice coming through the speakers, I look to the stage.

"Cot death..." the room falls silent, "... is what many refer to as the sudden and unexpected death of a baby. Sudden Infant Death Syndrome, which is more commonly known as SIDS, now falls under the umbrella of SUDI, along with other fatal sleep accidents. Sudden and Unexpected Death in Infancy. Many are unaware a baby can die at any time of the day or night from SUDI. Most die quietly in their sleep. Many of you here tonight have been affected by the sadness, still feeling some blame. There are safe practices which mothers are educated on when they have a baby, such as... always put your baby on their back to sleep. Never cover their head. Do not expose your baby to tobacco smoke. Make sure baby doesn't overheat or get too cold. Safe bedding. I can go on, but many of you have heard advice given by others and know the factors that increase risk. I look around the room, and for those affected, I see the devastation in your expressions. Guilt, anger, fear, blame, and despair. You did everything you were told, eliminated all known risk factors, and yet here we are, all feeling the heartache..."

Harrison shifts in his seat. Meg swipes a finger under her eye. It's quick, yet I notice.

"Tonight is not about educating any of you," his voice softens. "Support is needed for research. We also provide bereavement support and counselling. Ladies and gentlemen, please dig deep into your pockets tonight. Enjoy your meal and the wonderful entertainment. My mother once told me drinking makes you loose." That gets a low chuckle, which lightens the tenseness in the room. "If it makes you loose with your money, then drink up." He smiles and raises his glass. "I want to thank everyone for coming tonight and supporting a much-needed cause."

The crowd applauds. A rawness hollows out my gut on a level I was unaware I could feel. It's not good. And Alli being here is not what I expected. I'm supposed to have a clear head. Not this. The hefty cheque is evident I'm a valued supporter, but I'm investing myself on an emotional level. Something I can't afford to do. I go to stand and get some air before the main meal is served.

Harrison rests his hand on my arm. "Our table gets served first. I suggest you wait."

I nod and sit back in my chair. I can't risk looking at Harrison in case there's moisture in his eyes because it will be enough to break me. Picking up a fork, I twist it between my fingers. I glance up and let out a long breath when I spot Heather heading to our table.

"The Thunder memberships and signed apparel should raise a substantial amount in the silent auction," she says. "Especially now you've made the final."

"A win-win for everyone," I say, still twisting the fork.

"Don't even think about it," Harrison shoots at Megan when she looks toward the auction tables.

It makes me smile. "Megan, I can get you anything you want. You only have to ask," I say quietly.

Waiters arrive to serve the main meal. "Well, I only wanted to come over and thank you. I won't keep you from your meal." Heather leans in close. "We received your personal cheque. It's substantially more than last year."

"What can I say, I had a good year." I give her a subtle wink.

Heather places a hand on my shoulder. "Thank you, Darcy." I give her a nod before she sashays away.

My thought switches to food, and I opt for the steak and steamed vegetables. On the first mouthful, my gaze travels to Alli, and I watch her discuss something with Carli. God, she looks beautiful. Logic tells me to finish my meal and quietly excuse myself, so I can slip away and have an early, uneventful night as planned. Only my entire body is drawn to her like a damn magnet, and all common sense is slipping.

On the stage, the speaker announces the silent auctions and highlights my donation of the Thunder apparel bringing attention to the fact I'm a guest here tonight. I watch Alli's expression change. She slowly turns in her seat and surveys the room. She looks to Carli and shakes her head. When the waiter approaches their table, Alli unfolds her napkin and places it in her lap. Slowly, her gaze shifts as though she senses me. She tilts her head, and when our eyes meet, her lips part. I imagine her gasping the way she did in my apartment.

I give a slight nod.

Her smile is subtle, as though she's caught off guard, before returning the solitary nod. I imagine her saying my name in her head. It's not enough. I want to hear her shout my name when I make her come again and again.

Keeping my gaze lowered, I don't glance her way again until I finish eating. People at other tables are finishing their meals and moving about the room to inspect all the silent auction items.

"I'm going to say hello to a friend," I inform Harrison.

"If you're not back before dessert is served, I'm giving yours to Megan."

"Be my guest," I say and wink. I'm now considering an alternate dessert. One that involves my tongue and Alli.

CHAPTER 12

ALLI

"Are you going to go and speak to him?" Carli asks.

"He never told me he was coming. Only he had a thing tonight." Should I make anything out of it? Questions fill my head as to why he didn't want me to know.

"At least, he's on his own," she whispers.

I let out a breath. "How do you know?" I'm too nervous to look his way knowing—feeling—his eyes on me.

"He's sitting between two guys. Wait, he's standing. He's shaking hands with the guy next to him. He's leaving." Carli's expression changes while giving the live commentary. "Shit, he's heading to the back of the room. He's definitely leaving," she says with disappointment. "Hell, you'd think it was a game of dominoes the way heads turn."

My shoulders fall. "Good, now eat," I tell her. I slice into my chicken and take a bite.

"Wait. He's walking along the back wall. Oh shit."

"Shit?" I repeat with chicken in my mouth.

Carli swivels in her chair and picks up her fork. "Act normal."

I cough on my food before swallowing. Then I sense him behind me. When I glance up, I'm surprised to find all eyes at the table on me. All with a similar stunned expression.

I don't know these people. Some I've seen, but all are from different departments of the airline. Even the silver tree centrepiece dripping with shimmering Swarovski crystals fails to screen judging eyes.

"Carli." His voice wraps around me like a blanket. I stop myself from turning in my seat. I wait.

"Darcy," Carli drawls out his name. "Lovely to see you again. Congratulations on your win yesterday."

A heavy, warm hand rests on my bare shoulder. "Alli."

I swivel and look up to those eyes that tighten my insides and make my heart fibrillate. "Yes, congrats, Darcy. I'm surprised to see you here."

His brow furrows and then relaxes. "Likewise."

"Our airline is a major sponsor," I confirm.

He looks around the table and nods his head. "It's something close to my heart, and I attend the gala ball every year." Before I respond, he adds, "Do you mind if I have a word with you? Outside." I look to Carli. "After you finish your meal," he adds. "I have a few things to attend to first."

"Yes, of course," I say obediently.

Darcy nods to the table guests. "Enjoy the night, everyone." He strolls away, heads turning in his wake.

I turn back to questionable expressions.

There are a few nods then everyone gets back to eating and drinking.

The harpist takes to the stage. People move about the room upon finishing their meal. Carli bumps my arm. "I need the restroom."

Making our way around white-covered tables, we head directly toward the exquisite wooden double doors that open out to a foyer. Hanging overhead, a three-metre wide crystal chandelier glistens. It's remarkable, and for a moment, I'm dazzled, at a loss to how I missed its magnificence when I arrived. Then I recall the fluster of arrival and my concern of making a late entrance. Late because Gran suffered a 'turn'. A TIA the nurse had called it. A mini-stroke. Apparently, she's been having these episodes for a while now, and Pop hadn't told me.

"There's nothing we can do," Pop had said. "They happen. She needs rest."

I swallow down the worry building within me. Tonight was supposed to be about having fun and not thinking about *what-if?* Yet words of the last speech reached in and squeezed my heart. Acerbated my own internal battle, the heartache of losing loved ones, the fear of losing another. The difficulty of keeping a brave face when I'm everything but brave. It's the little things like pretty chandeliers I need to focus on, so I don't slip away into the dark hole of my thoughts.

Before Carli and I make it to the doors of the restroom, Darcy appears in the foyer.

"Ladies." His gaze wanders down my body.

"I'll go ahead," Carli says.

"Are you having a good time?"

I nod. "As good as these events can be." He quirks an eyebrow. "It's a good cause, so I don't mind."

"Yeah..." he pauses. "I had to speak with someone regarding the auction." He takes a step closer. "I intended to come and make an appearance then slip away quietly to have an early night."

"Big night celebrating last night?"

Darcy's brow pulls tight. "No, Alli. I had an early night. Went home after the presentations at the clubrooms."

I nod. Relieved. "You must be pumped about making the Grand Final."

His stares at me. The intensity making me take a step back. "More than I think you understand. I won't do anything to jeopardise my focus leading up to the game."

"Of course," I say quickly. When he glances at the staircase, I assume he's about to leave. Instead, he takes another step toward me.

"Are we still on for tomorrow?"

"Sure." *Did we plan anything?*

Darcy's eyes soften. "I thought we could catch a movie?"

I avert my gaze toward the restroom only there's no sign of Carli. "I'm not sure what's on at the cinema at present," I say and shrug trying to lighten the mood.

"We could watch a movie at yours... or mine." More people are flowing out the large double doors, and standing at two metres tall, their eyes drift automatically to Darcy. I notice it, and I know he does too. He leans in, so his mouth is close to my ear. "Come home with me?"

"I thought you wanted an early night?"

"I've decided I don't want to be alone."

Loneliness I understand. Darcy and I are heading toward dangerous emotional vulnerability. And we both have a lot to lose. And yet, we can't seem to stay away. "I'll let Carli know I'm leaving."

His eyes darken a little. A window to his thoughts. "I'll arrange for Valet to bring my car around front."

It's the second time I've been in Darcy's black BMW. It's all luxury, pure comfort, and I'm aware of my heart rate as though we're on a racetrack testing the car's performance at maximum speed. Yet, Darcy is driving at the speed limit, giving no cause to be nervous.

Only we're going to his apartment, not mine. He knows I have tomorrow off. And he doesn't have to be at training until ten in the morning. Every moment I spend with him is one step closer to admitting I'm falling for him.

The sex is becoming my *more*.

I run fingers along the door until I find a button. The window lowers and cool air blows on my face.

"Are you hot?" Darcy adjusts the settings on the air conditioner.

"A little," I say with my face directed to the window.

"Did you drink much? Maybe the food didn't agree with you. Sometimes the food can be rich at these events."

"I don't feel sick, I just need air. And I only had one champagne."

We drive in silence for another five minutes until the wire gates slide open to the underground carpark beneath his penthouse.

Taking my hand, he guides me to the elevator. We step inside with one other guy. His right arm is supported in a sling. Dressed in a white shirt, I consider the difficulty of buttoning it with one arm and grateful to him for the diversion. My eyes lift to his face. He's stunning and somewhat familiar. I would remember meeting a guy this beautiful and yet, I can't recall how I know him. Mocha skin glows against the white material of his shirt. Chocolate brown eyes meet mine, and I'm surprised by the sadness behind them. His gaze rises and locks with Darcy's. This guy is over six foot, yet Darcy towers over him. Something changes between them, and the beautiful guy straightens, composing himself.

He gives Darcy a nod. "Good win yesterday."

Darcy holds out his left hand, which is thoughtful since this guy's right arm is immobilised by the sling. "Thanks. Hope your shoulder improves quickly. The Aussies missed you in the test series."

"Thanks, man. I have surgery next week, so I expect to be back playing after Christmas." His gaze shoots to me.

I still have no idea who the beautiful man is. Regardless, I smile politely.

"Jardine, this is Alli. Alli, Jardine," Darcy says in a tone I should recognise him.

I keep smiling. "Nice to meet you."

The elevator dings, and the door opens at level four. "Best of luck for the final," Jardine says before stepping out.

"Appreciated." Darcy is smiling. "You have no idea who that was, do you?"

"Should I? I mean he looks familiar but..." The doors open to his penthouse.

"If you followed cricket." He unlocks the door pushing it wide to allow me to enter first.

"You know I don't follow sports."

Darcy punches in a code on the security pad. "Your brother lives in England. Before you say anything, he would know something about cricket. He would have heard of Jardine Kumble. He's one of the best fast bowlers in the *world*."

"Right. Then maybe."

Darcy places a hand on my back and leads me to the kitchen. "Can I get you anything?"

"A green tea," I say, sliding onto the stool and kicking off my heels.

He opens the cupboard and pulls out a cedar box housing a variety of teas. "You're in luck."

"So, Jardine happened to be here in your apartment complex."

"Yeah," Darcy says and shrugs a shoulder like he's surprised. "He's from Adelaide. Left around five years ago to play international cricket. Could be visiting family or friends while he's injured and has some free time."

"You've never met him before?"

"Nope."

"Yet, you spoke like you knew each other. Wait, I get it. It's a fame thing." Darcy shoots me a look in warning. "You have a code."

"Does it impress you?"

This time I roll my eyes, and he chuckles. He pours the boiling water into a china cup with a teabag and slides it near. Leaning his long body over the bench, he's close, too close, watching me sip tea.

"He looked sad, don't you think?"

"Jardine?" Darcy frowns. "I didn't study him that closely."

Looking over the rim of my china cup, I nod. "He did. I'm observant like that."

"Really? Can you tell what I'm feeling right now?"

Taking another sip. "Apart from what all guys have on their mind twenty-four-seven..." His lips twitch, and I know I'm right. "I think you're trying to distract yourself, so your mind doesn't weigh you down with thoughts about the Grand Final."

The arm leaning on the marble bench straightens bringing him closer until I feel his breath tickle my cheek. "And you're the perfect distraction?"

I place the cup on the bench. "Am I?" I whisper.

His hand reaches out and closes over mine now in my lap. "Yes," he rasps. "Does it make me a bad person?"

"Depends on how you use the distraction." I swallow, not sure why I have a need to ramble. "You spook me. Not your actions but more how I feel when I'm with you. It bothers me when I want to spend more time with you because you're my fix. And a fix is not healthy in the long term."

"No, it's not."

Lowering my gaze, I stare at my hands. My fingers tremble beneath his.

He squeezes my hand tight. "Are you cold?"

I shake my head.

His beautiful eyes are not enough to calm me tonight. Instead, they search my face for an answer. "What then?" The uneasiness in his expression is messing with my emotion, especially with everything that happened today with Gran.

"It's me. I get anxious easily. Get spooked. But it's okay. I know what to do before I—" I stop myself not wanting to startle him.

"Before you what?" His concerned gaze flicks across my face.

I swallow. "I have anxiety attacks. I rarely get them now," I add quickly. "Occasionally, I come close."

"Like now?" His eyes widen.

"No." I smile. "You make me nervous, but I'm venturing into something else."

"So, if you did have one," he begins. "What could I do to help?"

I give him a look that he doesn't need to worry even though I'm filled with warmth that he asked. "You breathe with me. Talk me through it, so I can hone in on your breaths and slow down my own. Then distract me by talking about something else and helping me think of other things."

He nods slowly.

"For some reason, it works. Gran used to do it with me when I was a teenager."

"So, you don't get them often now?"

"No. Being nervous around a sexy guy isn't enough to bring one on." I wink at him.

"No?" A long finger curls under my chin and raises my face until our eyes lock. Darcy opens his mouth, yet no words follow. We stare, breathe as the air heats between us.

Tipping my head back, I take everything he's offering. The passion dissolving my pain. Like a magician, he stops time and transports me to a bubble, to a universe where only he and I exist. His touch wipes my mind clear of everything except what his touch is doing to my body. From the moment I sensed him at the gala, the fire sparked low and deep in my stomach. With every touch, heat works its way up. His tongue slides over mine, performing its own kind of magic. I moan lightly, the flame coming to life. My heart thumps hard in my chest knowing where this is leading because it's not just a kiss.

Darcy's lips trail to my ears and bites gently on the lobe. "All I think about is you. You've left me desperate. Desperate to touch you, be inside you, so I can feel all of you."

Tender, light kisses dot my skin and then stop. Tilting my neck, I offer him more, myself accountable. He scoops me into his arms and carries me to the room of my *more*.

CHAPTER 13

DARCY

My damn heart is pounding like it's my first time with a girl.

I want to laugh at the absurdness, only I know I can't dismiss it.

There's a quality of innocence about Alli. Slowly, with every meet, I'm seeing the shield around her heart lower a little, and tonight all defences have yielded. Carefully, I place her on the bed as though her body is as fragile as her heart.

Innocent eyes stare up at me. I'm second-guessing everything. Cockiness has only camouflaged my vulnerabilities. Every fibre of my being wants her. Needs her. Knows what's at stake.

Hell. I'm staring at her lying on my bed. Her arm twists behind her back as she lowers her zip. Then I'm helping to dismantle her clothes. Those dark eyes stare up at me watching my face as I lower the bodice of the dress over her breasts. Creamy flesh bounces free, and I waste no time tasting her nipple. Sucking and toying until it swells between my lips. She gasps, and my dick flinches hearing her moan.

"Allow me," I say, helping to slide the dress over her hips and down her thighs. Tossing it aside, the silky material floats to the floor. Crouching to lean in and kiss Alli, she holds up a hand and stops me.

"I don't want to be the only one naked," she whispers.

Pushing up off the bed, I slip out of my shoes, throw my coat over a chair, and unbutton my shirt watching Alli watching me. My fingers refuse to cooperate, fumbling with each button. When I toss my shirt toward the leather chair, her lips part, and she says something under her breath, her gaze trailing down my chest and abs. My fingers work the belt where her gaze lingers, and my cock senses the need radiating between our bodies. Hooking fingers over the elastic of my briefs, I pull them down and step out of both underwear and trousers. Alli's eyes widen. Stroking myself in an attempt to calm my dick, I decide to wait a moment. Seeing her stunned expression turns me on even more. Alli licks her lips, and in one swift action, I'm hovering over her.

"May I?" My fingers linger at her panties. She gives one quick nod, and I'm sliding satin material down her lean thighs.

"You are gorgeous," I whisper, trailing one finger over her stomach toward her breasts. "Perfect," I say and kiss each nipple.

"I bet you say that to all the girls."

I know she said it in jest. It's enough to halt my thought. When our eyes meet, hers are apologetic.

Alli runs a hand along my face. Her touch is soft and yet it beckons me. "Kiss me," she whispers.

I kiss her in a way she understands. Reaching for her hand, I place it on my chest so she can feel how quick my heart beats for her. It's enough for the passion to lift a level where it's difficult to slow and pull back. My hands are all over her caressing her soft breasts, following the gentle swell of her rear, and along the taut muscle of her inner thigh. Concern crosses my mind how little meat covers Alli's body, then it evaporates when her thighs open permitting me to explore. My cock hurts it's so damn hard. I give it a stroke before settling beside Alli and giving her full attention. She writhes and bucks as my hand brings her close to orgasm. I kiss her tenderly as she moans and squirms with every pump of my fingers. Hell, I enjoy giving her pleasure. The moment she takes a deep breath, I lift my head and watch her eyes glaze as she comes.

Beautiful.

Even if her eyes were closed, I could watch the simple action of Alli breathing. The way her lips purse a little on inhalation, the gentle rise and fall of her chest. I study her face, take in every little detail. The sprinkling of faint freckles over her tiny nose. High cheekbones and a defined jaw. Her eyebrows are thin and light brown in colour. Running my fingers through her hair, I notice she's a natural blonde.

At my touch, her eyes open, and her chest expands to suck in more air. I kiss each breast when her chest rises. "Are you okay?" I ask gently.

"Gratified is a better word," she breathes.

Gratified.

My dick pulses.

Reaching for the condom in the drawer near the bed, I roll it on, aware she's watching. Fire flares in her eyes. I crawl over her and settle between her thighs. Pushing up on my elbows, I'm conscious of my size and weight.

I adjust her hips and push into her.

Alli gasps as I sink deep. Her eyes round and lips part. Eyes locked, I gauge she's not hurting. She nods once. I ease back and give her a moment before I push deeper this time. My body trembling withholding the urge to drive into her.

Alli's hand reaches up and strokes my jaw. "It's okay."

It's the green light I need. "Hang on to me." Leaning down I take her lips, kiss her gently while I thrust into her repeatedly. Her hands tighten around my waist holding on as though she's afraid to let go.

I'm trying to control the urge to fuck, hard. The holding back pushes me to the edge quicker than I intend. My breathing is loud, and no matter how many laps I have run on the damn field, it doesn't help me gain control. I'm lost inside of Alli. Her long limbs hug my body. Fingers dig into my back and heels into my hamstrings. Alli wrapped around me goads me on. She cries out. Hell, I didn't think hearing my name on her lips would give me so much pleasure. It pushes me over the edge, and her name fills my head, my every thought, my every touch.

She is my all.

"… you," I whisper, collapsing beside her. It was the end of the sentence. The first two words trapped in my throat.

I know what I feel.

Alli is under my skin, in my blood.

Rolling onto her side, her finger traces the outline of the tattoo across my chest.

I fling an arm across my eyes and try to block out the emotion overcoming all logic.

I'm falling. Fast.

Too fucking fast.

Focus.

Two. More. Weeks.

It's all I need, and then Alli Bradley can destroy me.

ALLI

His room is quiet. A subtle light shines through the floor-to-ceiling windows despite the curtains pulled closed. I'm tempted to walk out onto the balcony and stare at the ocean because I can. I imagine the night sky to be clear, and the moon full, because in my mind, the night is perfect.

What I'm feeling lying beside Darcy is beyond perfect.

My skin buzzes with excitement, and yet, I'm content. Content just to listen to the sound Darcy makes in his sleep. His breaths are slow, long, and rather audible. If I were trying to sleep, it would keep me awake. But I'm not.

Darcy curls into me from behind. His strong arm rests over my waist. I don't want to move, and not that I could from the sheer weight of his arm, for the new lightness in my chest. I'm relaxed in a fulfilled way, not a want to sleep way. My breaths are as deep as his, and I'm indulging in the warmth from having a body close to mine, holding me tight.

Last night was special. I would like to believe it was special for him too. Common sense tells me otherwise. If I allow myself to *think*, the bliss will shatter. I have always believed you can't get hurt if you don't let someone in. If you lose someone you don't love, the pain won't be as bad. Darcy and I are not so different. We both have our barricades up, so we don't get hurt. He's doing the same thing except his method is different. A smile creeps across my lips in appreciation of the skill he has perfected over time, and yet last night, there were moments he looked as though he was coming apart.

Because of me.

If only it were true.

Gently stroking the hand resting on my stomach, my eyes shut, and I only feel. Where our bodies touch, every sensation makes my body glow.

For one night I can allow myself this luxury.

I wake alone.

Grabbing a blanket from the end of the bed, I wrap it around my shoulders shrouding my body. The kitchen is quiet. There's an empty glass on the sink. Something yellow on the marble catches my eye.

A sticky note.

Didn't want to wake you.
The fridge is full, help yourself.
I'll be back around 1. X

The blanket around my shoulder becomes a lead weight. I sink onto the stool and tear the note from the marble and read it again. My heart shrinks a little. It's only eight, and I remember him mentioning he didn't need to be at the club until ten. I spin around and stare at his empty apartment questioning why he would leave so early? I don't want to be here alone for five hours. Quietly, I berate myself for believing Darcy wanted to wake up beside me. Returning to his room, I grab my gown and shoes and dress quickly.

There are people who need me.

I can't be here, pretending.

Keeping my head down, I stride past reception. Piercing stares penetrate my skin as I scurry toward the Uber waiting out the front.

How many girls have done the walk of shame out of Darcy's apartment?

I swallow down the hurt and croak out directions to the driver.

The silence makes the ride home more awkward with the sound of my breaths and muffled sob filling the cabin. Hell, why doesn't he turn up the volume to his crap radio station? He pulls into my drive, and I dash toward the front door before any of my neighbours catch me in a ball gown at this time of day.

Inside, I pull at the gown, peeling it off my body as though it were covered in spiders. I run the shower and stand under the warm spray until the tightness in my chest eases.

DARCY

Pulling off my boots, I toss them into my bag with force. My boots are not the reason I kicked four balls out on the full, another two kicks over my teammates head. Jenks is shouting some sort of macho bullshit across the change room to Bulla. They exchange words in jest revving the other up. We have fifteen minutes to shower and be upstairs in the meeting room.

I don't check my phone because I'm a coward.

It took all my self-control not to wake Alli. She looked so peaceful in *my* bed, lips slightly apart and breathing slow. The sheet had slipped down her arms, so I pulled it high over her shoulders, kissed her cheek before I left. It was a special night for us both, and I killed the after moment. The longer I stayed, the more I wanted her. I don't expect her to be there when I get back. I'll give a reason for fleeing the bedroom pretending it's not a big deal. In two weeks, I can do as I please but not now. If training was anything to go by, I made the right decision.

I sit up front in the meeting room, beside Ferg, the vice-captain. I'm a leader, and today I let my team down. Coach walks up to me and pats my shoulder once. He's scowling. "I expect everyone to have a bad training day leading up to the game. Better it be now than closer to the big one. Whatever you've got going on, deal with it." Our eyes meet. I know he would have heard rumours and sees through me.

I'm distracted.

Last night I was so fucking happy I should have trained my best. Yet, my conscience is warning me not to let Alli in. My entire focus needs to be on one thing. The one thing that has driven me over the past ten years. It all comes down to one day, and in twelve days, the ultimate football dream is in reach. I'm royally fucked because Alli has already penetrated barriers, and I feel her in my blood. She's like the fucking ocean crashing over the rock wall protecting the esplanade. The tide resides but pools of water have trickled over and down every rocky crevice, seeping into the tiniest holes, weathering away the toughest layers. She has permeated my soul, and I'm losing grip on what's real.

Walking to the front of the room, Coach stands beside the whiteboard, game plans filled with X's and O's. Words are scribed on the side.

First to the ball.
Protect the player.
Fight to the end.
Make a contest.
NEVER GIVE UP.

I stare at the board and feel every word, forcing my thoughts to focus on what's important.

Coach makes a sound to snare everyone's attention. "I've spoken to the guys who were travelling to Melbourne for the Brownlow medal count. They're no longer going. We don't need our week disrupted days before a game that we have worked our arses off for an entire bloody year. The Magarey Room will be set up for our team and guests... and the media. Your partners are welcome because I know I've upset a few of the ladies by cancelling when they already have their dresses and appointments organised. You blokes know how I feel about this, and your wives' and girlfriends' grumblings are not going to sway me when there are more important things at stake. The cameras will live stream our football club for the Brownlow to the nation, so I expect appropriate behaviour."

Considering I was reported and found guilty earlier in the year, I'm not eligible for the medal. As captain, I'm expected to attend. I've never bothered taking a girl to the medal count because, in my opinion, it's more about the girls frocking up than saluting the best bloody player in the nation. But that's me and many disagree, especially Sando's girlfriend.

"Doc and Ferg, I expect you to keep matters under control on the night, and the curfew stands. No one is to go out after, and no alcohol, but I don't need to remind you men on the rules. There will be plenty of time to celebrate in another twelve days."

When Coach finishes his spiel, I head to my car along with the other players. Ferg walks alongside me. "Everything okay?"

"Yep." My car beeps when I unlock it. I open the boot and throw my bag in.

"Got anyone special going to the game?"

"Nope."

"Heard your parents are coming?"

"Yep." I give him a long look before climbing into the driver's seat.

"See you tomorrow, Doc."

CHAPTER 14

ALLI

I don't bother drying off my hair. I dress and grab a banana. After a couple of bites, I toss it aside.

Snaring my keys from the bench, I drive along the esplanade before going to Pop's.

Sculptures line the beachfront. Art standing before the sea. In a matter of minutes, I park the car, and taking the sandy path, I admire each piece, studying the artist's work and wishing I had the courage to do something like this. Metal is out of my league, although pottery or ceramic I could do after dabbling with clay in my teens. After thirty minutes of perusing and breathing easier, my erratic thoughts have slowed enough to return to my car and head to Pop's house.

When I pull into the driveway, Pop is sitting on the steps of the veranda staring at the lawn. His gaze lifts, a faint smile crosses his lips. He walks across the lawn to greet me, each step exaggerated in the long grass.

I could mow it for him.

Today.

Now.

"I thought you were coming later?"

"My plans have changed. Have you eaten? Morning tea?"

Pop shakes his head. "I need to shop. Not much in the cupboard."

I rummage through the cupboard and find plain flour and vanilla essence. He has plenty of butter and jam, so I start to make jam cookies. Pop fills the kettle. Half an hour later, I take warm cookies and a pot of tea to the table in the back garden in the warm sunlight.

"Last night I left not long after you when Evelyn fell asleep. I wanted to tell you about the turns, but I didn't want you to worry."

I nod. "I know. It was a shock, that's all."

"There's nothing we can do. They happen."

I nod again, taking a sip of tea, hoping it will ease the lump in my throat. "Before we go and visit today, I'll mow your lawn."

Anything to keep busy and not think.

"You don't need to, love. I'll do it later. It's a time thing."

Like the dishes on his sink.

Time escapes us all. I blame myself for how little time it took to fall for Darcy. Now, I'm feeling a pain that's all too real.

"I want to. Remember when you used to let me help you? I do know how to work your mower," I say quickly.

Pop smiles as though he's remembering back to when I was young. When Gran was well.

We head outside and utilise the next hour by raking leaves, clipping shrubs, and pruning the flowerbed. The scent of mowed lawn and flowers squished on my hands is enough to lift my mood a little.

When we arrive at the nursing home, Gran is sitting in the shade under her favourite tree. She waves out to us, although it doesn't mean she recognises Pop and me as family, merely people walking by. She's always been a friendly, polite lady.

"It's a lovely day," she sings.

"It is." Pop takes the chair beside her and gives a nod to the nurse standing nearby.

"So lovely I'll go make us some tea." I indicate for Pop to stay with her and orientate Gran if need be.

I return with a pot of tea and china cups, place them on the table beside my phone, and an Instagram message notification lights the screen.

> **Darcy:** *Training took longer than I expected. I'm sorry I missed you this afternoon.*

I ignore the notification until Gran has finished her cup of tea. She is smiling, and I don't want to ruin the moment messaging back and forth.

When I leave Gran's side to visit the restroom, I send a quick reply.

> **Me:** *I'm visiting my Gran. BTW, I had a good time last night.*

Hopefully the last part of the message will imply I'm cool with everything. The way my heart sinks, I know it's a lie.

> **Darcy:** *So did I.*

I know he did. I was there. Yet, evasion is all too easy for him. I head back out to Pop and Gran forcing a smile.

Gran waves at me as though I've just arrived. "Hello, dear. Lovely day, isn't it?"

My chest tightens a little. "It is. The garden looks lovely this time of year." It's the same conversation I had with her earlier.

Pop stands. "I'll get the photo album."

Before I settle in next to Gran, my phone rings. It's Nate. It must be six in the morning in London.

"Nate," I say in a high voice, forgetting where I am for a moment.

"Hey, gorgeous, how are you?"

"Fantastic after hearing your voice." I smile. "What's up?"

"I have a date for the engagement party. Any chance you can come? What am I saying is I really need you here. I need members of my family to be beside me on the night. And ask Paige by all means."

I cough. "Wow. When?"

"Who is it dear?" Gran asks snagging my attention.

I withhold from telling her the truth. "It's my friend, Paige." I angle my body away from Gran. "I'm sitting outside at the nursing home, so I need to keep my voice down. I don't want to confuse Gran any more. Pop's headed to her room to get the photo album. Have you told him yet?"

"No, but when he gets back, put him on. No better time than the present. Could he make the trip?"

Even if Pop wanted to attend, I doubt he'd leave Gran. "I'm not sure," I murmur.

Pop walks up and places the album on the table. "It's Nate," I whisper. His face pales a little, and I want to reach out and hug him. "He wants to speak with you."

Pop nods once. I hand him the phone. He walks a short distance away and out of earshot. I block out his conversation and talk to Gran, opening the album and pointing to the photos she likes. The same photos I show her every time I visit.

Moments later, Pop is standing over me with his hand outreached offering me the phone. He's smiling. I take it and walk to the exact spot Pop stood seconds earlier. "So, what's the date?"

"Three weeks."

I gasp. "You're kidding? How can I be organised in three weeks?"

"You work for an airline company," he says and chuckles. "If anyone can do it, you can."

It all sounds wonderful, and I could do with a short break. "Give me a few days, and I'll let you know."

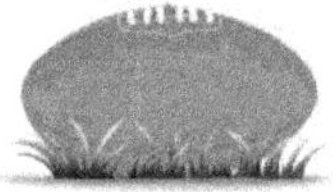

The following night I'm sitting at Paige's dining table. We both have our Macs open and a take-out noodle dish to the side.

"It's doable," Paige says with a smile ear to ear.

"I want to. Hell, I want to."

"But?" She shoots me her best scowl.

"Gran… I'm afraid something will happen while I'm away."

"You can't live your life waiting. You have to take the opportunities when they come."

I swallow, trying to rid the ball of fear growing in my throat. "I can't be like that. You know me. I hate surprises."

Paige squeezes my hand. "I know. It's time for change. I'm going to come with you. We'll be fine. Your grandparents will be fine."

I want to believe her.

"How are things between Darcy and you?"

I look down at my hands in my lap.

"What did he do?"

"Nothing."

"I know what *nothing* means." She stands and goes to the cabinet and pulls out two wine glasses.

I wave my hand. "I have an early start and really should get going. I wanted to speak to you about all this. If you can get the time off, I'll look into flights at work tomorrow."

Paige pours herself a glass, and I agree to only one, hoping it will take my mind off Darcy.

"I'll confirm tomorrow with an update. I can't wait to call Nate and tell him."

CHAPTER 15

ALLI

After a stopover in Perth last night, I arrive home exhausted. Throwing my suitcase in the corner, I kick off my heels and flop onto the bed. I'm thinking about Uber eats, something healthy-ish. Scrolling on my phone, I sit up when his message appears.

Darcy: *My parents will be at the game. I will try with them. Thought you'd like to know.*

A few words although it tells me more. Tells me he'll try because he knows it means something to me.

Me: *I'm proud of you.*

Darcy: *Don't compliment me yet.*

I smile.

Me: *What are you doing?*

Darcy: *Watching a movie. Staying low.*

He doesn't seem his usual self. I don't know why I sense it with a couple of messages, yet I do. Instead of replying, I unbutton my shirt and pull on a T-shirt. Leaving on my uniform skirt, I remove my pantyhose and slip on Birkenstocks. I'm rushing so I don't change my mind. I grab my keys. I don't think, I only drive.

The concierge is staring at me. I sit in a suede leather chair and open Instagram.

Me: *I'm in the foyer*

I don't get a reply. The receptionist is far too busy to notice. My heart is racing, my head is telling me to leave. I check the phone again. This time I log into Facebook and call him on messenger.

It's damn time we exchange numbers. Or is this why he doesn't give out his phone number. Acknowledging it's stalkerish behaviour, I decide to end the call and leave. Only he answers before I do.

"Alli?"

"Hi. I'm here. I don't know why, I just am. Can you buzz me up or do whatever you do."

He pauses, and my stomach falls and smacks the white tiles at my feet. "Okay, go to the receptionist."

I glance over as the last person in line walks away. She's on the phone. Her eyes meet mine. She says, "Yes," repeatedly, hangs up and summons the concierge.

"Who are you visiting?"

"Darcy Rayne." I'm eyeing the concierge's white shirt. Not a single visible crease.

"And your name?"

I don't want to look at his face only I do for a fleeting moment. "Alli Bradley." In that second, I didn't miss the way his eyes subtlety judge, and I wonder how often this happens.

"Follow me."

Inside the elevator, the concierge swipes his security card and takes me to level five. I step out, and the doors close behind me. I walk down the hallway toward Darcy's room, and it opens before I'm ten feet away.

He stands before me in track pants. No top. His tanned chest bare.

My mouth goes dry.

"This is surprising." He folds his arms over his chest. Muscles ripple and bulge.

I stop at his doorway and allow him to peruse me. "I have a feeling something's wrong. I wanted to check on you. Make sure you're okay."

Strong arms flinch and unfold. He steps back, pushing against the door with his shoulders to open it wider. "Come in, my little psychic."

I step around him. "Well, are you okay?"

He closes the door and walks to the couch. Only now I notice how imposing it is. Black leather and long enough for Darcy to lie on it comfortably. How the navy and red cushions are stacked at the end, I gather it's what he was doing.

"Hey, Google, turn off the television." Seconds later his television switches off. He's watching me. "Hey, Google, play my favourite playlist."

"You can't control everything," I say and barely hear my own voice.

His brow pulls to a tight V. "I know."

Drake plays through the speakers, loud enough that I have trouble hearing Darcy. He walks closer to the dome object on the display table. "Hey, Google, turn it down to level three."

The music softens.

It doesn't matter because I'm fixated on his abs, his biceps, and his shoulders. Hell, I don't know where to look. Everywhere is solid muscle, dents, and contours. I'm mesmerised, yet I sense him watching, knowing I'm staring at him.

"Why are you here, Alli." His tone drips with sexual provocativeness.

I glance up to eyes challenging me. With every step closer, I struggle to breathe. "I told you," I rasp. "I thought there was something wrong."

"So, you rushed here still in partial uniform." He's standing in front of me. Towering over me.

"Yes," I croak.

"Does it look like there's something wrong?"

"Don't," I murmur. "Don't pretend with me. I can sense it with you."

His large hands rest on his hips. The exact spot where the V arrows down. Tearing my gaze away, I look back into eyes searing mine. I don't know what's worse, only I know I can't be looking down to witness the rising of his cock. It's going to happen, I know it, even without special powers. The air crackles between us. He's like a caged lion calculating when to attack.

"Something is bothering you."

"Of course something is bothering me. Parents who couldn't give a damn are suddenly interested in parenting. And everything I've worked for the past ten years rests on us winning in ten days."

I nod in acknowledgement.

"Ten days," he says louder. "It's not a long time."

"I know," I say quickly realising he's annoyed with me.

"All I need to do is focus on the goal. Visualise us winning until there's no other option."

"Yes." I have no idea what to say to him.

"So, why aren't I?" he almost growls it.

"Because I'm here?" I cross my arms to hold them steady.

Darcy glances to his feet as he shifts his stance. "Right," he says under his breath. When he looks up again, there's hunger behind his eyes.

"I'm sorry. I was genuinely worried."

"And you wanted to help?"

"I'm sorry," I say louder and step around him ready to head to the door.

One hand grips my arm and halts me. "I can't because all I think about is *you*. I want to fuck you, Alli. Every damn night."

My chest tightens. A number of questions race through my mind. Is he using me? At this point, I don't care because I want him to. "Will it help?"

His nostrils flare.

He doesn't have to answer.

My hand twists to behind my skirt where I start to unzip.

His eyes hood. "I'm not talking about the slow type. It's fucking."

I jut out my chin. "I. Know."

He pulls my T-shirt over my head. My bra is unclipped and tossed aside in seconds. He leans down and kisses me hard. Nibbling on my lips between kisses. He lifts me up, but the tight-fitting skirt inhibits straddling. He carries me a few steps toward the kitchen bench. With our lips still fused, slowly he allows me to slide down his torso and over his thick erection. I gasp when it fuels my need.

My feet touch the ground, and he spins me around.

"Hang on."

"Hurry." I waggle my rear as he finds the fine line zip. He curses, and I figure his fingers are too thick to ply it from the seam. The hem of my skirt is pushed up and scrunched around my waist, my G-string lowered and flung aside. I go to look over my shoulder and stumble when my hips are pulled back and my thighs pushed wider.

Fingers push inside, and I groan, rocking my hips back, seeking him.

"Christ," he mutters. Lips press to my ear. "You want this as much as I do."

I tilt my head back to rest on his shoulder. "I do."

A wrapper tears, he moans a little before his cock pushes all the way in. I scream a little. He waits for me to relax, and then I nod. He starts slow, allowing me to move my hips with his rhythm, then he places a hand on my back to still me, and his thrusts quicken. I'm panting with every movement until my hips are jerked back, and he pounds me hard and fast, balls slapping.

The speed and intensity obliterates my senses until I can barely stand. "Darcy," I moan, my insides shattering when I orgasm. One hand wraps under my waist to support me. He's hunched over my back taking all of me as he forces himself deep and hard one last time and groans as though it's painful to come. We stay like this a moment. His head on my shoulder. Thick arms wrapped around my middle.

"You are my undoing," he murmurs.

I can't rally up the energy to respond.

He pulls out and walks to the bin. Waves his hand over the lid, so it opens. He disposes of the condom and looks up at me. I glance at his torso, naked, tanned, and hard. His thighs are like a gladiator's, long powerful muscles glistening with a layer of sweat.

I adjust my skirt sans panties. "Do you feel better?"

"Do you, or do you want another round?"

I know what he's doing. "No." I find my bra and T-shirt and dress while he watches. He stands there naked as though it unnerves me. It doesn't. He doesn't. I understand what he needs.

Control.

Because I also need it. Knowing he loses all sense of it when he's with me, gives me a power I was blind to.

"You look less stressed."

His nostrils flare again. "So, why do I want to fuck you again?"

I won't allow his words to push me away at a time he needs me most. "You can. Tomorrow night."

He frowns. "I thought you were working."

"I am. A red-eye, but I finish early afternoon."

He nods.

I find my clutch. "So, do you want my therapy?"

"Therapy. Is that what we're calling it." He smiles a little before slipping into his track pants. "I'll walk you down."

"No. I'm fine, thanks. I know my way out."

He comes to me, wraps his arms around my waist, and kisses the top of my head. "I'll see you tomorrow night."

"You will," I confirm. "If we do this, I want your phone number. I'm not going to stand in the foyer to be judged."

Darcy lifts his chin assessing me. "You come tomorrow at eight. I'll be in the foyer waiting. You'll have it before you leave."

The following night, Darcy is sitting in a chair in the foyer waiting, as promised.

"You're late," he says when I walk up to him.

"Bill me."

That gets a smile. He's wearing a white shirt and dark jeans. His eyes look bluer tonight.

"How was your day?" His tone is light, and I sense his mood has definitely improved.

"Good. All the passengers behaved themselves. It makes easy flying with no football players."

He smacks my rear and nods to the elevator.

"How was your day?" I repeat the polite nicety. Truth was I thought about tonight, about being with him, all day. I turn and look up to eyes gleaming with excitement.

"Trained like a pro."

"You are one." I laugh.

"I've been training like shit. Things were getting to me. Today was a new day."

Doors beep and open. We step into the elevator. "Sounds like my therapy is working."

Darcy picks me up, and I straddle him, not caring if the doors open on the next floor. He kisses me like it will be our last. Another ting. My back is to the doors. He walks with me like it's second nature to him. He stops and lowers me to open the door.

I lift a finger and trace my tingling lips. "I take that as you agree?"

"You know I don't like to break routine."

"So, this is a new routine. Can you keep it up for another nine days?"

He chuckles. "I doubt you could."

"I might surprise you."

He leans in close and kisses my ear. "You do. Every day."

I walk to his balcony and look to the ocean. The calm water an indication warmer weather is on the way.

"Do you want a drink?"

I turn. It's a formality. We don't need formalities. He needs to fuck me to clear his mind. It's the way it has to be for another week.

"I'm good, thanks." I start to unbutton my blouse.

He pauses, watches me. I keep going until I'm standing there baring my all to him.

"Go into my bedroom and wait for me there."

I do as he asks and walk around his huge bed tailor-made for him. The curtains are open, so I press the button to close the thick grey material. It's darker. Safe.

The door opens, and he pauses in the doorway. His silhouette moves. "By the window," I whisper.

My eyes adjust. He unbuttons his shirt. Then his jeans are kicked aside. "Get on the bed."

I crawl to the centre and wait.

"Lay on your back."

I do it. Soft lips press between my legs kissing my clit, caressing my sensitive spots, jumpstarting my heart into a quicker rhythm.

I moan and lift my hips. "I don't need foreplay. Not tonight."

He stills, and I sense him hesitate. Shit, I'm telling him what to do. I inhale a breath.

Thick, long fingers push inside of me.

I gasp and buck with the intensity.

He hovers, fingers still controlling me. I try not to squirm beneath him, but it's useless. I writhe with his touch. Climb quickly to an orgasm, ready to explode.

He stops and removes his fingers before I come. "I want you to feel all of me. I want to feel all of you."

"What?" My head is fuzzy after being denied the pleasure.

"Do you take contraception?"

"Yes," I whisper.

"Should I use a condom for other reasons…?"

"No," I rasp out. "Do you have anything?"

"What do you think?"

What do I think?

Club doctors are thorough, and I'm sure the players are checked regularly for STDs. He's not stupid or risky.

He trusts me.

And I trust him.

I reach down and take his cock in my hand and guide it to my entrance. He pushes in slowly, lowers his lips and kisses me. His kiss, gentle. His thrusts, tame. I take his lip between my teeth and bite down. It's a trigger. Darcy rears up, and his thrusts intensify. He's pounding me, and I'm building all over again. He slows, continues to caress my shoulders and neck with subtle kisses. Wrapping ankles around his back, I lift my rear like I'm riding him. Darcy's thrusts quicken. I build for another orgasm. I call out his name, and he finds his own release not long after. I turn to him when he collapses beside me. Stroke his face until his breathing slows. Arms wrap around my waist, and I feel his entire body slump onto the bed beside me.

We relax into a mould together, a perfect fit as reality returns. Only it's not normal. Lying here with Darcy is far from my normal. I run my fingertips over his skin and wish for us to stay like this.

"You know I have a spare ticket to the Grand Final. I would like it if you were there."

I don't stop stroking him to answer, "I can't," I croak. "I would love to watch you play, but it's too late to get leave and a sick day would be obvious."

"You could say it's an emergency."

Closing my eyes I roll to kiss him. "I'll try."

"Thank you," he murmurs.

I expect him to stir, ask me to leave.

Only his arm gets heavier around my waist, along with the sound of deep breaths. I lie awake a little longer until my own body melts into the mattress.

My phone beeps with a message. The sound distinct, even in sleep. A distant one when my clutch is in another room. I open my eyes to darkness. Unaware of the time, yet aware of the empty space beside me. I climb out of his bed, tentatively, and grab the top coverlet to wrap around me. My eyes adjust to the brighter light when I open the door to the kitchen lit up like Times Square.

I'm surprised to find Darcy *naked* and standing behind the island bench. His phone in one hand, a glass of water in the other.

"I fell asleep. I'm sorry."

His gaze sears mine.

Something is not right.

"I can go if you want."

He nods to my phone then places both of his hands on the bench and leans forward as though he's tired. Weak. My phone is lit up on the marble, and it's not where I left it.

"I think it's time we exchanged numbers." Irritation laces his voice.

"Now?"

"Yes. Now," he says louder than normal.

I pull the cover tighter around my shoulders and reach for my phone. There's a message on the screen. An unknown number, and when I read the first few words, I know it's not intended for me. "I've received these messages before, and I don't know who they're from." I glance up while explaining myself. "I'm sorry if it woke you."

"It didn't." His voice cuts through the air of the room.

I put my phone down and look up. He's slumped forward, head hanging. Hands fisted on the bench. I want to go to him. "Darcy…" I whisper.

He shakes his head and looks up. "How long have you been receiving the messages?"

It's there, sadness I've never seen before.

"Maybe two years. I don't know really. I don't respond to any."

"Read it."

I hesitate. Other times guilt fills me knowing the message is not meant for me. I shouldn't be sharing.

"Read. It." He annunciates each word.

Panic thumps through my chest. I swipe my eyes to clear my vision and open the message.

Unknown: *I need to share a secret with you since we told each other everything—*

"Told being past tense," he interrupts.

He has his phone in his hand. I inhale a breath and before I resume reading, Darcy continues to read from his phone.

"There is this girl. She gets me like really gets me."

I glance down to my phone, and it's word for word.

"It's taken me years to let anyone in, but she's different." He stops reading. His gaze remains lowered as though he doesn't want to look at me. "I don't need to finish it because you have it in a message. I don't know how the fuck you do or why you never texted and asked me to stop."

"I knew…" the sender was sad I wanted to say. I shake my head. "I'll delete all of them."

He shrugs, pushes away from the bench. "It's done. No need to exchange numbers now."

"Darcy." I take a step toward him.

He rubs his palms over his face. "I need you to go."

"Darcy, please…" He shakes his head.

My clothes remain scattered across the floor. He doesn't look up once while I dress. A ball of emotion grips my chest and bubbles up in a small sob. Snatching my clutch from the lounge, I swipe my nose with the back of my hand and walk toward the door. "You told me there was no one I should be worried about."

This time he glances up. A storm whirls in his irises. "I assumed you'd wouldn't be concerned with the dead."

The tone of his voice slices at my chest, opening a scar that held my heart together. "I'm not at fault here. You texted me," I cry out.

"And you never stopped it. I thought I was talking to a ghost. You have no idea how betrayed I feel." The look on his face crushes me.

"I'll come tomorrow, and we can talk."

Darcy shakes his head. "We'll talk about this after the final. I can't deal with anything else. Every time you leave, I'm thinking about stuff I shouldn't be. At least not for a couple of weeks."

"I don't want this to ruin us," I rasp.

I want him to say it won't.

"And I don't want it to ruin everything I've trained for over the past ten years."

I stand at the door and wait a moment longer. "I only wanted to help because I know you'd be there *for me* if I needed you."

He glances at me, but it's guarded. "I'm not talking anymore, Alli. I need to sleep."

As soon as the door closes behind me, the tears stream down my cheeks, continue all the way home until I'm in bed. In two hours I need to wake for work. I'm exhausted, pushing myself to the limit—for him.

I tried.

Expecting to hold onto anything or anyone meaning something to me is a sure fail.

Why does history always find a way of repeating itself?

CHAPTER 16

ALLI

Saturday night I walk through the terminal holding on to the last drop of energy inside of me. I want to collapse on the floor. Crawl to my car. And then close my eyes and breathe.

I make it to my car and lean back on the headrest. After a few minutes, I reach for my phone buzzing on the seat beside me. My chest tightening, hoping it's a message from Darcy. Wishing last night to be a big misunderstanding.

One voice message registers.

"Alli, it's Aubree. Please call Blue Skies."

A chill washes over me. I press the window so it lowers a little to allow some air into the cabin.

I press 'call back' and wait.

"Blue Skies Nursing Home, Aubree speaking."

"Aubree, its Alli. I missed a call from you."

"Alli," she says, her voice calm.

My heart continues to thump because I know staff are well trained. "I just finished work."

"I wanted to let you know Evelyn has been transferred to the hospital. She had a turn and fell and is having X-rays and a series of tests. Thomas is with her, and I reassured him I would let you know."

"Thanks. I'll head up there now."

I don't think, only drive.

Rushing to the information desk, I'm directed to the medical ward on level eight. After speaking to the nurse, she leads me to an empty room.

"You can wait here until your grandmother returns from X-ray. We expect to keep her in at least overnight. There are magazines on the bed table."

I pace the floor, too afraid to stop. I'm sick to my stomach, close to curling up in the corner and burying my face in my knees. After ten minutes of patrolling a dark window, I jump when the door opens. A nurse wheels Gran in, and Pop is not far behind. I go to him and pull him into my arms. "What happened?"

"She stood to go to the toilet and collapsed," Pop croaks. "They said her heart is *weak*."

Clenching my teeth, I swallow hard determined not to crumble in front of him. "She's in good hands here."

The nurse gives directions, and Gran is transferred to her own bed. She's smiling and showing no signs of distress. I notice a purple bruise above her right eye. "Was she unconscious?"

"Out for only for a minute. Didn't break any bones. She was lucky this time."

This time.

Gran sees me and smiles. "Aaliyah."

I stare at Pop in amazement. "You had us worried." I go to her. I lean over and give a tentative hug scared I'll hurt her. "Can I get you anything?"

"No one has fed me. What I'd do for a plate of roast beef."

I look at Pop, and he shakes his head. "They gave you sandwiches after your ECG, remember, Evelyn?"

"Sandwiches," she scoffs. "What does a lady have to do for a decent meal?"

"How about I bring you a plate of roast meat tomorrow?" I pat her hand. "Some for you and a plate for Pop. How does that sound?" The idea of cooking a heavy meal turns my stomach, yet it's the least I can do for my grandparents.

Two days later, my kitchen reeks of stale roast meat from the dirty dishes left in the sink. Last night I couldn't face eating something I cooked, although it was worth it to watch Gran eat every last piece. The leftover meat is in a container for Pop. After I clean up, I'll take it to him. Gran is being transferred back to the nursing home today, so Pop and I will wait and visit her then.

I arrive at his house a little before lunch. The garden looks neater since I mowed the lawn. I remind myself to purchase more freesias to plant. Supplying Gran with flowers from her garden requires more maintenance than Pop can provide. It's a little something I can do to help.

After picking a bunch of sweet peas from the garden, I drive Pop to the nursing home. Gran's face lights up seeing the flowers, and it makes it all worth it. Especially since her face is paler today. I reassure myself it's from being shifted about over the past two days.

It doesn't take long for Gran to drift to sleep while she's sitting in the chair. Her head falls to the side, and I place a pillow beneath her neck for support.

"Have you booked your flights to London?"

My attention shoots to Pop. "Yes. Although, I'm afraid to leave now."

He waits a moment before answering, "Evelyn would want you to go." His chin dips before continuing, "She always hated your brother and you being separated after we promised to keep you together."

"Nate was an adult when he left." I say his name softly, so Gran doesn't hear. "It had nothing to do with *us*." I include myself in the scenario. The path he's taken in life was best for him. If only I could be certain of my own journey. Still, I would rather be here with my grandparents watching over them like they did me. It's why leaving now when Gran's health is deteriorating makes it difficult for me to visit Nate. If something happened while I was gone, I would never forgive myself for not being with her, holding her hand like she did mine on many an occasion.

"I want to go." Pop swallows. "But I can't."

"I know." I reach out and place my hand over his resting on the wooden arm of the chair.

"I'll get a card, and write him a letter so you can give it to him."

"He'll appreciate that."

"She wanted to see him one more time." He looks pointedly at Gran. "I hoped he would come home before she forgot."

"She wouldn't recognise him now. Most days she struggles to recognise us," I add in a quiet voice.

"She would in her heart." Pop turns his hand over and squeezes mine. "And it would also be for him."

"I was going to ask him to come home for a visit. So you can meet Rebecca."

His eyes plead with mine. "If anyone can convince him, you can."

"He's stubborn, but it's time."

"Both you and your brother are stubborn," he reminds me. "Like your father."

I squeeze his hand and smile. "In a good way."

"Yeah." He sighs. "Because you all take after Evelyn. And she's perfect."

DARCY

The room reeks of menthol. An aroma that irritates some does the opposite to relax my mind. Tonight I need to trick myself into believing I'm not prepping for a game to actually get some bloody sleep. Yet, I know it will be broken sleep with Cleo icing my hamstring every bloody hour.

It's the third time in my ten years at the club I'm required to stay the night in a special room for injured players. A room designed for medical staff to give treatment throughout the night.

"Take the ice bag off in fifteen. Leave it on the table, and when I come back next hour, I'll collect it," Cleo says.

"Is that your way of being nice?"

Cleo folds her arms over her chest. "I thought you could get some rest."

I nod even though I'm hurting like a bitch. Cleo worked my lower back, glutes, and hamstrings with her strong hands to relieve some of the pressure. It's not her fault I lightly strained a muscle a week before the big game. She's doing her utmost to ensure it doesn't stop me from taking the field to play the game of my career. My mood is a combination of frustration and anger. I'm lucky to have her stay overnight and help. She's compensated well by the club, but Cleo gives the players her undivided attention and earns every dollar she's paid.

"Did I say, thanks?" She narrows her eyes at me. "I apologise. I appreciate what you do for me. It's—"

"I know." She throws me a blanket. "Keep warm, Rayne. Can't help you if you get sick as well."

I sink down under the covers and pull out my phone from my pocket. I still haven't responded to my father's earlier text. He can wait. I scroll through the messages. There would have to be at least fifty in the last hour. Some from my teammates asking how I am. Acquaintances asking if I could score them tickets for the game. And several social media messages from girls I no longer have anything to do with. I deleted that list long ago.

Cleo switches out the light before shutting the door. The darkness stirs thoughts to the surface. Thoughts about Alli, and the last time I saw her. Naked in my bed. My dick thickens mulling over that night. Hell, she must hate me. I type one word. It sits below the messages I sent to who I thought to be someone else. Mixed emotions rise in my chest. I send the solitary word not knowing what else to say.

Me: *Hey.*

The screen turns black waiting. I'm an idiot. She would be sleeping.

Alli: *Hi.*

Maybe she isn't. Maybe she's barely slept the past few nights like me.

Me: *I'm sleeping over at the club. The physio is treating me through the night. I can't sleep.*

Alli: *Neither can I.*

I have opened the box.

Me: *There are many things I want to say only it will have to wait. The timing sucks. I feel like time is playing me, and I won't win whatever way I chose to go.*

Alli: *It is what it is.*

Her response is short and full of wisdom. The messages cleared nothing, and now my thoughts are cloudier than ever. I've managed to block out the hurt, but it's the betrayal I struggle with. Emotion I don't know how to handle. Yeah, I was stupid to believe the messages were lost in cyberspace. Mobile phone numbers are recycled. When no-one replied to the first text years ago, I thought maybe it wasn't recycled. So, I stupidly presumed I was talking to a ghost. Saying stuff I wouldn't say to anyone else. I need Alli to know I wrote those texts because I was incredibly lost, and had no one to talk to who would understand. My entire gut was twisted as if it was wringing out every sad drop, and writing those messages helped in some fucked-up way. It was impulsive in the moment. Erratic and stupid when loneliness wears you down.

A fucking idiot.

Cleo knocks quietly before entering.

"You don't need to knock, Cleo. I know it's you." I roll onto my stomach ready for the ice.

Cleo flicks the lights on to the dim setting. "Giving the heads up in case you're immersed in—"

"For fuck's sake. Give me the ice."

"Don't take it personally. I know what guys are like."

I flinch when the ice bag touches my skin. "Guys?" I say between clenched teeth waiting for the cold burn to ease a little.

"Maybe it's me? I seem to attract the wrong type."

I turn my head on the pillow so I can see Cleo's face. "I didn't think you'd get much time to date during footy season."

"I don't, that's the problem. And don't offer to hook me up with any of your friends. That would be like throwing me under a bus."

I chuckle. "Wouldn't dream of it. In a week, you'll have more time, so..."

"Nope." She sighs. "Well, yeah, I won't be so time poor, but a friend has asked me to look after him exclusively." I shoot her a look. "Not like that," she growls.

"A footballer?"

"Cricketer. He's having surgery on his shoulder and coming back here for rehab."

"Jardine?"

"You know him?"

"Not well. Bumped into him at the Bay wearing a sling."

"Yeah, well, he's into my friend, and it's complicated."

"I'm sure it is," I say now feeling tired.

She smiles. "Don't want to bore you. Get some rest because I won't," she jeers.

She turns the timer for another ten minutes. "Take it off when this rings." She picks up the used ice bag and leaves me in the dark.

"See you in an hour," I moan.

CHAPTER 17

ALLI

After an overnight stay in Sydney, Carli and I are at the front of the plane ready to greet passengers as they board the flight to Melbourne.

Business class passengers queue to board. Two men dressed in business suits are seated first. Then a tall gentleman hands me his boarding pass, and his unusually tall wife hands her pass to Carli. My heart skips a beat when I read the name—*Mr Daniel Rayne.*

The height thing could be a coincidence along with the surname, but when I look up into the familiar blue-green eyes, I realise there's a high chance Daniel Rayne is Darcy's father. My fingers tremble as I hand back the pass. "Good morning, Mr Rayne. Your seat is in row 1 seat A by the window."

"Thank you," he says in a gruff tone. A tone similar to Darcy's when we first met. Only now I know Darcy has a softer side.

Carli's tone rises when she says, "Mrs Rayne," and I know she's thinking the same thing. Carli gives me a wide-eyed knowing look before smiling to greet the next customer.

More passengers board, and in a robot action, I read the name and seat allocation and direct them accordingly. My mind is stuck on Darcy, realising his parents are heading to Melbourne for the game. *When is Darcy leaving?* I know he spent the night at the club, and I promised myself I wouldn't mull. Yet, here I am worrying.

My fingers have trembled for days. I hope in a matter of days he forgives me and reaches out. Otherwise, what we had meant nothing, and it's more than I can cope with right now.

It's after seven when we arrive in Adelaide. I make my way to Pop's house. It's too late to visit Gran. By now, I imagine Pop to be sitting in the front of the television watching a show on the ABC network. In another hour, he'd be in bed.

I don't bother to go home and change. I'm thinking about Pop and hope he's eating. I understand how easy it is not to eat when your stomach's in knots. After smelling airline food all day, I can't stomach any myself. I'm coping fine. It's my grandparents I worry about.

Pop answers the door in a flannel blue-striped dressing gown. Long flannel pyjamas creep out below along with matching blue slippers.

"Thought I'd call in on my way home and check how Gran was today." He shoots me a wary look as though he knows I'm also checking on him.

"Had a better day today." He leads me to the kitchen and flips the switch on the kettle. I notice a blown light bulb.

"How long has that light been out?"

"Ah… a few need replacing. I'll get to them soon. I can see fine in the dark." He grins at me. "Your Gran made me eat carrots and blueberries all my life."

"I remember her at meal times watching over us to make sure all coloured vegetables were eaten."

"Only then did you get dessert."

I groan. "I couldn't eat another bread and butter pudding if you paid me."

Pop spins to look at me. "They were the best. What I'd do for one now."

I look around the kitchen and realise all the dishes are clean. No sign of food lingers in the air. "What did you have for dinner?"

"Made two sandwiches this morning before I went out. I ate one for dinner."

"And the other?"

"I'll eat it tomorrow night."

"It's not enough," I say in a calm voice. "You need more than a sandwich."

"Aubree has the kitchen staff sneak me a hot meal for lunch. I'm okay."

I smile knowing Pop has some pleasure in being sneaky. "You don't always like what's served to Gran. You said so yourself."

"Guess I'm hungry enough to eat it."

"My point. I'm going to call Meals on Wheels and ask if they can help."

"I'm fine. If I want something, I'll go shopping and cook it. I don't want to waste time away from Evelyn."

"Then I'll cook up a batch of meals and freeze those for you."

"As long as you eat some yourself." Pop cocks a brow at me. "Don't think I don't notice. You hide away under loose dresses."

He points to my uniform. "I know I'm not the only one not eating."

"You know I have Mum's genes," I say quickly. "And I'm not the one I'm worried about." Pop stares at me but doesn't say anything more.

I lean over and give him a kiss. "I better go. I finish earlier tomorrow, so I'll call into the nursing home in the afternoon."

Pop runs a hand up and down my arm. "I love you. And so does Gran."

I stiffen. It's the first time in a long while Pop has said the words.

"I love you, too. See you tomorrow."

DARCY

"Welcome to Melbourne. The time is eleven o'clock, and the temperature is a fine nineteen degrees."

I ignore the rest of the captain's speech thanking everyone for travelling with the airline.

"Hope it stays like this for a few more days," Dustin says as he stands to retrieve his carry-on luggage.

Coach shoots out instructions before we disembark the plane. "Avoid the media and any cameras that will be in your face when we walk through the terminal. Fans have made the trip from Adelaide, and many will be there to greet us. You may stop to sign autographs, pose for pictures, but then swiftly move on."

The fans were there and more than we anticipated. After handing a kid his pen, I glance up at the line of fans and notice her in the background. She's wheeling a small overnight case behind her. Two hostesses walk ahead of Alli. She's not laughing with the other ladies and appears to be deep in thought. Miles away. Her gaze shifts, and she's looking at my teammates. Something crosses her face, and she dips her head, so I can no longer see her expression.

Shit.

"Excuse me," I say to the kid, and I step out into Alli's path.

"Hey." She looks up.

"Hey." Her gaze lowers.

I don't like that she's nervous around me. I want to reach for her hand then several flashes catch me off guard. A television camera zooms in. *Fuck.* "I wanted to say hi. We can talk later…" Her eyes widen. What a dumb arse thing to say. Only I can't stop and dwell because Alli and I are attracting a crowd, and my coach is glaring at me. I stride toward the escalator. Coach stands with arms folded over his chest waiting for me.

"What was that about?"

"She's a friend and flown numerous times with the team. She wanted to wish us luck."

But she didn't. Not once.

"We're good?" He circles his finger between us, questioning if my head is where it should be.

"Yeah. We're good."

I wish I could say the same for Alli and me.

ALLI

After mulling over Darcy half the night, it seems as though I've barely closed my eyes when the ring tone of my phone wakes me. My fingers fumble in an attempt to locate it with my eyes still shut. I open one eye and groan.

Three in the morning!

I sit up when I read *Blue Skies Nursing Home* across the screen.

"Hello," I croak.

"Alli?"

"Yes."

"It's Marion, the registered nurse on night duty."

"Hi." I swallow. My heart thumps against my rib cage, sensing what she'll say next.

"I wanted to inform you Evelyn has been transferred to the hospital. We called an ambulance and she should almost be there. One of the nurses found her unconscious. Your grandfather is already on his way."

"Thank you for letting me know."

I spring out of bed.

In a rush, I pull on jeans and a jacket and head out the door, not bothering with my hair. The hospital is only a ten-minute drive and yet, it feels like an hour by the time I pull into the car park. I rush into the Accident and Emergency Department and find Pop sitting near a wall, hunched over, his face in his hands.

"Pop." I take the seat beside him.

He glances up and composes himself. "Hi, love. You didn't have to come when you have work tomorrow."

"I want to be here. I want to be with Gran, like you. She'll be scared when she wakes and realises she's not in her room."

Pop stares at his hands on his knees. "Yeah."

I know what he's thinking, and we can only pray Gran does wake. Another half hour passes before a doctor walks through the waiting room doors and calls for Mr Bradley. We both stand. He leads us to a small cubicle sectioned off by a curtain.

Gran is sleeping, and by looking at her nothing appears wrong. I take a deep breath and allow my shoulders to relax a little.

"We suspect Evelyn had a stroke. The degree unknown until we receive the test results. She has uttered a few words although she didn't make sense, and her dementia makes it difficult to assess her. We hope when she sees you, it may orientate her to the surroundings. We'll keep her in a few days until we know more. Stay by all means, but I suggest you go home and get some sleep and come back in the morning."

Pop glances at me. "I'll give her a kiss and come back in a few hours," I tell him.

"What about work, love?"

"Gran is more important. They'll understand."

I barely sleep when I get home, so after a few hours, I shower and return to the nursing home.

Gran has been transferred to a single room. I'm not surprised to find Pop sitting beside her.

Over the next four hours, she opens her eyes twice, stares at Pop and me, then her lids shudder close. Keeping my voice low and steady, I talk to her about Nate and how happy he is. Tell her he's going to be married, and she'll soon be a great grandmother. Someone once told me hearing is the last sense to go. Even unconscious people can hear what's happening around them. I want her to be informed on everything in the chance if something happens she will take it with her. When Pop leaves to use the restroom, I tell Gran about *him*.

"The stupid thing is I love him," I whisper. "I know you're laughing at me because I never liked sports. Still don't. But I like watching him even though the game scares me, and I'm afraid he'll get hurt. I didn't tell you before because he's the type you warned me about. You know, the one where you could stare at his beautiful face all day. Allow his strong hand to hold yours for hours because you feel safe when you're with him. When you're not, you worry." I pick up her hand and gently stroke it. "I know he *cares* about me. I think you'd like him."

"Like who?"

I look up at Pop. I didn't hear him walk in.

"A guy," I murmur.

"You've been seeing someone?" He positions his chair on the opposite side of the bed so Gran is between us. He sits crossed legged and takes Gran's other hand, glances up ready to hear my story.

The hurt I withheld from revealing to Gran, surfaces. The pain like a knife slicing my gut, tearing me apart. Wrapping one arm around my stomach for support, I clear my throat. "Not really. Well, in a way…"

Pop smiles. "You like him?"

I nod.

"What's his name?"

"Darcy."

Pop nods back. His vague expression has my shoulder's relaxing.

"Met him on a flight."

"You hear that, Evelyn? Our girl met this guy on a flight. You knew it all along, didn't you?"

I smile at the way Pop believes Gran set the whole thing up. Pop continues to ask questions, and I describe Darcy's appearance, avoiding the football aspect, only mentioning he travels a lot. I describe a fairy tale because deep down, I believe Darcy and I are no longer real. Gran and Pop deserve the fairy tale. When I next glance over at Gran, she's lying there, eyes open, listening. She smiles as though she understood everything I've said.

"Hey." I stand and kiss her.

"Welcome back, old girl." Pop kisses her on the lips.

Grans eyes dart between us and around the room. "I'll get the nurse." I head to the door and freeze in my tracks at the shrill in Pop's voice.

"Alli!" Machines chime and beep noisily around us.

I rush back to the bed to witness the light disappear in Gran's eyes. I take her hand in mine. "Gran," I rasp. A beg.

The door whooshes open, and the nurse hits a red button on the wall. Within seconds, staff surround her bed, and Pop and I are ushered out of the room into a waiting area. We sit opposite of each other with neither of us speaking. I stare at nothing but the floor or wall. I honestly don't know what's worse—having someone you love ripped away without warning, or watching him or her slowly deteriorate?

I can't allow my thoughts to wander, and yet tears stream my cheeks. There's a pain in my gut. One that's instinctual sending warning signals to prepare me for the worst. I suck in more air, holding back the shaky breaths that lead to sobs. *No.* I keep telling myself it won't happen. She will come back from this. It's just another turn. She won't leave us.

She can't.

I say it in my head, silently pleading to her.

Ten minutes later, the door swings open. I see a white coat and stand. Pop stands with me. The doctor places a hand on Pop's shoulder. "I'm sorry. There's nothing more we could do."

I burst into tears. Flinch at the crying of a tortured animal, and realise it's me.

Pop's arms squeeze around me.

I'm falling.

His voice is like a faint echo above the dark hole my mind has already entered.

"It'll be okay," he whispers.

I wish I could believe him.

CHAPTER 18

DARCY

Journalists clutching notepads occupy the majority of the seats in the media room of the luxurious Melbourne Hotel. Television cameras aim at the table holding the premiership cup, the cameramen ignoring the flashes of handheld devices.

Bill Stansborough, media director, directs me to a table where the Falcon's captain, Justin Pavlich, is already seated. There is no love lost between Pavlich and me. In two days, we'll be vying for the gleaming silver cup. We sit either side of the silverware like it's an apple from the Garden of Eden. Only it's height is the length of my torso. Golden leaves don the base. Teal, white, and silver ribbons, the colours of my team, are tied to the long handle closest to me. Gold and brown on the other. I'm staring at the trophy like it's a magnet to my eyes, taking in all of its glory while withholding a need to reach out and touch it.

Victory is so damn close I can taste it.

Dean Farlow coughs and introduces himself. His voice quivers. A journalist I haven't met before. His question is slow and long-winded about the better team on the day. Pavlich answers first, cuts to the chase, boasts about his team's fitness and winning six straight games to get here.

"We've won eight straight," I say with a level voice. "And our winning streak isn't over yet. The boys have never been more ready… physically or mentally."

John Boin raises his hand to speak. He's been around the traps for years and directs his next question to me. "What will it mean to you and the Thunder to take the cup home to Adelaide?"

"You've harped on this before, John," I say wryly, and it gets some chuckles. "We have worked solid on and off the track. During preseason, Coach set new goals, a clear direction to bring the Premiership Cup home to our city. We are true to the game and our preparation has been flawless. I know what I have to do. The team knows what it has to do, and the coaches know what they have to do. We *arc* ready."

"What about your hamstring?" Dean Farlow adds. "There were rumours you're not one hundred percent fit."

"Wouldn't be on the team if Coach had any doubt," I say firmly. "I am ready mentally and physically."

When I pause, another hand raises. "Steven Casey, ESPN. You lost the first three games this year, and everyone dismissed you being a premiership contender. It's also your first, and in fact, your young team's first Grand Final since the Thunder last won ten years ago. How will your lack of finals' experience fair against the Falcons who have played four out of the last six premiership games?"

I nod, unthreatened by his question. "Earlier in the year, we were trying out new game plans, using the first few rounds to execute those plays. For us, it wasn't about winning, but to get it right. It worked. Our execution is effective, our team is physically strong, and our younger guys are prepped. The last ten years for me has been a lead-up to this game. We have never been more ready. We don't look at it as lack of experience, but as an edge on the opposition because my guys want this more."

The last comment causes a few stirrings. The next question is directed to Pavlich. I'm quick to zone out and block his negative comments. My eyes drift to the back of the room, and I stiffen when I find my father leaning up against the back wall.

How the hell did he get access?

Our eyes meet. He gives me a swift nod of approval. Hell, going by his black suit, you'd think this was one of his board meetings.

I swallow hard, unsure of what to make of it. He assumed my football life stood for nothing. He is now witnessing it with all the grace and blessing of the country.

The remainder of the interview with the press blurs as I tear my thoughts away from my father and focus on what is at hand. I can't allow him to get in my head.

"Good luck, gentlemen, and may the best team win." Bill walks over and shakes Pavlich's hand, then mine. Security leads us past the rows of seats and into the foyer. Before I have taken my first step toward the elevator, my name is called.

"Darcy. I was hoping to have a word." Dad holds out his hand. I take it and give a firm shake. "Your mother and I want to see you before the game. Do you have time tomorrow after the parade?"

"I'll check with the team manager on our commitments. I'll give you a call."

"Do you have time now?"

I note the time on my wristwatch. "Team meeting in an hour, but I hoped to get a bite to eat first."

His phone is yanked from his pocket. "I'll call your mother to meet us in the lobby. Our shout."

"You don't need to pay for my food."

"I know." Two words that hold so much meaning. He wants to. He also acknowledges I've made my own path in life and don't need his money."

"There's a café down the road that has great Vietnamese rolls."

"Haven't you eaten lunch?" His brow pulls tight.

"Yeah. This is a snack." I give him a grin. "I need the carbs."

"Well, for your mother's sake, I hope they offer more than carbs." I smile. It's been years since we've talked like this. He speaks quickly into the phone then disconnects. "She's on her way... and so is Clare." He says it with a smile.

I haven't seen my kid sister in months.

I give him a nod. "I'm glad you're here."

Dad pats my back. A gesture of understanding. "Likewise. It's why I wanted a word. To apologise—"

"No need," I interrupt. I don't need thoughts to be emotional this close to the game.

We turn to leave then stop in our tracks when a camera is pushed at us. "Your father, Darcy?" Not a smart observation. Obvious really, when he's the only man in the hotel almost as tall and looks like me. Before I answer, he adds, "Can we get a photo of the two of you?"

Dad shoots me a wary look. I note the apprehension in his eyes, not for him but for me. "Sure," I say and give Dad a nod.

He snaps our photo and asks for his first name. "What are you going to write, Derek?" I prod. Derek has been known for his controversial articles.

"Your father is wishing you luck before the game. Not a lot of space left in the editorial, Rayne."

I give him a warning look. "Fine."

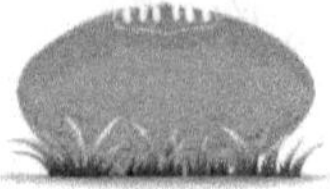

Overhead, the blue sky indicates no rain on the outlook for which I'm thankful if I'm to sit in the back of a ute, while meandering the city streets of Melbourne. Balloons and streamers cover each car chauffeuring the players in the appropriate team's colours. Friday is a public holiday in the city that lives and breathes football, so the fans have come out in the hundreds of thousands, donning their team's colours in playing tops, caps, and scarves. Banners wave high and flags flap in the gentle breeze as we make our way along the crowded street, waving and smiling, mostly at the kids.

There are a few boos, yet most clap even though the Thunder is not the home team. We are not the favourites to win over the experienced Falcons. When we reach a stretch of road lined with our fans, I stand and hang on to the back of the car. Dustin, our newest rookie from Renmark, is paired with me. It's his first year in the big league, and I have been watching the awe cross his face. Even though Rhett, his famous brother, played for the Blackbirds, he never played in a Grand Final. Ironically, Dustin is inexperienced, yet playing in the biggest game football can offer. He stands beside me, the only two in the back of the utility vehicle, and the first of our team's cars. Turning the corner, Thunder fans scream and cheer when we approach.

"Shit, there are thousands of Thunder fans," he says as though he can't believe it.

"More will be at the game tomorrow." I thump his back.

I wave to every kid that calls to us, point at them, and note the pride in their fathers' eyes. My heart is beating hard. We didn't expect this. Not this many fans to take time off work and travel to Melbourne to be here supporting us in the Grand Parade. I keep waving, embracing their support, my heart swelling with emotion. We turn a corner, and more silver and teal greet us.

"Bloody unreal," Dustin murmurs.

"Yeah, it is."

Because I've waited my whole life for this.

The team rallies in the media room for a meeting before heading downstairs for dinner. The air crackles with excitement. The guys endeavour to keep it low key, but in a room where we all share the same nervous anticipation, voices fail to hide the enthusiasm.

Coach calls for calm. He waits until the room is quiet. "Curfew stands. I want everyone rested for tomorrow." His eyes scan the rows of seats before him. "We will meet in the dining room at seven for breakfast. Bus will depart at—" Coach looks my way when *Run the World (Girls)* by *Beyoncé* tunes out in my direction.

Beside me, Dustin trembles holding in laughter. Then I realise my phone is vibrating in my pocket. I yank it out. "Cockhead." I remember being a lad caught up in the fun of pranking teammates. He took my phone to take snaps at the parade and must have changed the ringtone in a moment my guard was down. And it was switched off until this morning. I curse, blaming myself and hurry to silence it since Coach doesn't tolerate boyish antics. My fingers hover seeing the name on the screen.

Alli.

I hesitate, but there's no way I can take her call.

"When you're ready, Rayne," Coach's voice booms out.

"Sorry, Coach." I slip it back into my pocket and elbow Dustin before straightening in my seat. Plotting my revenge falls flat because I'm thinking about Alli and why she would call the night before the game. She doesn't know my schedule, so she probably wanted to wish me luck, since she didn't say it at the airport.

Coach continues his speech on team expectations.

I visualise his words, or at least I try to. My thoughts wander to the night Alli was in my bed. Hell, I can visualise her easily. The soft curve of her breast. The way her lips part when she smiles. The citrus, flowery scent of her skin. I take a deep breath, wishing it were Alli's scent I was inhaling and not the sports deodorant Dustin has sprayed over his clothes. My phone vibrates once in my pocket. A message. My fingers twitch wanting to retrieve it, only I can't. Not today. Not when she's already in my head.

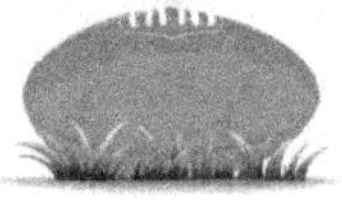

ALLI

After reading over the eulogy Paige helped me write, I push the piece of paper across the table toward Pop to peruse.

"You didn't have to do this today," he says in a low voice.

"I know. Every minute gets harder." My throat burns holding back tears. Tears that come easy.

I didn't sleep last night. Cried, but not into sleep. Only cried.

My chest is hollow as though someone has ripped out the remainder of my heart.

Paige rests a hand on my shoulder. "I'm heading out to grab dinner. Any requests?"

I shake my head, and she gives me a sharp look before turning to Pop. "Chicken and chips?"

"Don't want to put you out, love."

"You're not, Mr Bradley." Paige grabs her clutch. "You want to come for a drive?"

I feel like shit and look like it. No way am I heading out. "I'll stay in, thanks."

Paige has been by my side since the sun came up. I waited for the first sign of light before informing her. Chickened out of calling. I couldn't. Couldn't say the words. Even now they stick to the back of my throat. Not saying the words doesn't change the truth. I'm struggling to handle the reality because if I face it, I know I'll come unstuck.

I'm yet to call Carli. Next on my list since I called in sick, and she might hear it from someone else.

I push the eulogy aside.

When the door closes behind Paige, I head for the bathroom. I stand there a moment staring at my phone. My vision blurs, and I scroll past Carli's name and stop at Darcy's. After several rings, it goes to voice message. Closing my eyes, I listen to the calm of his voice. I press the end button and stare at my phone. What would I have said to him? I shake my head and wish he wasn't the person I want to be with right now. All I want is those long, muscled arms to wrap around me and pretend the world is okay.

Me: *Only wanted to hear your voice.*

I press send.

A stupid text, yet I don't know what else to say. Taking my seat at the table beside Pop, I keep checking my phone while he browses the photographs splayed across the white tablecloth, a small pile to his left, the ones he intends to use at the funeral.

I know Darcy's preoccupied, but all I want is a reply. Something to show me he cares.

Today, I need him to show me.

I'm staring blindly at a blank screen when it lights up.

Nate's name appears. "Finally," I murmur. Last night I left a voice message to call me back regarding Gran. Nothing else.

Pop glances at the phone. "Do you want me to talk to him?" I want to fall to my knees and bow my head. Pop has been my rock, staying strong when I'm the one who should be consoling him after losing his soul mate. He cried at the hospital, but since then, he's got on with what can't be avoided.

"I'll talk first," I croak out, my voice already faltering. "Nate," I rasp.

"Hey, Al. What's going on? You're still coming, aren't you?"

"I... Gran... died."

"What? W-When?" His voice cracks on the last word.

"Yesterday."

"How?"

"A stroke. The funeral is Tuesday." I rasp out every word.

Nate doesn't say anything for a few seconds, and it feels like minutes. "How's Pop?" His voice is low, flat.

"He's been strong." I glance at Pop, and he's looking at me as though he knows we're talking about him. Pop holds out a hand for the phone. "I'll put him on."

"Nate."

Tears cascade down my cheeks. Pop rubs my arm before standing and walking outside to talk to Nate. I know he believes he's saving me from the pain of hearing it all again, but nothing can stop it. The pain is unyielding, searing my chest like a katana sword. Pushing up from the table, I walk to the sink and start washing the pile of china mugs. I've been at

Pop's house since nine. I don't really want to leave because around him, I'm better. At home, I'm lost, a refugee.

In a matter of minutes, Pop enters the front door. "He won't be coming to the funeral." He hands over the phone and takes a step back, a stony expression crossing his face.

My stomach drops knowing Pop's upset. I take the phone from Pop and turn away before I talk to Nate.

"You're not coming?" I say incredulously.

"It's not that I don't want to. I *can't*."

"Can't or won't."

"Can't. Cut me some slack, Al. I'm not a defiant teenager anymore."

"Then what?"

"I had a DVT." He doesn't have to explain the medical condition to me since it was part of my training. "Spent a few days in hospital two weeks ago. Not a big blood clot, but the pain in my leg was indescribable. I didn't want to worry you until I got the all clear. I'll be on the drugs a while longer."

"And you can't fly," I whisper, acknowledging.

"Not for another two weeks, and that makes it close to the engagement party. The timing really sucks, I know."

Time has its own law. It plays havoc with plans. One day it's on your side, the next it's like an opponent. "I need you here," I whisper.

"I'm so sorry, Alli-girl." A sob escapes my lips hearing the name he called me when we were kids. "I can't risk it."

"I know."

"As soon as you get here, I won't leave your side. Promise."

"I'm not sure I can come, leave P..."

Pop looks up before I finish saying the words. He gives me a pointed look. "You have to go. I want you to. So, would Evelyn."

"I don't want to leave you," I whisper. "You could come now..." I take a deep breath when Pop shakes his head.

"If it were another time."

"Alli, he's right," Nate says. "The timing is off. Another month or so and nothing would stop me getting on that plane. I want to be there. Hell, you have to believe me." I nod even though he can't see me. "I loved her, too."

I close my eyes and visualise Gran's pale face moments after she passed.

"Alli, you have to come. I need you to come," he croaks. "I need family here."

"Okay." I sniff and wipe my nose. "I'll call you later."

"Tomorrow. Call me tomorrow, Al."

I end the call as Paige walks in the door with dinner. The hot greasy smell turns my stomach, and then I'm heading to the bathroom. My stomach heaves yet nothing comes up. I keep heaving, knowing I have to stop myself since I haven't eaten anything all day. I sit back on the cool tiles and wipe my mouth. Black dots join in front of me. I lie down and close my eyes in case I pass out. I stay here a moment enjoying the nothingness until a quiet tap on the door disturbs the serenity.

"Alli. Can I come in?"

"Coming," I call out to Paige. "I needed a minute."

Taking a deep breath, I walk out. Paige is serving dinner onto three plates. "No more for me," I say and stop her from piling fries on my plate. "I'm not hungry."

"You've barely eaten." She stops when I glare at her. "I'll put it here."

"Really appreciate you doing this," Pop says. "It smells great."

"You're welcome." She glances at me.

Knowing she's watching, I pick up a piece of chicken and chew it slowly. It doesn't want to go down, so I keep chewing telling myself to swallow. When it finally slides down my raw throat, I nod at her. "I also appreciate you being here and helping. Only I'm not up to eating."

"Try, Al. You have to keep going."

I nod knowing it's not only food to what she's referring.

CHAPTER 19

DARCY

Twirling the ball between my fingers, I focus on Coach yelling out directions in the change room.

"Be first to the ball. Find your man. Attack the ball." He points to his scribble on the whiteboard and taps his marker on *No 50/50 balls*. "We make it sixty-forty. Or eighty-twenty. Make your transfers count. No passengers. Everyone contributes. You men have worked hard to get here, so go out there and make it bloody count. Back yourself and believe."

"Back yourself, and believe." The team shouts back.

Outside, the crowd roars in the stands above. Flames explode near the entrance we're to run through in a matter of seconds.

Boots clink on concrete running through the underground tunnel. Our club's song sounds out as we jog onto the field, fans screaming in support. Ninety thousand devotees to the game. The hairs on the back of my neck stand to attention. My body tingles with raw emotion.

This is what we play for.

This is our moment.

We gather at the banner and wait for everyone to group. "The game gives back to those who believe," I shout to my men.

"Back yourself and believe," they roar.

Chest out, I burst through the banner, ripping crepe paper apart. The noise is deafening. Experience tells me not to look to the stands, not to focus on the crowd. For a stolen moment, I do and take it all in, absorb why the adrenaline pulses through my arteries ready to fight. My gaze circles the oval and lands in the member section where my parents are seated. Air whooshes out of my lungs in relief. I've made peace with my dad, and I'm elated they can share this slice of history with me. My only regret is Alli is not here to meet me after the game. To take me in her arms and tell me she's proud.

Next year, I tell myself. Head down, I bounce the ball onto the grass, and stride out the next thirty metres testing my hamstring.

It's halftime, and we're down by seventeen points. The Falcons' experience showing in the centre with on-ballers snagging sixty percent of loose balls. My tap-outs have been accurate, but the younger lads are standing flat-footed and allowing the Falcons' rovers to swoop in and intercept the tap.

Coach throws his pen at the wall. "What's the use of practising plays if your execution is passive. This..." He bangs on the whiteboard to his scribbling. "First to the ball does not mean stand and wait for the fucking thing. Doc is winning the ruck, but you men have to move your fucking arses and jump on it. Dustin. You have to play in front of Lawson. Give him nothing."

Thoughts in the back of my head push forward to my pre-game preparation. My knee bounces as I run through my routine. Same breakfast. Same jocks under my shorts I wear to every game. Clare's horseshoe key ring sits in the pocket of my training bag. I'm drinking a red Powerade. Nothing is different, yet something is amiss. I try not to contemplate my parents being here as unlucky.

My skin crawls as though a ghost is sitting next to me.

My knee bounces faster. I take another swig of the red liquid.

Focus.

"Doc, use your voice more. Direct the plays." I nod at Coach. "You're still in this. Get your head in the game and go out there and show the bastards what we're made of."

The boys chant back.

I can't fix this on my own. Coach is right, I have to direct my men. I believe in my team. Not many teams as young as ours get an opportunity to play in a final. These guys don't take it for granted. They have worked hard. Coach gave us a great plan, and we need to go out there and execute it, then the game will give back to us, and the scoreboard will take care of itself.

At the end of the third quarter, we matched them goal for goal, but we were still down by seventeen. After each ruck, I reach for my hammy. It's tightening up and affecting my kick. Fifteen minutes into the last quarter, we're only down by eight points. I sub out. Cleo orders me to lie prone on the grass as she works her fingers into my hamstring. I cringe as her fingers push deep into tense muscle. From here, I watch the ball sail out of the centre to the forward line. Jenks marks in front of goal, and the crowd erupts. Teal and silver flags wave through the air, stop when he lines up for goal. Fists clenched, I hold my breath following the curved arc of the ball spinning in the air toward the white posts.

A bloody behind.

Fuck.

"You done?" I shoot at Cleo.

"Yep." She smacks my thigh. "Go."

I'm bouncing on the spot at the interchange line waiting for Jenks to relieve me. "Doc," the specialist ruck coach calls out. "Go to the forward line and put Dustin in ruck for the next bounce."

I frown at him, and although I have faith in Dustin, it's crunch time, and I have smashed the ruck all game. Jenks runs past me and taps my hand—my legs hurl me toward the goals. "Dustin," I shout. "You're up." I point to the boundary line. At eighteen, Dustin is nearly as tall as me. He's lanky and still needs to work out in the gym, but his limbs are Gumby-like, bending like rubber even though he's not green. An odd technique, yet those long arms reach high for the ball and flick it to Cooper.

Cooper drops it on his boot, and it sails toward me in the goal square. I leap from behind a Falcon player and take the ball. My feet have barely landed on the turf. I'm off balance, yet I notice Max in front, alone. My opponent releases me, and I handball it to Max. He's quick to drop the ball on to his boot, and it pierces the centre goal posts. It all happens so quick, I'm still regaining my balance. I turn to witness flags waving in the stands. The goal umpire snaps two fingers out front signalling the goal. "Yeah," I scream out. My teammates sprint from all sections of the field to hug and pat backs, Max and I centre of the huddle. I point to Cooper and Dustin, in commendation.

Minutes are left on the clock.

We're one point down.

The deafening roar of the crowd fades. Replaced by a sharp ringing in my ears, and the thud, thud, thud in my chest. A new source of energy surges through my body watching Dustin line up in the centre circle ready to ruck. He has to get the ball down to me in the forward line as fast as possible. I'm pacing and edging closer to help out. I want to be in that damn circle and winning the ruck to ensure the ball gets in the hands of a Thunder rover. It's out of my control, and it's damn killing me knowing the clock is ticking. Everything I've worked for comes down to the last seconds of this game. I've been true to the game. Given it my heart, blood, sweat, and tears. Proved the doubters wrong. With seconds left on the clock, I'm losing the calm to fight or flight. I'm held back like a boxer when his opponent takes to the ropes. I want to shout, *give me the damn ball.*

I'm bouncing, jab stepping watching as Dustin takes the ruck and taps the ball to Cooper. He takes off, heading straight down the guts towards me. Bounces it once. Twice. Then puts it on his boot and it arcs toward me. I jostle with my opponent, both pushing to get the better position. It comes down to physical strength, who will stay on their feet and maintain balance as the ball falls from above. Out the corner of my eye, I notice the Falcons' captain tear in from the side as though he's going to take the mark in front.

Fuck! No, you don't.

I push forward, leaping high. The ball drops, bodies crunch, fists rise, and I manage to get fingertips to the leather. Air whooshes out in loud grunts of exertion around me. I topple, vaguely aware of bodies falling with me. My eyes were fixed on the ball, and over everything that was happening, sheer determination allowed me to land with the ball as I crash into the ground and on top of another player, my back crunching as I roll.

From the ground, I raise the ball from my chest, the whistle sounding, and somewhat relieved when legs and arms uncurl from me so I can stand. Pushing up to my knees, I'm tentative.

Unfolding slowly. Urgency takes over to take my kick and get on with it. Coach's voice is in the back of my mind reminding me to stay calm. More thoughts push forward of what this goal could mean.

I block it out and concentrate at doing this one job.

Kick the ball through the centre posts as though I'm at training and done it thousands of times before.

Lining up with the goals, I jog forward taking my time as I think of balance, timing, and execution of the kick. It sails high and long... and straight through the goal posts.

Whistles sound, teal and silver flags wave. I stand rooted to the ground waiting for the goal umpire to signal and wave the white flags that matter most. In my head, all sound is muted. I'm standing alone on the field. Waiting. Praying.

Two flags wave.

A goal.

Tension rushes from my shoulders.

I scream out and punch the air.

My teammates come from everywhere to jump on my back, rub my head like I'm an eight-year-old, and smack chests with me.

I'm laughing with them, rallying in the glory for a few seconds until I acknowledge the game isn't over. There is still time for the Falcons to kick another goal and retake the lead to end our victory dance.

Taking my position in the goal square, I'm forced to watch Dustin take control of the ruck. "C'mon, kid, you can do it," I murmur. He goes up and down when the Falcons' ruck knees him in the stomach. *Shit.* Dustin's on the ground, and the ball lands in a Falcons' on-baller's hands. He takes off, breaking free of our defender's tackle. He boots it downfield to their forward player, Hendry. Hendry is awarded the kick twenty metres out from goal.

"Bloody pick up your man," I yell.

Then the siren sounds.

Both hands pull at my hair as I moan loudly. Players fall to their knees knowing the result will depend on this one kick. Slowly, I walk to the centre, watching Hendry stall, pull up his socks, angle the ball at the goal and jog slowly toward the white posts.

He kicks the ball—it spins, keeps spinning toward the goal and hits the post!

Fans roar, the sound booms across the field. I sprint to the centre, jump on Cooper's back, hug him, hug every player I can reach.

Dustin is up, all pain forgotten.

Tears are shed. Tears of joy. Laughter, elation, regardless of the exhaustion coursing through my body.

We fucking won!

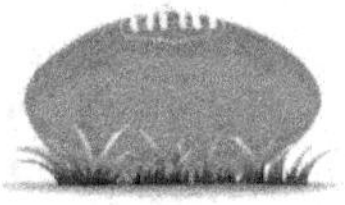

ALLI

The seconds it takes to become conscious from a deep sleep, those seconds my brain signals to wake, my body retaliates, turning to lead even though my lids are still closed.

My eyes won't open. I want to stay in the dream where my heart is light yet full, and Gran is still alive. Rolling over, I shiver and pull the duvet over my shoulders. Prying one eye open, I peek at the time. Nine-thirty. I groan and curl into myself.

Last night Paige called Carli and filled her in on why I'm absent from work. I took two weeks leave, so I don't have to go back for a few days after I arrive home from London. Paige relayed the message that Carli will call in later tonight when she finishes her shift. I don't want pity. I want to stay here in my dark room and hide.

My phone vibrates on the bedside table. I moan again and consider not answering it but change my mind when it could be Pop.

Darcy's name appears at the top of the screen. I suck in a breath, hesitate.

"Hello," I croak.

"Are you sick?"

"No. I'm... not having a good day."

"It's mid-morning. Bit early to be making assumptions about your day." He slurs the last few words.

"Have you been drinking?" Words catch in my scratchy, dry throat.

"What do you think, Alli? We won for fuck's sake. Bloody won when many thought we wouldn't."

"Oh, right. Congrats," I say trying to sound enthused.

"Congrats," he snickers. "Thought you could've sounded a little more excited.

"I know it's a big deal, but—"

"Yeah, it *IS* a big deal! It's everything I've worked for. All I've ever wanted. The reason I haven't been to bed yet and drinking with my mates."

"I'm happy for you, I am." The emotion in my voice betrays me.

"Yeah? I'll let you go about whatever it is to make your day better. We're flying home this afternoon, so the team can continue celebrating with the fans in Adelaide. I'm heading to a supporter's lunch now with the fans who made the trip to Melbourne."

"Enjoy it all," I say softly. I can't tell him the truth. I don't want to ruin anything for him.

"Right..." He takes an exasperated breath. "Nice talking to you. Thanks for your congratulations."

With the heel of my hand, I wipe away tears. Maybe if I got drunk, the pain mightn't hurt as much.

I'd do anything right now not to feel.

DARCY

Marty, our team manager, insists we drink coffee before boarding our flight.

I snort. As if it will help us sober up. "No one is to order any alcoholic beverages. No drinking until we arrive in Adelaide. The last thing I need is one of you blokes being kicked off the plane for indecent behaviour."

"I'm sure the hostesses will understand," Jenks shouts.

Hostesses.

I freeze, then remember I had talked with Alli and assume since she was having a bad day, she wouldn't be working. The team is on a high and talking loudly when we board. Before take off, I notice Carli talking with passengers at the back of the plane.

This is a chance to get some shuteye because as soon as the plane lands, we'll be back in full swing, celebrating and heading to the stage to be presented to our fans.

I remain awake and wait.

Minutes later, the beverage trolley wheels along the aisle. "Anything for you, Darcy?"

"Water, thanks."

"Congratulations, by the way. You all played well."

"You saw the game?" I want to ask if Alli was with her.

"I did. It was fantastic to watch."

I wait a moment before quizzing her. "Did Al watch with you?" I say it quietly so not to get any ribbing from the blokes.

Carli shakes her head. "No. She's…" Her voice falters. "I'll talk to you later."

I fold my arms and settle back in my seat. Carli's expression confirmed what I already know. Alli wasn't interested in watching my game, and I'm glad I'm not seeing her for a couple of days. Nothing is going to dampen the festivities.

The plane thuds when the wheels hit the runway jolting me out of a sleep. I sit up, look around, and notice the rest of my team stirring. We file in line to disembark the plane, passing the captain and Carli, thanking passengers for choosing the airline. Carli stops me.

"You need to call Al," she whispers.

"Why?"

"She's not good. Her grandmother died, and the funeral is tomorrow."

"Shit." I'm not sober enough to remember what she's telling me. "I'll call her later." My fuzzy brain makes a mental note.

One that gets lost with more celebrating.

By ten o'clock that night, I can barely stand and fall into a taxi heading into the city. Cooper falls in after me. I retrieve my phone to call Dustin and check where the rest of the team is headed. Only I can't read the screen. There's a text. I have no idea who it's from. Whoever it is can wait.

I'm not ready to quit partying yet.

CHAPTER 20

ALLI

I've never been one to wear black.

Yet, for days, black has harmonised my every thought. The world playing out under thick dark clouds in my own apocalyptic movie.

So, today I wore black.

This is my first funeral service since my parents' death, and I couldn't view their bodies since their remains were a charred mess.

No matter what I felt then, nothing could prepare me for this.

In a mental list, I've noted everything in the tiny room which isn't much of an observation. One wooden table covered with a white doily, a crystal vase holding three white calla lilies, a brown, wooden cross positioned in the centre of the wall behind me, and a red cedar coffin pushed against the far wall enclosing the most important person in my life.

With each tentative step, I hedge closer until I'm staring down at my grandmother's pale face. My hollow chest opens, and I feel like I'm falling into a rocky crater, a dark hole. A black mass. Then I notice her cheeks are brushed with rouge, her eyes made up like I've never seen before, and lips a soft shade of pink. She looks at peace. Content. And it throws me. I look closer as though searching her coffin holds answers. Lace sheets tucked in under her chin hide the rest of her frail body barely filling the coffin. A single red rose, the stem the length of her chest, adorns her.

I want to take her hand in mine, tell her I love her, will never stop loving her.

I shiver, the coldness filling the hollow cavern of my chest. "I'll never forget you," I whisper. "You're my inspiration. Every time I watch *Lucy*, I'll think of you." There's a gentle knock at the door behind me. Before I leave, I lean down and kiss Gran's cheek. When my lips meet her ice-cold skin, I jerk back. I stare at her face, and in this moment, realise she's an empty shell of a body. I look around as though her spirit is in the room with me. "Please, Gran, if you're here... stay with me." Tears drip from my chin. "I need to know I'm not alone." I unclip my necklace from around my neck, the one she gave me on my sixteenth birthday. A sterling silver cross and chain. "You need to take this, a piece of us both to stay with you always. I love you." I choke on the last words as more tears fall.

A second knock has me backing away from the coffin. I pat my cheeks and open the door.

"Sorry, Miss Bradley, it's time to take your grandmother to the front of the church."

"I understand," I tell the funeral director. "I'm... all done here," I whisper.

I check my phone and realise I've been in the private viewing room for thirty minutes.

I squeeze Pop's hand during the eulogy and watch him wipe his eyes once.

My eyes run like a tap.

Paige hands me a tissue for the twentieth time, wraps her arm around my back.

The priest signals, and I make my way to the stand. My breath coming out in little pants.

Fingers tremble as I unfold and straighten creases out of the piece of paper.

"Exceptional. My grandmother was ex... exceptional," my voice cracks, and I stop. Take a deeper breath and gulp water from the glass on the wooden stand.

"A matriarch and a believer, teacher, and guide. Evelyn believed dreams came true and nothing should hold you back from achieving those dreams. Never fear." I look up and note Paige's parents sitting a few rows back. I smile bleakly when her Mum gives me a nod. Behind them, Carli blots her eyes with a tissue.

"My mentor and comforter even before the day my parents died." I keep my head bowed, afraid to look at Pop. "Both my grandparents stepped up in a time of need, and Gran taught me to listen. Seek out answers to questions I buried deep in my heart. How to cope." I swallowed the lump in my throat. Recall the words she would whisper if she were with me now.

"Her constant loving presence shaped us." I smile at Pop. "And her supportive words, words filled with love, will remain with us forever. I recall them when I need to know she is still with me, an angel on my shoulder. We will miss your cooking, singing, hugs, and those stern looks." I smile now because my friends knew not to argue with her. "Miss the days we sat and watched *I Love Lucy* together. The days where you taught me to garden… and make pots from clay to nurture seedlings." The list of Gran's skills rolls off my tongue, and I glance up, look beyond Carli. Alongside her are Sammie and Georgia who also work for the airline and nurses and staff I recognise from Blue Skies Nursing Home, including Aubree. Further back some men from the bowling club where Pop used to bowl a few years ago. Otherwise, it is a small, private service.

"You impacted many lives, influenced, and shaped me." As I talk about her influences, I can't help feel some anger toward Nate. Part of the grief response, maybe. If I'm being honest, it's because I need him here for support. I take another sip of water. "I wanted you to be immortal. Hoped never to be here saying these words. Afraid of a life without you." Discreetly I wipe a tear, lift my gaze to Pop. "Your love and knowledge woven in tapestry, now completed. You will continue to inspire me… us. Admire you for your strength and how you battled a frightening disease knowing how it would affect us, not just you. Your strength is what guides us to listen and to live with courage in our hearts. The place in my heart where I will keep you. I will try to be strong, every day, for you. We will miss you for the rest of our lives."

I fold the note and walk the few steps back to my seat. The quiet room escalates the clicking of my heels on the tiles. Pop takes my hand as I slide in beside him. He sniffs. "She would be proud."

I bow my head, and in the moment, try and feel Gran's presence, imagine her smiling face.

The priest blesses the coffin, and then the congregation, four gentlemen step forward to wheel the casket along the aisle and out of the church to the hearse. Days ago, I stopped feeling sensations outside my body, numb to the external pain, only to bear the ice filling my core. I put one foot after the other, my head down as Pop and I walk behind the casket.

October sun heats the ground, and dry dirt powders into small dust clouds as feet stomp the area near the gaping hole in the ground. We gather near the priest who waves people closer as they arrive. There's not much room for a crowd with other graves merely feet away. It's a new part of the cemetery, and I only hope the grass grows as green here.

The priest commences a prayer, and I link my fingers with Pop's. He talks about Gran's life, her love for her family. Pop trembles beside me holding everything in. He leans forward and then someone is there with a chair. His composure crumbles as he sobs into his hands. I kneel beside him, cry with him with my head on his shoulder. We watch her coffin lower, and I say my final silent goodbyes.

"Farewell, my love," Pop rasps out, and I lose the last thread of sanity, lowering my head to Pop's lap and sob. The kind that scorches your throat and slices your heart as it steals your last breath.

A hand rests on my shoulder.

The funeral director passes us both a glass of water. I take it, and when I hand back the empty glass, my gaze darts to the small crowd behind us, and I see *him*.

DARCY

"What are you doing here?" Aubree whispers after she oversees the look Alli gave me.

"Later, Aubs," Hunter says under his breath.

What am I doing here?

I woke an hour ago, after finally hitting the sack around six this morning, and after two full days of partying. My eyes were barely open when I scrolled through the long list of congratulatory messages on social media, stopping at Carli's.

Carli: Alli's grandmother's funeral starts at 1 p.m. Burial service on Goodwood Road at 2 p.m. Alli needs you!

I vaguely remember Alli's phone call. The alcohol blurring the past two days into a continual celebration where time meant nothing. Staring at the text, I remembered the look on Carli's face, and something registered, told me to be here, regardless of my throbbing head.

Nerves had hit me while walking over to the small congregation at the southern end knowing I was late. Seeing the only hearse parked to the side didn't take much to figure I was at the right place. When I saw Hunter, the captain for the Blackbirds standing with his wife, I hesitated I got it wrong. But then *she* turned, locked eyes with me, and obliterated my heart. Her pale, gaunt expression knocked me for a six.

My heart thuds in my ears, a deafening drum. While she was suffering, I was partying. Realisation sets in, clawing at my chest. She needed me, and I was on a high from winning, too drunk to care.

What an arsehole.

I swallow down the lump in my throat and loosen the top button of my shirt. The priest signals for everyone to take a rose to drop into the grave, say their last goodbyes. Hunter and Aubree file in line and I follow, since it seems the right thing to do.

I've been to four funerals in my life, two in my teen years, which I barely remember.

One was Kelsey's.

I'm lost at what to do for Alli. When it's my turn, I take the rose, drop it over casket, and say a few silent words.

I didn't know you, but I wish I did. Seeing Alli this upset, you must have been a special lady.

In a fleeting moment, I glance her way, our gazes lock, her bloodshot eyes widen, those heart-shaped lips part, and she mouths, "Thank you."

I sense her grandfather staring at me. I give him a nod, and follow Hunter to the back of the group. The priest invites everyone to the house on the grounds for tea and coffee to salute Evelyn's life.

Evelyn.

Fuck, it's time like this I wish I wasn't seven foot tall. I want to shrink in shame. The group divides as everyone begins making their way across the lawn. Stepping forward, Aubree gets in my face. "What are you doing here, Darcy?"

I know Hunter from years back playing football, and when we all had partied together before he met Aubree. Now they are married with kids, and by her tone, she doesn't trust me.

I stare her straight in the eye. "I've been seeing Alli."

She gasps. "I don't believe it." I shrug. "You're hardly her type." I shrug again. She huffs before walking away to speak to some other ladies standing nearby.

My gaze levels with Hunter. His eyes silently question. "How do you know, Alli?" I ask.

"I don't. Aubree works in a nursing home. Alli's grandmother was a resident the past three years. Listening to Aubree this morning, Alli and her grandmother were close. I don't usually attend funerals with her, but she asked me to come to this one. Said she might need support because she knew it would break her heart seeing Alli upset."

I nod.

Hunter cocks an eyebrow. "You like her then."

I shift my feet. "Yep."

"Wouldn't be here after winning a Grand Final otherwise."

I rub the back of my neck. "Don't I know it. I'm struggling. Barely slept. The high has kept me going."

"Yet, you're here."

"I am."

"Then you need to go over to her, mate."

I undo another button beneath the tie. "I'm not sure she wants to see me."

"My guess is she's going to need you."

Aubree interrupts before I can say anything else. "We should head over," she says to Hunter.

And I follow them.

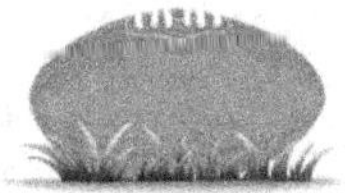

Everyone is getting ready to leave. I'm grateful for the coffee boost, and to Hunter who stayed with me at the back of the room. Any joy I was feeling this morning has dissipated. For the past hour I have watched photographs of Evelyn flash up on a big screen, pictures of a younger Alli, and her brother. It dawns on me he's not here. The photographer. I sense she's worried about her Pop, staying by his side as they talk to guests.

After Carli came and spoke to me, thanked me for coming, the nausea set in. My gut is tight. I can't help steal darting glances at Alli while Hunter talks about the game. Every time our eyes meet, she looks heartbroken, and I doubt anything I say will fix it.

"Dustin played well for a youngster," Hunter adds.

"He did. Something he'll remember for a long time." I loosen the tie from around my neck, my throat thickening as I watch Alli meander closer.

"Rhett was bloody proud. Couldn't stop talking about it. Only eighteen months ago he thought he was going to lose his brother to drugs. Coming to Adelaide, and getting a gig with the Thunder was the best thing that could have happened to him."

I remember Rhett and Dustin had lost their father in a tractor incident on the family farm. We all have internal struggles, and some of us lose the ones we love which threatens our sanity. So, we search for a fix to ease the pain. Mine was sex. Dustin took soft drugs. "The club ensures the right people are around him to help him stay on track."

He remains silent for a moment. "You know, my biggest regret is not winning a premiership."

I stare at Hunter. His team, the Blackbirds, may not have won a premiership when he was captain, but they played in finals games, and he won many accolades, including the most prestigious medal in the country. "Yet, you won a Brownlow."

Hunter's brow pinches. "Yeah, the year I married Aubree. It's what love does to you." He nudges me, and I look up. Alli is coming my way. "I better find Aubree and get back to the kids." He shakes my hand and strides off to leave Alli and me alone.

As soon as she's close, I take her into my arms and hug her tight. Fuck, she's all bones.

"I'm a little surprised to see you here."

I kiss her forehead. "I'm sorry. I didn't know…"

"It's okay." She steps back. "Who told you about today?"

"Carli sent me a text."

"Thank you for coming." She says it so politely it almost sounds rehearsed.

"Is there anything I can do?"

She shakes her head vehemently. "I'll be looking out for Pop for a while. I mean after I..." She gives me a look. "I'm going to London on Wednesday for Nate's engagement party. The timing is wrong, but Pop insists I go. He doesn't want to come. Too early for him to leave yet..." her eyes well, "... and I'm afraid to leave him alone." She wipes her eyes. "I'm suppose to fly over there and be all happy for Nate. I don't think I can."

"I can come with you," I say so quickly I surprise myself.

Her eyes widen. "Paige will be with me. It's Pop I'm worried about."

"If there's anything I can do for him, let me know?"

She smiles. "Thanks. We'll be fine."

I fold my arms over her, and my breath hitches.

"Thanks for coming, Darcy," she whispers.

She pulls back and nods as though she'll be fine.

She's not. We're not.

And my gut clenches in regret.

Tuesday consists of more interviews and sponsor commitments. Hell, I'm looking forward to a few weeks' break. The celebrations have not slowed. I've pulled back on the beer, to have my wits about me when I visit Alli. My gut has been in a tight knot since yesterday when I walked out of that damn sad room, saw the pain in her eyes when she whispered goodbye. As soon as Coach finishes his final address to the team, I'm in my car driving to Alli's.

When she opens the door, I'm surprised to find her dressed in an old sweater three sizes too big. It's not the sizing that surprises me—the weather in October is not sweater weather.

"Are you sick?"

"I feel the cold." She hesitates and then opens the door wider. "Sorry about the mess. I'm leaving tomorrow."

"I know. I'm hoping I could stay with you until you leave. I can drive you to the airport."

"That's not necessary. Besides I was going to spend the morning with Pop before my flight."

"I can still drive if you need a lift. Have you eaten dinner?"

"I'm not hungry, thanks."

I'm starving and skipped dinner to come straight here. And Al looks like she hasn't eaten in days… weeks. "My shout. Want to order in?" She shoots me a look, and I know I'm pushing her boundaries. "A movie?" I'll say anything to stay. I look to the television at *I Love Lucy* paused on the screen.

She doesn't say anything, so I keep talking.

"I know we need to talk about what happened, and that I owe you an apology—"

"Don't." She holds up her hand. "I can't do this now. We can't pick up where we left off."

I swallow hard. Adjust my voice. "You need to know why I reacted the way I did."

Alli stiffens and then she shakes her head. "No, I don't. It's none of my business. I'm really tired, Darcy. *Really tired*." She bows her head, and my chest tightens at the way she almost folds in the middle.

I go to her and guide her to the couch. "Sit a minute. Breathe," I remind her. "You don't need to say anything."

She lays her head in my lap, and I stroke her face. I'm not sure she wants me here only right now she needs someone, and I'm not going anywhere.

For the next hour, I sit still, allowing her to rest in my lap. Let her be. The television is muted, a black and white rerun of her Gran's favourite show. The quiet room has given me a moment to consider what I want. Every time I gaze down to her pale face, my chest clenches because I don't know how to fix us.

I didn't do this, but I contributed. Failed to be here when she needed me the most.

It's ten when I gently wake her. "Hey," I whisper. "You should go to bed. I can stay."

I help her off the couch and support her to the bedroom. I don't bother undressing her, but simply assist her to lie under the covers fully clothed. I strip down to my jocks and climb in beside her. Hold her, so she knows she's safe.

"Relax, and go to sleep," I whisper. "I'll stay as long as you need."

Hooking an arm around her, I keep her close to my body. I don't wake until the tapping of a pipe in the wall indicates someone's in the shower.

I check my phone and jump up. Hell, I should have woke before Alli. I tap on the door and wait before I enter. Alli turns away to cover herself with a towel. My gaze lowers to her rear, to thinning butt cheeks. The sight of her frail body knocks the wind out of me. "What do you feel like for breakfast?"

"With going away, I don't have much in the cupboard, sorry," she says over her shoulder. "Only gluten-free bread in the freezer."

"Perfect. I'll make us toast."

"I'm not hungry. Make enough for yourself."

I ignore her and place four pieces in the toaster. I know she likes hot tea, so I boil the kettle. It takes her fifteen minutes to eat one slice of toast. But she eats it.

"You don't have to watch over me," she says. "I know you have places to be."

"I'm not watching over you. I want to be here." She jerks a little at my tone. "I'm sorry, but unless you tell me to go, I'm staying."

Alli gives me a look, one telling me she's going to do that. Only her expression wavers, and she looks away as though I'm dismissed.

"I'll come with you." I'm serious, and her eyes widen. "I could tell your brother I'm his greatest fan."

For the first time, she laughs, only the once, and it does something to my heart. She stands to take her mug to the sink. "There's something seriously wrong with you."

I grab her arm and pull her into my lap. "And it's all your fault." Then I lower my lips to hers, and kiss those damn lips I've wanted to taste for days. Alli is stiff in my arms, and then she relaxes, her kiss taking over, the passion building.

She pulls back and stares at me. "I can't do this. I have to go and see Pop. And Paige's mum has offered to take me because Pop doesn't like airports. So…"

"Do you want me to leave?"

"I think it's best we say goodbye now."

She needs her space. I, of all people, understand that. "Okay."

She nods, and I lower my lips to hers only she springs out of my arms. "Darcy…" her gaze darts away from mine.

"It's fine. I understand." I do, yet my gut is telling me otherwise. "I'll see you when you get back."

She nods even though she doesn't look up.

I see myself out. As soon as the door closes behind me, I want to punch it because I've realised how much I've fucked up.

CHAPTER 21

ALLI

I turn up the air conditioner, but it's not enough. "I'm not going to make it." I reach for the spew bag. Paige leans over and takes my hand in hers and squeezes until my fingers stop shaking.

"I have Valium," she whispers. "Take one."

"I'm trying not to take any sedation."

"Waiting for things to get worse?" She cocks an eyebrow at me. "You're already stressed."

I turn away from Paige. "I'll take it in a few hours if I need."

She nods and adjusts the screen in front of her business-class chair.

I must have dozed because I wake in a sweat, my heart racing. Paige pulls her earpiece out. "What's up?"

Silent tears flow without warning. "A bad dream. Pop fell over and broke his hip, and there's nothing I could do to help him because I'm stuck up here in the middle of nowhere."

"He's fine, honey. Try and calm yourself," she says softly.

Calm myself.

After taking the sedative she offers, I settle back in my seat and pull the blanket over my shoulders.

I wake when warm towels are offered to freshen up. My shoulders are lighter, and I'm somewhat refreshed. Paige's red eyes hint at her lack of sleep.

"Did you sleep?"

"Not much." Her mouth opens wide in a yawn. "Watched four movies instead. Figured I'll sleep in a comfortable bed while you get quality time with Nate."

"Still a princess."

"At least I'm in the right country."

I laugh a little and then stiffen when the trolley comes into view.

Paige reaches over and touches my hand. "You need to eat something. I don't want you passing out on me. No food and stress isn't a great combination." Her eyebrows arch in a pleading way. "I'm worried about you."

"I'm fine," I whisper. "I'm scared I'll puke if I eat. I just can't."

"Then we're stopping to get something to eat on the way to Nate's."

Paige didn't bother to shower before curling up on the Queen bed in Nate's spare room. As for me, I couldn't wait to shower and dress in clean clothes.

Sitting at the kitchen table, I gaze around his kitchen pondering his life here. There was no hiding disappointment when I received Nate's text telling me he had to work, couldn't get out of it. He hid the door key and told me where to find it. Nate promised he would only be a couple of hours, and then he would take me out.

It's been years since I visited, and this is my first time in the apartment he shares with Rebecca. It's odd seeing her things, and yet I admire her taste in furnishings. My stomach warms seeing Nate's photography on the walls, knowing she's also proud of my brother.

Their place is different to what I imagined. Not modern and sleek but more country and homely. The kitchen wooden benchtops run the length of the wall, and a long rustic wooden table is pushed along the opposite wall. No chairs match in a stylishly shabby way.

I've managed to eat a banana and apple, and my mood has improved. Paige is right. I'm going to need energy for this trip, and I'll have to force food down even if my brain tells me I don't want it. I keep telling myself I need to eat because I don't handle stress well. I have to try...

Keys jangle on the other side of the door, and I perk up, a smile ready on my face. I strain to keep it there when a tall female appears on the other side.

Long dark waves fall over her shoulders, and then I'm met with the most incredible green eyes. She smiles, and her whole face lights up, and it's clear why my brother fell for this girl. "Hi. I'm Becca. You must be Alli," she says in a distinct British accent.

"Hi, Becca." I stand and meet her halfway. We hug quickly, awkward almost. "Thank you for allowing us to stay with you."

"Oh, it's my pleasure. I'm so excited to finally meet you. Nate talks fondly of you." She gives me another squeeze. "So, have you eaten? I know Nate said he'd be here, but he always runs late." We both laugh at that. "He won't take long. I don't want you to starve."

"All good, I've already eaten so no hurry."

"Well, I'm going upstairs to change. He said he's taking us somewhere special for lunch, and he won't even tell *me* where."

I watch Rebecca climb the stairs, each step in elegance. She's wearing a tight-fitting navy wrap dress. I survey myself and consider changing out of jeans. Unfortunately, the only decent dress I packed is for the party, so jeans it will have to be.

At that moment, the door swings open. I'm staring at a blond guy, eyes reminding me of my own, eyes holding back emotion, and then I lurch myself at him. "Alli." He says it with so much love and meaning. "I've missed you so damn much."

"Me, too." Of course, I'm crying, tears soaking Nate's button-up shirt. My hands tremble, and I hold onto him with a firmer grip trying to take control of the emotion soaring through my body. His arms tighten around me, and he's so much stronger than I remember.

His chin rests on the crown of my head. "I'm sorry I couldn't be there, Alli-girl. I really am."

"I know," I croak. I pull back and swipe my nose. "It was really hard. And Pop…" I shake my head.

His hand runs along my cheek, and he's staring as though he's feeling every word. "I was going to take you out for lunch with Becca. How about *we* go, and you can tell me about it. It will do you good to talk."

I nod and sniff in an unladylike way. "Would she mind? I mean she can come."

"You and me today. Give me a minute to go explain."

Five minutes later, Nate strolls down the stairs wearing a clean shirt with a sports jacket slung over his shoulder. His blond hair is messy yet stylish, his jawline sharp and strong. He really should be on the other side of the lens. He stops and takes my hand. "Ready."

"Is Becca, okay?"

"Yeah. She was a little disappointed, but she knows she'll have time to get to know her future sister-in-law." He winks at me. "Besides she's tired, and is thankful for a chance to lie down."

"Ah, is she another princess like our Paige?"

"No," he says quickly. "She's... tired."

Nate leads me outside to a black Land Rover. "Nice wheels."

"Yeah. Perfect for work when I'm on those tiny roads and for lugging all my camera equipment."

I giggle because only now I notice his accent.

"What's so funny?"

"You. You sound... like a cross between a Brit and an Aussie. It's an odd accent." He shoots me a look. "I like it," I add and laugh again.

"Wait to you meet Becca's parents," he says in his best British impersonation. "You'll need to concentrate when her father speaks."

"Well, I'll do my best," I tell him trying to sound posh.

He laughs and veers the car onto the road. "At least you're smiling."

"Yeah."

"It's my duty to make sure I see more of those before you go home. I want your visit here to be a happy one, not one to reminisce on the past and feel guilty for whatever it is you think you should feel guilty about."

I lower my head and stare at my hands in my lap. "You haven't been home for a while. It was hard watching her slip away and barely remember us."

"I'm not doubting it. But whose fault was it? Not yours or Pops. It's *life,* Al. It happens. Life goes on. The sun continues to rise and set. Today's another day, and I want you to think of it as taking a new step to a better future. A brighter one. Not because Gran is gone, and you won't have to witness her fading away anymore because you should remember. Only the good times. Happy memories. I want to help you. 'Cause honestly, I'm scared I'll lose you, too."

"What do you mean?"

"I know you've never carried weight although you could use a bit now."

I glare at him. "You know nothing about me."

"Yeah, I do. You're a lot like me only we used the lack of control in our lives by other means. Me with drugs, you with food."

"I don't—"

"I understand. And I can help by telling you the things I did to set my life on track when I came here. You have to let the shit go." He runs his fingers through his hair. "You can't dwell on sadness and loss, or you'll turn into that person."

I sniff as a tear falls to my cheek. "I already am that person."

"No, you're not. I won't let it happen even if it means starting over in a new place. And lesson one will start today. Lunch with me, your favourite brother."

"My only brother."

"Irrelevant. What do you feel like for lunch?"

"I'm not hungry," I whisper.

He's quiet a moment. "I know somewhere you'll enjoy. It's called Raw Treats. The food is naturally good for you and tastes amazing."

I smile knowing he's doing it for me.

DARCY

The address is in my phone.

Whipping the gear stick into park, I stare at the faded red brick cottage, the dated green tiled roof needing a lot of work.

I check the message I sent Hunter again. The one where I asked for the address to Alli's grandparents. At first, Aubree refused, said it was against work policy until I reiterated Alli mentioning her Pop needed the help.

I hit the steering wheel with my palm. It seemed like a good idea to help her Pop. So, why am I having second thoughts on meeting an old man?

An old crimson Nissan is parked in the driveway. A hissing sound comes from the watering system on the flower garden below the elevated veranda. Two wooden chairs and a table are positioned in front of a small window. The wood so weather-beaten it's difficult to tell the original colour. I take each step slow and notice a teacup and saucer on the round table. The door swings open, and I stop before I take the last step up. Her Pop stares at me a moment before recognition crosses his face.

"Good morning, Mr Bradley. I want to offer my personal condolences. I hope I'm not intruding." I wait, not game to take the final step even though this man is more than a good foot smaller than me, and his frail body half of mine.

He steps out of the dark doorway, closes the screen wire door behind him. His gaunt, pale face remains stony. Bloodshot eyes meet mine. He nods. "Alli is not here."

"I know. I wanted to check in on you while she's in London. Check if you needed help in any way." I swallow knowing the words came out all wrong.7

Lines deepen around his eyes. "Did she put you up to this?"

"No. She doesn't know I'm here. I do know she's worried about you and was afraid to leave you."

"Seem to know a lot about me when I didn't even know you existed," he grunts. "Take a seat." He points to the outdoor table and sits opposite me. "Can I get you anything? Do you drink tea?"

I smile, adjust my size to the small chair and hope it doesn't collapse beneath me. "I do, but I'm fine for the moment."

"So, what do you do?"

I scratch my jaw before answering. Consider using words that attract a lesser judgement. Acknowledge straight honesty is in my best interest if he's anything like Alli. "I play football for a living."

He gives me a sideward glance, maintaining a squint with his face in the line of the sun. "Thought it was you. You've been in the papers quite a bit."

His tone lacks praise, and I get his wariness. "Yeah. I haven't given Alli the support she needed of late, and I apologise. I didn't realise your wife was ill."

"Just how well do you know Alli?"

I swallow again. "Not well enough to be here asking for your acceptance, but I want that to change. I want to be part of her life. I care about her."

Mr Bradley drops his elbows to his knees and slumps forward, stares at the garden. "How long have you two been seeing each other?"

"A few months."

"And you didn't know her grandmother was deteriorating?"

"I knew she visited the nursing home frequently but not any details."

He turns his head and familiar brown eyes meet mine. "Does she feel the same way about you?"

"She did. I sense she's pushing me away because she's hurt. And if I can be honest with you, I'm concerned about her weight."

He stares at me for too long.

Hell, I've said the wrong thing.

"She gets her genes from her mother's side, but her weight loss through stress she gets from me." I nod and add nothing more. "But I've noticed it, too. Tried to say something, and she tells me not to worry. I don't know what to do for her. Her grandmother knew those things."

I rub my palms over jean-clad thighs. "I want to help. Both of you." His brow pulls tight. I push on, "I want to help you with chores around here. I know it's tough at the moment to concentrate on other stuff, and I now have extra time on my hands."

Mr Bradley wipes his hand over his mouth contemplating my words. "My first reaction is to tell you to *buggar off, I'll be fine*, only I'll be no different to my granddaughter."

"In no way is it my intention to be intrusive or rude."

He offers a single nod. "My gut tells me you're going to be around whether I like it or not..." He visually sizes me up. "And this could be a way for me to get to know you better without my granddaughter screening you."

My shoulders relax. "I'd appreciate the opportunity to get to know you, Mr Bradley. I'm reasonably strong, so I could help—"

"Son, I have eyes. Why don't you come on inside, and I'll make you a cuppa."

CHAPTER 22

ALLI

Purple and gold helium balloons conceal the ceiling. Laughter fills the long hallway of Becca's parents' home. Paige hands me a champagne glass, vintage saucer-shaped filled to the brim with the expensive stuff. I take a sip so it doesn't run over my fingers before she drags me outside to a large marquee at the rear of the house. I glance up to the fairy lights strung to the trees and heart-shaped lights hanging off every low hanging bough.

"It's so romantic," Paige draws out.

I should be more excited, but I blame exhaustion after two full days of sightseeing and jetlag. My brother is happy and in love, and I have to be happy for him.

Paige guides me to a group of people around our age and introduces us. All eyes are on me when she announces I'm Nate's sister. I take a sip and allow the cold bubbles to ease my dry throat.

"What do you do in Australia?"

"Do kangaroos really hop around your city streets?"

"Have you ever held a koala?"

"Are you in the photography business like Nate?"

I barely have time to answer one question before the next is fired.

"No. I'm an flight attendant."

"Domestic or international?" A guy beside me asks.

"Domestic."

He smiles, and I like how it reaches his brown eyes. "So am I. Here in the UK, I mean. I'm Aaron."

I smile and take another sip. "Pet peeve?"

"Passengers that use the call button like hotel room service. Yours?"

"Same."

Our conversation continues comparing our work environments until crystal chimes to get everyone's attention. "This should be interesting," Aaron says with his glass to his lips, the notion to Becca's father ready to make a speech.

"Two years ago, a young, ambitious Australian photographer worked with Rebecca on a shoot where she was the model. They worked well together..." he pulls a face and everyone laughs, "... so he asked her to model for him in future shoots. We were not sure about this guy. After all, he came from *down under*." A few more people laugh. Odd. "A year ago, they moved in together, and, well... we accepted he was here to stay." He glances at Nate, a serious expression crosses his face. "Many of you know Nate lost his parents in a plane crash when he was young. He came to London to rebuild his life, and we're thankful he met our Rebecca. Caroline and I love Nate like he's our own son, and now we are proud to officially welcome Nate to the George family."

My mouth falls open with reality hitting Nate has another family. And it feels like he's less a part of ours because of the distance. Tears sting my eyes. Nate's gaze finds mine, and he shakes his head in a subtle way. I raise the glass to my lips and gulp champagne to ease the lump burning my tonsils.

Vaguely aware of hands clapping, I watch Nate as he hugs his future in-laws. He clears his throat before he takes the microphone. "Thank you, sir. It means a lot. Firstly, I want to thank everyone for coming to celebrate our engagement. You're here because you have touched our lives in some way. I'd like to thank Mr and Mrs George for arranging the party, and family and friends who helped decorate to give it a special touch. Most of all, I'd like to thank my beautiful sister, Aaliyah, and her friend, Paige, for making the trip from *down under*." He shoots Mr George a look, and everyone laughs at the way he says down under. "It's a difficult time back home. My wonderful grandmother, Evelyn, passed only a week ago, and my grandfather wasn't up to making the trip. I'm so thankful to Alli for being here under the circumstances. Her love for me is endearing, and I adore her with all my heart." My gaze shoots to Rebecca, her head is down, her fingers flicking. "I could go on all night, only we are here for the new love of my life. The one who light's up my world like the brightest star on the darkest night." He loops an arm around Becca's shoulder. "Since we have you all here, we'd like to share another announcement." He waits, and the silence kills me. "Becca and I are going to be proud parents in May."

Hoots and whistles sound around me. The clapping gets louder. "Are you okay?" Paige whispers.

"Yeah," I rasp out. "I don't know why he didn't tell me... I mean..." I shake my head silently counting the number of times we were alone the past two days and yet, he never uttered a word. I stare into my wine glass because right now, I can't look at Nate.

"Well, this changes everything," Mr George says over the mic. "The wedding will be early next year."

Without looking up, it's clear to me Mr George is the one in control of his daughter. This is Nate's fate. It resonates—you can't run from your past, you need to face it. Nate's happy, and it's all that matters. More importantly, he didn't run from me. He didn't leave me because I didn't mean anything to him. He loves me, but this is not where I belong. I turn to Paige and whisper, "I'm tired, and ready to go home."

"Yeah." She rubs my back. "Know what you mean."

DARCY

In two days, I have ticked chores off my list.

> *Mowed lawns.*
> *Plans drawn up by landscaper to redesign the front garden bed.*
> *Garden borders laid and soil delivered with flower punnets ready for planting.*

Dropping my name in conversation helped escalate the job priority. Minimal cost because of my name. Ironic really.

The bigger jobs are progressing. Today painters are recoating the exterior, touching up the heritage features, and replacing the old bullnose veranda. Mr Bradley initially refused, saying the cost was too great for these renovations. My convincing abilities to sway his decision were aided by his emotional fatigue.

He removes his hat, wipes a hand over thinning hair, and smiles while peering up at the veranda. "She's looking good. Reminds me of the day Evelyn fell in love with this ol' place."

"To finish, we could do with a new table setting for the porch, one with an extra chair."

He opens his mouth, then his expression changes with understanding. "An extra chair. Presumptuous of you to think I'll be inviting you over for tea."

"I was hoping for a beer, or two."

"I see. And I suppose I'll need something sturdier than this." He points to paint-faded chair with notable rot.

Rubbing the side of my jaw, I decide to play along. "I don't want to influence your selection, but yes. That is if I were to be invited." I jingle my keys. "We could go now."

Mr Bradley assesses me. "You're doing a fine job of keeping me busy while Aaliyah's away."

Aaliyah. I'm still not used to hearing her full name, and my heart picks up a beat. "It was my plan."

We set off to *Bunnings.* "Do you shop here much?"

"Nope. Haven't done anything to the house in years. I used to like to potter, you know before Evelyn became sick."

"I understand."

Mr Bradley surveys me. "She never mentioned you until a few weeks ago. She was telling Evelyn about you right before she passed. The conversation wasn't meant for me to hear. I wondered if you were even real. Then I saw the look in her eyes at the funeral, and I knew. But there was also something else. I have to say this. She puts on a brave front, yet she breaks like china. There are only so many times you can glue china back together."

"By not being here for her when Evelyn died was out of my control to a degree. I'm sorry I didn't call. I won't hurt her again."

"I don't blame you for anything. Although, you might want to explain it to Aaliyah.

When you double someone's wages, an unachievable job finishes in miraculous time. Connections to my fathers business also helped. Sitting in my car out front of Mr Bradley's, I admire the renovation. The paintwork outside is complete. The bullnose veranda looks a million dollars. The old cracked cement is replaced by limestone pavers.

My car beeps as I lock it. The last of the petunia seedlings sit along the garden bed ready for planting. Mr Bradley bought six punnets yesterday insisting he wanted to do some planting himself. Said it was therapeutic.

He appears at the side gate. "Looking good," he says and smiles. "You want a cup of tea?"

"Please. I'll sit in *my* chair." I wink at him and walk to the new four-seater table setting on the veranda.

After taking a sip of his tea, Mr Bradley places his cup down and crosses his legs. "I don't know how I'm going to repay you."

"It's not about you owing me."

"If I'm being honest, I woke up thinking what the hell did I agree to? Taking advantage of your generosity because you can afford it and because you're sweet on my granddaughter."

I smile. "I'm more than sweet on Alli."

"Call it what you want. I was wrong to accept. It's not that I'm ungrateful, it's actually given me a lift, but... it's not right. I'll pay you back."

"I'm not the nice guy you think I am. Consider it an agenda. If you like and accept me, it will make it easier for Alli to say yes."

His eyes widen. "Say yes to what?"

"Being my girl." I grin at him using words he would understand.

"Well, I hope she feels the same way. Otherwise, you might change your mind about the repayment."

My gut reacts at the thought of rejection. Clenches in an odd sensation. "If it's okay with you, I'd like to pick her up at the airport then bring her here and show her the house."

Mr Bradley peers at me over the rim of his cup. "It's okay with me, but I want to warn you, she's not big on surprises."

CHAPTER 23

ALLI

Gran used to say, '*the world is my oyster*'.

By using my youth to achieve what I wanted in the world never truly resonated until now.

It's not about being selfish as my Gran was an altruist.

My work as a flight attendant served a purpose.

It shaped courage in understanding the nature of my fear, and control came from within.

I look to my right as Paige stretches out in her bed then she jerks up, causing tendrils of hair to fall across her face. "We're still in the air. You slept well, princess."

She yawns in an unladylike way, then eyes my empty plate of food. "Did I miss breakfast?"

"Buzz, and they will bring it to you. Business class, baby." It could be the last time I travel in class for some time.

"I need to use the restroom first." She throws off the bed covers and saunters down the aisle leaving me to my own awakened thoughts.

I have enough holidays to spend quality time over the next month with Pop. Enough time to contemplate the direction my life should take. My shoulders lift, and it's like my mind senses my guard is down because *he* slips easily into my thoughts.

I'm not sure why I'm working hard to keep him out. I need to consider if his presence has a positive influence. There's no denying the attraction, especially by the way butterflies flutter in the pit of my stomach when I remember the nights we spent together. No other guy has affected me in this way.

Lust or love?

Part of me believes I've already fallen for him.

The past few weeks has taught me if I'm to contemplate a relationship with *anyone*, my dreams, and goals need to be clear. I need to know what *I want* in life. I'm aware happiness isn't measured by having a certain guy in your life. If you're married or single, love and contentment has to come from within.

I let out a sigh of relief when the pilot announces our descent, and we'll be landing in less than an hour.

The line in customs feels like an eternity. Paige stops to purchase perfume, and then we emerge through the doors to reality, and to Paige's mum waiting on the other side.

She stands from her seat, and the tall gentleman beside her stands also.

"Did you know he was coming?" Paige asks, clearly surprised as much as me.

"No." I smile at Darcy.

"Mum." Paige hugs her mum.

Mrs Longley smiles eagerly. "I can't wait to hear all about the engagement."

She nods in Darcy's direction before wrapping her arms around me and squeezing tight. "Quite the surprise, Alli."

"Yes. Quite." I release her and step to Darcy.

He scoops me close, so I'm pressed up against his chest. Kisses the top of my head. "I've missed you."

I'm thankful he didn't kiss me here in front of everyone because as soon as I step back, I notice an audience. Children hedge closer holding pens and paper, small boys bounce from foot to foot. Some are wearing the Thunder caps and tops. Phones rise high. I step back for fans to take his photograph. Darcy turns, his eyes are apologetic. He offers me his hand to stand beside him.

I shake my head. "I can't do this. Not now."

Darcy's gaze ping-pongs from his fans to me.

"Darcy," Paige intervenes. "Go ahead. We'll wait outside. It will give us time to get some fresh air."

"I won't be long, Al. Only a few minutes."

"Well, aren't you the sneaky one," Mrs Longley says to me. "Could've warned me. I would've put on some makeup."

"As if you need it, Mum," Paige remarks. It's true. Paige is a younger image of her mother. Long, blonde hair, blue eyes, and olive skin. Her mum looks fifteen years younger than her actual age. "Besides, Alli had no clue. More to the point, how do you think we feel? We didn't even bother to shower."

Automatic doors slide open.

I inhale fresh morning air. "Ah, it's always good to come home."

I hug Paige farewell when her mum points out the direction of the car.

Paige glances over her shoulder. "He's here already," she warns. "So, we'll leave you to it. Call me, okay?"

Paige and I had talked in depth while waiting around for connecting flights in airports. She confessed how some of my behaviour scared her. I could finally tell her what I was feeling, what really scared me, and why I had acted in a certain way. We have always had an understanding, although I know she's not the only one I have spooked of late.

"Catch you later, Darcy," Paige shoots over her shoulder.

Darcy takes my case, which I'm thankful. I have enough time to close the car door when Darcy leans in and kisses me. His lips are soft, warm, and demanding. It takes merely seconds for Darcy to make me lightheaded, losing all coherent thought to the way my body reacts to his.

I manage to pull back. "Sorry…" I cover my mouth with a hand. "Airline toothpaste doesn't quite make the cut."

Darcy chuckles. "There's nothing that can stop me wanting to kiss you right now."

I smile, but I can't allow him to charm me, lull me into a false sense of security.

"So, where to first?" Hazel eyes sparkle then he steers the car onto the road.

"Home. I really need to shower."

"Do you want to go to your Pop's first?" He smiles as though it's not a problem for him.

"No. I'll see him later. I want to rest a bit."

There's a hint of disappointment which surprises me.

We listen to Darcy's playlist for the remainder of the ride home, only making light conversation about the weather or traffic. We pull up at my house, and I talk first. "You're not going to like what I'm about to tell you…" I speak quickly before I change my mind. "I need some time on my own. To heal."

He kills the engine and faces me. "What are you saying?"

I reach over and touch his hand. "I like you, really like you, but I'm so messed up. I have to get my shit together. There were days when I needed you and—"

"I was committed to football." His eyes soften. "To a Grand Final, which you've barely acknowledged if we're being honest." He says it so gently as though he's the one asking for understanding.

My throat burns. I push the emotion down and straighten in the seat. "I'm not talking about then. No one knew my Gran was going to be taken from us. I'm talking about me needing you. You became my only happiness." His brow pinches. His hand stills beneath mine.

I push on. "Now that Gran has passed, I need to find some joy within myself, and I need time *alone* to sort through personal baggage and find what makes me happy. What gives me pleasure? If you're around clouding my thoughts with a false sense of security, I won't be able to think clearly."

He glances down to my smaller hand covering his. "False sense of security? I'm not going anywhere."

I offer a weak smile. "Thank you for saying that, but I need to do this. Please understand…"

Darcy turns his gaze to the window. He removes his hand from mine and grips the steering wheel. "I know it's-not-you-it's-me speech when I hear it."

"It's not…"

He refuses to look at me. His knuckles are white on the wheel.

I open the door, remain seated a moment longer waiting for him to say something. "I'll call you, I promise. I need time."

He glances at me sideways. Lips pinch tight and his brow furrows. "How long?"

I shake my head slowly. "I don't know."

Darcy turns his gaze to the road.

I get out, open the back door to retrieve my small case. Before I close the door, I acknowledge my deep feelings for him. I have to stick to my guns in order to get ahead with my life. In the moment, it seems right to say something. "I want you to know, I—"

"Don't say it," he interrupts. "Don't."

When the door closes, Darcy accelerates, leaving me alone on the sidewalk. My suitcase lands with a thud, my shoulders slouch watching him disappear. Muscles around my chest constrict knowing it's possibly the last time I will see him.

CHAPTER 24

ALLI

Twelve months later...

"Are you done yet?" I look across the glossy wooden slat table to Pop. "We better go." I check the time on my phone, and although we're not late, I'm on edge.

"Almost, love. No need to panic, we have plenty of time." He sips his tea then sets his cup in the saucer. "One could believe you were eager to get rid of me."

I snort. "I'm going to miss you like crazy. I don't want you to be late. You know what I'm like with these sorts of things."

"The boat won't leave without me."

"Ship, Pop. It's a cruise ship." I laugh. Deep down I'm excited for Pop to be heading on his first holiday in years. I wanted to go with him, introduce him to people, only he was determined to do it alone. Said I would cramp his style. I laughed because it's not about him meeting a lady, only people. And this cruise is styled for retirees not twenty-somethings like me. I hand him back his phone, one he recently learned to use. "Call me anytime, okay? Take loads of pictures. Don't worry about the quality, I'll edit them in Cairns."

I'm meeting him in Cairns before flying home together because I know he won't cope flying alone. The cruise takes seven days to reach Cairns, and I doubt he'd handle another seven days on the water for the return trip, so we opted to fly home from there. Pop can get a little stir crazy not being able to get outside and in the garden, so I'll head to Cairns on the weekend.

It's been one year since I took up my new job as a waitress—in an inner city restaurant—while studying part-time. I'm looking forward to spending some downtime wandering the art and craft markets or soaking up the northern sunshine until the ship arrives.

In an attempt to relax, I lift my feet to rest on the chair opposite and set my gaze on the petunias already blooming in Pop's neat garden. My heart fills with pride remembering Darcy helped to do all of this. The renovations have made life easier for Pop, and he enjoys every minute in the garden. When I called and thanked Darcy, he dismissed me like the gesture meant nothing. We have barely spoken since, bar a couple of texts. And now that I no longer work at the airline or hang out at nightclubs, our paths don't cross. Yet, occasionally, I turn on the television and watch him doing what he loves, stare into those eyes looking back at me on the screen, and butterflies take flight like every other time I'm met with that steely glare. The glare is not directed at me, but I know what it means, understand his enthusiasm, and take joy knowing he's happy, successful in the game that has set his path and future.

My future wasn't so concrete.

Thoughts linger if I made the right decision. My brain tells me yes because I'm happy. My heart disagrees.

Every day.

Because every day there's some reminder of what could have been.

"You know the extra chairs weren't intended for your clod hoppers," Pop says, bringing me out of a daze. "Wood's still shiny, and I'd like to keep it that way."

I roll my eyes and remove my feet from the jarrah chair as directed. It's not the first time he's made a dig about the empty seat. Didn't hide his disappointment when he heard I didn't give Darcy a chance. Now he ribs about not getting any grandchildren from me. "Everything ages," I shoot back. Then I grin at him. "Can you hurry up and finish your tea?"

"Heard from your brother lately?"

I sigh. "Yeah. Jace still isn't sleeping. Nate's grumpier than you on the phone." I make a clicking sound with my tongue, and Pop laughs.

Pop came with me to Nate and Rebecca's wedding in January, and he didn't cope well with the flight. He was still grieving, going through the stages, and had an anxiety attack on the plane. He's still embarrassed and scared it will happen again. We had to sedate him on the trip home. Nate and Bec's son, Jace, was born in late May, and five months later, he's still waking frequently through the night. The downside of me not working for the airline is I no longer get cheap flights, so I didn't have the money to make the trip back so close to the wedding. Pop flatly refused.

We hope Nate will keep his promise and bring Jace home to Australia for a visit. However, with Becca developing post-natal depression, Nate's had to juggle work and caring for Jace as well as looking out for Becca. They hired a nanny a couple of months ago to care for Jace during the day, and I hoped life would get easier for both of them. Thankfully, social media and Skype unite us like we're part of his growing up.

Pop downs the last of his tea and stands.

"Finally." I wheel his case to the car, then follow Pop inside to check his light switches are off and the door is locked. I don't offer to water his garden because Darcy covered that by installing an automatic watering system.

"You're all set."

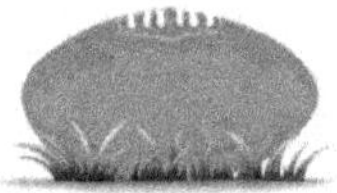

Holding my phone high with the cruise ship in the background, I take a selfie of Pop and me and post it to Instagram with a simple hashtag #seeyouincairns. My account has been dormant for months, like my life was put on hold. After waving goodbye to Pop, I head home with mixed emotions. I'm sad and yet happy for him. He was already joking with a group of ladies sitting near us before he boarded. He has come out of his shell the past six months, and it's been a relief to watch him living and not wallowing away mourning Gran. He loved her without a doubt, yet his liveliness surprises me. At times, I wonder if he's taken a leaf out of Gran's little life book and doing it for me, to prove there's more to life than living in grief for the loved ones you have lost.

I have also taken a leaf out of Gran's book by working in a restaurant surrounded by food. Another plunge. The hospitality experience as a flight attendant helped me to secure the job. The food at Lombardi's restaurant is amazing, and the staff is social getting together regularly. I never thought I'd enjoy carbs as much as I do now. I change into my work uniform, black trousers and a black shirt, and head into the city to work the late shift. Doesn't hurt as my young, Italian boss is easy on the eye. I now have a thing for man buns.

Unfortunately, he's already taken, but eye candy is free and harmless.

I walk through the back entrance, closing the door gently that leads into the kitchen of Lombardi's restaurant. I pop my head into the adjoining office where Oliver, my boss, is seated behind a desk.

"Here she is." He smiles. "Thought you might have pulled a sickie so close to your holidays."

"I haven't taken a sickie yet," I tell him.

Oliver scratches at the shadow of whiskers along his jaw. His dark eyes survey me. "No, you haven't. Guess it's time we sign you on as a permanent employee and not casual." He pushes a yellow envelope across the table toward me.

I walk over to the desk and open the envelope with my name on it. "Are you serious?"

"Very."

"You have no idea how happy this makes me." I struggle to contain a wide, cheesy grin.

"Well, a few of us are hanging around later when things quiet down. To have a drink with you," he clarifies, and beams a contagious smile at me, one that captured his fiancée, Tessa's heart. "Jardine and Ava will pop in as well."

"Oh..." All of a sudden I'm feeling special. Ava and Jardine are co-owners of Lombardi's, and Jardine is the star cricket player I ran into the time when I was with Darcy at his apartment. I've never mentioned it, and I doubt he remembers me. "That's so nice. Well, I better get started so all my chores are done for when everyone arrives."

Oliver checks the time on his watch. "You're not due to start for another thirty minutes."

"It's all good," I chirp and walk out of his office with a spring in my step.

It surprises me more when Oliver puts up the Closed sign at nine-thirty before the last of the diners leave. Most of the staff is here, including Molly, whom I'm close to as we both study Creative Arts and Design at the same university. Molly is majoring in fashion design. I've taken the visual arts pathway, majoring in sculpture, something Nate encouraged me to pursue.

"What did you decide on for your major piece?" Molly asks as she sits beside me, a glass of pinot on the table in front. She holds up the bottle. "Want a refill?"

I wave a hand. "I'm driving."

"You're not driving home," she insists.

I pause a moment while she holds the bottle mid-air. "Sure." I push my empty glass toward her. "I'll catch an Uber." I gulp down a mouthful before answering her first question. "I decided on a mosaic face mould using lightweight cement and Italian glass. It has a touch of Picasso." I laugh at my fake modesty. "What about you?"

"This year I designed a men's line as my final presentation. Shirts in colourful floral prints and pinstriped suits with a large collar line. The parade is in four weeks, and my model can no longer help out. I can't afford a proper model so now I'm looking for a guy under six feet, slim build. Happen to know anyone?"

"I wish I did." Glancing around the room I realise the staff must know someone who can help out. "Have you asked the guys here?"

Molly shakes her head vehemently. "They're either too large or..." she screws up her face, "... not model material."

I laugh once. "I didn't mean for them to be your model." Although Jardine and Oliver are fine looking men, they're definitely too tall and too broad in the shoulders for the requirements. "They might know someone."

Molly looks up to Jardine. A vague expression crosses her face with her mind ticking over. "Maybe... I'm embarrassed to ask."

"I'll ask." I call out to Oliver and Jardine and wave them over to our table. "Molly needs a favour."

"This should be interesting." Oliver raises his brow and folds his arms over his chest.

"It's not work related. She needs a guy to model for her."

"Well, why didn't you say so?" Both guys joke about them being perfect for the job, and Molly and I both groan in unison.

Ava joins us, eyebrows arched.

"Molly needs a model for her men's fashion line. He needs to be under six foot and small to medium build."

Jardine and Oliver stare at me.

"And these two twits are offering their services?" Ava pats Jardine's puffed-up pectoral muscles from hours at the gym.

"You didn't say—"

"You didn't let us finish," Molly quips back to Oliver. "Seriously. Do you know of anyone? I'm desperate."

"My mates aren't medium build." Jardine apologises. I certainly didn't mind when he brought them into the restaurant to dine on occasions.

Ava turns to Oliver. "What about some of our school friends? Didn't Adrian come back here to teach? He was always small in stature although a good looking guy."

"You thought he was good looking?" Jardine is clearly appalled.

"He has a strong jawline and deep-set eyes. He'd be perfect."

Molly nods at Ava. "Do you have a photo?"

Ava smiles. "Oliver, you follow him on Instagram, right?"

"Yep." He pulls out his phone and brings up an image then passes his phone to Molly. She takes a screenshot and then enlarges the image.

"You're kidding me," Oliver groans. "It looks like I'm bloody stalking him."

I pull out my phone at the same time and snap a quick image of everyone around our table to post on Instagram.

Allibradley
Celebratory drinks with these guys #Lombardi's #lovinglife

Then I slip my phone back into my trouser pocket.

"Can I have his number?" Molly asks. Oliver gets it up, and while she types on her phone, I pour myself another pinot, feeling chuffed.

Ava announces to Jardine they should leave considering their young son is home with the sitter. They're leaving on the weekend for a month for Jardine to play cricket in India. Ava is excited as it's her first visit there, and since Jardine's famous grandfather is Indian, she's excited to take their son and learn about his heritage. Apparently, I presented my resume at the right time a year ago because Ava was taking more time off. Although, I believe things have not always been rosy between them. I have never asked questions since it's none of my business, but I do remember the sad look on Jardine's face the day I saw him in the foyer.

Jardine hands Ava the keys to their Audi.

"Congratulations again." Ava rises to her toes to hug me. "It's great having you on board. I'll see you when we return home."

"Thank you and enjoy your holiday. India sounds fascinating."

Ava turns to Jardine, but he's now talking to a group of tall guys in the doorway. One wishes Jardine luck on the cricket tournament. Ava turns back to me and shrugs. "He knows everyone. Enjoy your holiday. Cairns is beautiful."

I smile with anticipation of lying around by a pool. "I've only been there overnight or on weekend stays, so I'm looking forward to relaxing."

Ava stares at me. Only I note the respect behind her eyes. "I admire that you're travelling alone. I would've done the same if Jardine never came back into my life."

"I appreciate you saying that."

"Hello, Alli," a deep voice comes from behind Ava, wrapping around me like tentacles holding me still.

I turn to meet pools of green and blue, gleaming under the door light. "Darcy," I breathe more than say. "It's good to see you again."

His beautiful eyes narrow a little at my words before his gaze darts across my face as though he's searching for honesty. Something changes in his expression because beneath the surprise, there's hurt. He conceals it giving a curt nod before turning back to Jardine. "Good luck, mate." And then he's gone.

DARCY

Yesterday I was talking about heading to Byron Bay with my teammates, then after scrolling through Instagram and seeing Alli's post in Cairns by a pool, I booked a flight and a room at the same hotel as the one in the photo.

Every decision made over the past twelve months had been carefully calculated. Those made on impulse stemmed from experience. Barely any alcohol, no women, and near perfect stats.

I owned my life.

In the off-season, football game plans are absent. No club constraints for another two weeks. The freedom pushes my careful control against a thin web of restraint. Now, perfectly distracted by a certain blonde, previous plans have disintegrated.

"Would you like to upgrade to an apartment by the pool, Mr Rayne?" The receptionist doesn't give me a second glance. Another reason why Cairns ticks boxes. Surrounded by passionate rugby league supporters, many Aussie rules football players are unknown.

"Sure, why not."

After handing over the key card to my apartment, she slides a folder including brochures on local tourist attractions. "Enjoy your stay."

I follow the map to my room that overlooks the pool. Decorated with noteworthy art and statues, it's filled with visions to admire. Luxurious, yet an empty room housing objects holding no warmth beneath fingertips.

Sliding the glass open, I step out onto the balcony. My body zings, though I'm not sure what I'll even say if I see *her*. Hell, I haven't even considered how she'll react.

Hairs stand on the back of my neck at the memory of Alli dismissing me.

I would have walked over hot coals to please her.

It's been a year, and there's been no call apart to thank me for the renovations or the one call she said she would make when *she was ready*.

Wiping my damp forehead, I'd forgotten about the intense humidity up north. I change out of jeans and head down to the pool for a quick dip.

The palms trees rustle in the warm breeze. There are at least two-dozen sunbeds around the pool with most of them empty considering it's nine in the morning. I do a quick assessment and continue on with no sign of her.

Tossing my phone, key card, and towel onto a sunbed, I wade in and immerse myself in cool water. No better way to clear my head and map out my defensive plan of attack.

CHAPTER 25

DARCY

Yesterday I made a decision to ignore all calls, especially those related to footy because I'm on vacation. When my phone vibrates on the towel beside me, and I read Clare's name, I know I have to take the call.

"Hey, kiddo, what's up?"

"I'm no longer a kid so stop calling me that."

"You're sixteen."

"Exactly."

I chuckle.

"Sorry I missed you a couple of weeks ago. I thought you were staying longer in Sydney since it's your offseason."

"Yeah. Had things to do back in Adelaide. I'm now in Cairns."

"With your team?"

"No, they're in Byron. How long are you staying in Sydney?"

"Only the weekend. I have school, remember. Mum said you'll be home for ten days over Christmas."

"Yeah, we made plans."

"It'll be a good Christmas. I've forgotten what it's like to have the four of us happy and all together."

My sister has matured. "Yeah. Well, I'm not staying on the phone chatting while you go all gooey on me."

She giggles. "I just wanted to let you know I'm sorry I missed you."

I smile, and look up and into the gaze of brown eyes, to Alli standing on the other side of the pool. A towel slung over her arm, delicate feet frozen to the spot.

"I have to go. Talk later, *Clare*." I've been calling her kiddo for years.

Acting nonchalant, I place my phone on the adjoining table. Honing my peripheral vision, I see her place her towel on the furthest sunbed. She strips down to a white bikini, the one in her Insta story. The one I partly blame for the reason why I'm here. For a year I banned myself from stalking her on social media. Weakening after the night I saw her at Lombardi's.

Alli wades into the water. Hell, she looks great. There's already a golden touch to her flawless skin. She has more meat on her than the last time she bared herself to me. Waist deep, she disappears under the water only to surface at the edge near my sunbed. She wipes water from her eyes before placing both elbows on the tiled edge and fixes her gaze on me. Honey eyes assessing.

We remain like this a moment, both silently appraising the other.

She tilts her head slightly to the right. Something I've remembered she does before she asks a question. "Is this a coincidence?"

I sit forward maintaining her gaze. "No."

She wrings water out of her hair, which has now grown below her shoulders. "I thought not. At least you're honest."

She holds no panic in her voice, only a calmness attracting me more. "I've always been honest with you."

"But not to yourself. I wondered how long it would take for you to show me you cared. I'd almost given up." She pushes off the wall with her feet, watches as my expression falters, then spins over and dives under the water.

What the fuck?

I dive in, reach her in seconds.

"What?" I barely manage to keep the frustration out of my voice. "You told me to stay away while you healed. That you would call when you were ready."

Alli wipes water from her face. "You never told the complete truth. I often had to decipher what you needed that differed to what you said to me. Sometimes you'd say what you thought I needed to hear."

I shake my head as though it will unscramble thoughts. I want to scream at her, but there are young families making their way around the pool.

"You said—" Her piercing gaze stops further words.

"You promised you would call," I say between clenched teeth.

Alli tilts her head. "You promised me you would be there for me."

I'm glaring at her knowing I wasted damn time not going to get her like my instinct commanded.

She floats on her back, teasing me. So close, yet untouchable. "You play for respect. You earn it. You want me? Then you have to earn me." She flips, giving me one last glance before swimming away.

I want to grab her by the foot and drag her back. *Earn her?* I tried to show her what I'd do a year ago. Wiping my hands over my face, I hope something will magically make sense to me.

Hell.

I tried to buy her respect with financial generosity.

Only now it dawns on me.

Idiot.

She saunters out of the pool as though the ball is in her court.

I turn away.

She has no idea how hard I will play.

No idea how far I will go.

Or does she?

Now I know what she wants makes the strategy so much easier.

Game clock starts now.

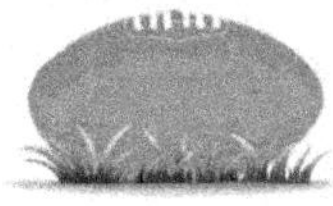

ALLI

Considering how calm I acted in front of him, I'm practically running to my room.

I turn, half expecting Darcy to be following, relieved and disappointed he isn't.

I don't stop until I'm in the shower, calming my thoughts, calming my heart. He surprised me, and then I surprised him—and myself—with how I handled it.

I'm not going to play games with him. I'm done with facades and lies, and yet, I feel like I played the biggest move to date.

It's the truth. Direct and honest.

After everything that happened, he didn't even try to win me back. Admittedly, I had told him to stay away, and he respected my wishes. But hell, with football, he's all about not giving up until the siren sounds, and he didn't even try once! And it hurt.

There are four days until I meet Pop to fly home.

Four days for Darcy to convince me he's worth a second chance.

Four days for me to believe it.

And yet, he's already earned a tick for taking the risk by coming to Cairns.

Impressive, yes.

Winning my heart won't be as easy as I'm no longer accepting risky behaviour as an act of love.

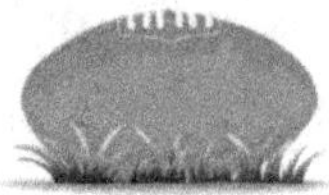

An hour later, my phone buzzes before I can make it out the door. Darcy is calling me. Well, that's a first.

"Hello."

"Hey. Can I come to your room? To talk?"

"I'm not giving you my room number, and besides I'm heading out…" I pause a moment. "Remember how you never liked to give out your phone number because people might stalk you?" It sounds like I'm playing him, only I'm not. Just stating the rules. Because rules apply when it regards my happiness.

"Do you want company?"

"You don't know where I'm going."

"Where are you going?"

"For a walk."

"Where?"

"Along the esplanade."

"If you would like my company, then I'll meet you in the foyer in ten."

"Fine."

A lie. I am far from fine. I'm no longer relaxed. Trying to act confident around him has my heart beating not at a resting heart rate.

When the elevator doors open, there's no sign of Darcy in the foyer. For a second, I consider leaving without him until the second set of elevator doors open, and he strolls out wearing black and white board shorts and a black tank top. My mouth dries ogling those bicep and shoulder muscles, parches as my gaze fixes on the pattern of his tattoo. Looking closer, I notice he's added to it, something I missed at the pool since being preoccupied with the entirety of his presence being in the same place as me. When our eyes meet, I melt a little, the heat a reminder of what one look can do. I hand him a brochure of the sculptures, anything to divert his gaze.

"Is this what you're into?"

"Maybe." I keep walking out of the foyer to the palm-lined path leading us to the resort gate. I swipe my card for the gate to open. It's mid-morning, and the sun is already beating down. Humidity exacerbating the heat. We both slip on sunglasses, and Darcy curses.

"Forgot my cap."

"There are market stalls along the way. Be a tourist." I hide a smile since I've only ever seen him wear designer labels, although most are endorsed brands by the club or his sponsors.

We reach the path meandering along the esplanade, and I stop to take photographs on my phone of each of the metal or steel sculptures. This time I notice Darcy looking toward a playground of kids, screaming with joy.

"You like kids?"

He turns to me. "Of course."

Another surprise.

"So you want them someday?"

"Someday, yes. I was thinking how about my cousin holidaying with his family. His son is now one. I was sitting next to him and his then-pregnant wife at the ball," he says it as though I remember the night. I only remember what happened after. "They lost their first child to SIDS." His chin dips, and I sense him recalling it all.

"They're lucky to have another," I say softly.

"Yeah." He rubs the back of his neck and glances over to the playground. "Although, they live in fear every day."

"Understandably," I say in a soft voice. I want to reach out and touch his arm. Instead, I keep walking, looking at my brochure to where the next sculpture is positioned on the waterfront.

"Where to next?"

"A little further. It's a few kilometres on the round trip. Not too late to turn back if you've changed your mind."

He laughs. "Because it's too far for me?"

"You're wearing Havaianas," I point out.

"And I'll barely notice because I'm with you," he says teasingly, although I sense some sincerity. "Thought you'd be running the distance, not strolling."

"A lot has changed in a year." I eye him carefully. "For one, I don't run anymore."

"Did you injure yourself?"

"No. I'm trying other things. Becoming more in tune with my body."

"Like what?"

"Walking for instance. Taking life at a slower pace. Taking in my surroundings... and yoga."

I can sense his mind working, ticking over everything.

"Why did you quit your job?"

I stop, and he stalls next to me. "I like that you're here, but I don't want the questions today."

"It's been a long time, Al. I'm sure you have things you want to ask me."

I did. It's taken a lot of energy to move on and put the past behind me.

"Ask me anything. I'll tell you anything you want to know."

I want to know about *her* and why he reacted the way he did. Only now the truth scares me. I can't change the past, and by the way I'm feeling with him this close, it's a glimpse of the old me who survived on cortisol and adrenaline. I take a deep breath of salt baked air and focus on the oxygen filling my entire body.

"Not today, okay?"

A bearded lizard scampers across the path, and I jump and laugh at the surprise.

"They don't bother you?"

"Lizards are cute. Snakes are a whole different ball game."

He nods as though he's taking mental notes. "Spiders?"

"You'll hear me scream."

That brings a smile. We keep walking, and it's easier now that the tension in the air has cleared.

We pass more people and notice them staring. More so to Darcy. It continues with every person. It's either the locals checking out whether we're tourists, or I assume they recognise him.

"Do you ever get used to people ogling... the whole fame thing?"

"It's not fame. I had to get used to it a long time ago."

"What do you mean?"

He looks out to the ocean, avoiding my gaze. "As a kid, people treated me like a freak." He shakes his head as though no one understood. "Kids would stare because I towered over all my classmates. Even the tallest kid only came up to my chest. As time went on, I grew at an abnormal rate. You know how it is with boys and late development compared to the girls. Adults expected more of me because everyone assumed I was older. It was suggested to my father to take me to basketball, so I played for a while. The smaller boys ran rings around me and made me look like a fool. My centre of gravity was continually shifting with growth, my feet were huge, which made buying shoes a bigger problem. I was slow and lanky. People laughed at me running down the court."

He stops and looks at the grass where markets are setting up for the afternoon. He leads me toward a tent. I say nothing as he buys a cap, a cheesy one with a kangaroo. I want to smile, but I'm still digesting what he's telling me. He positions it on his head and continues on.

"I assumed you were always treated like a gladiator," I say in a soft voice.

He shoots me a sideways glance. "The adoration came later, and I milked it like any teenage boy would. Only I didn't stop. Not until you reminded me we all have an Achilles."

We walk close enough for our fingers to brush occasionally. On the last swing of my arm, his fingers loop with mine, and I don't fight it.

"My childhood groomed me. My father taught me never to back down and to find another person's weakness. We all learn from mistakes and become the better person."

I'm not sure if he's talking about his present or past self. "When did you start football?"

"Later. My mother was a champion netball player, and she liked basketball especially for me to play college ball in America. So, I continued playing, for her. I made national junior team, and the game became all about me. 'Get the ball to Darcy under the ring.' Because once I learned to shoot, who was going to stop me? I had to get faster to keep up with the guards. In year nine I started to play football for fun. By then I was well coordinated for a tall guy, thanks to basketball." He glances down to gauge my interest. I nod so he continues. "The coach gave me one-on-one training and taught me how to mark and kick. It was like I was born to play. Mum was horrified and said an injury would ruin my basketball career. And a chance to play college ball in the states.

"Dad wasn't big on sports anyway. As for football, he said it was a thug's game and unknown to the rest of the world." His hand goes behind his neck. His telltale sign something's bothering him. "I'm like my father. Stubborn. So, I continued to play football, and sure enough, word got out to the district clubs and one picked me up. Groomed me over a couple of years, and the next minute, I'm in the Australian league and admired by the nation." I groan at his light bragging, and his hand tightens around mine. "The rest is history. Long story short… people up here follow rugby. More than likely they have no clue who I am. People always stare because I'm a freak of nature. I accept it. I use it to my advantage. So, yeah, I have to get used to it because if it's not one, then it's the other."

"Maybe they're thinking what is that beautiful woman doing with *him*?" I bump my shoulder against his arm, and he chuckles.

"It would be my first thought." He smiles, and I remember how much it brightens his face.

"Points to you." I indicate to the next sculpture after sliding my hand from his. A large shell shimmering under the bright sun. It's a telescopium made with Chillagoe marble tiles, iridescent and phosphorescent glass mosaic tiles. It's visually pleasing to look at and exactly what I was searching for to gain inspiration for my next piece.

"It's stunning," I say out loud and bend for a closer inspection. "I love how the artist has created this pattern."

"Is this what you've been doing?" His attention is on me, not the sculpture.

Taking a side step to inspect the mosaic, I intentionally put space between us. "I'm studying at uni and loving it. I work at Lombardi's to make ends meet." He nods satisfied. "So, now you know what I've been doing this past year."

"I like talking to you like this. It feels—"

"Right." I shrug. "Except a lot has changed. We can't pick up where we left off," I say it gently, not adamantly because I don't want him to stop trying. I want to hope there's enough between us for a fresh start.

We find a café and stop for coffee before we head back. Darcy asks about Pop, and I reveal how much he loves his updated renovation.

"I never did it entirely to win you over," he clarifies. "I saw how distraught you both were at the funeral and know when money can help in more ways than one. I enjoyed spending time with him. Got on like a house on fire. Even bought myself a chair for the outdoor setting." He grins at me. "Yet, I respected your decision. Understood you needed space." He leans in closer. "What I didn't appreciate is you secretly wanting me to come after you when you gave me a clear message to stay away. If I'd known..." He leans back in the chair, those hazel eyes boring into mine. "You acted as though you hated me."

"There were days I did."

He folds his arms. "I waited for your call."

"I didn't think you'd be single long."

A muscle ticks in his jaw. He's staring at me, though I sense frustration building. "Did Carli mention anything to you?"

I shake my head. We only keep in contact once a month, but she never mentions Darcy except if he was on her flight. Never details, out of respect.

"The Christmas after, I headed to Europe. Hit the grog and partied hard. But something inside me snapped. Knowing if I ever got another chance, I had to be a better man."

"Darcy, I—"

"It started with footy. We had to perform harder to succeed again. I had to improve my personal game. So, I stopped going to clubs. Stopped picking up."

I pull a face. "A big change for you."

"No. Because I first stopped hooking up when I met you."

His ice-cool demeanour doesn't change. I don't know whether to believe him.

"We should head back," I say changing the subject.

"Too much to digest?"

No games I remind myself. "It is."

He seems happy with my answer because he stands and follows me out of the café.

"What do you have planned for tonight?"

"A yoga session. Then maybe another dip in the pool."

He checks his watch. "I need to go for a run. Seems like we both need to clear our head."

CHAPTER 26

ALLI

It's seven, and the pool is quiet. The sky has turned pink, the colour sedating the earth. Staring up at its beauty visually helps to ease some of the tension. I wade into the pool and float, find the calming thoughts generated in my yoga session.

The water muffles all sound. I focus on the simplicity of breathing.

Of being.

It works until thoughts of the day creep in.

Walking hand in hand with Darcy. Hearing about what it was like for him growing up. Acknowledging he also had a tough time as a kid. And the memory stayed with him.

My conscience tells me we're alike. That I should give him another chance.

Common sense tells not to let down my guard.

I'm in a good place.

Keep the doors locked.

Yet, my body buzzes even when I hear his name.

Breathe.

Focus on the water lapping at my cheeks and jaw, framing my face.

Breathe.

I drown out the excited voices of children in the barbeque area beyond the pool fence. Hear the click of the gate as it shuts. Open my eyes and stare at the burnt orange sky while catching movement to my left. I flip and find Darcy placing a towel on a sunbed.

He stares at me but doesn't say anything. Lowers himself slowly until he's sitting on the end of the chair.

I paddle for a moment before realising he's not going to interrupt. I allow my legs to float to the surface. Tilt my head, and close my eyes. Test my mental strength. Deny his presence. Focus on my whereabouts in a tranquil place. A hammock swaying between coconut palms on a sandy beach.

My heart beats faster, louder behind my ears.

Focus.

My brain yells it.

I spring up and wade to the opposite side. He beats me there, stands before me, imposing, demanding.

"Did you enjoy your afternoon?" He lowers himself to the tiled edge.

"Yes. Did you come for a swim earlier?"

"I did. Kids everywhere. So, I went back to my room and waited for you."

"Waited?"

He points up to the rooms overlooking the pool. "I was having a beer on the balcony."

"Right. You're in one of the luxury suites."

"Want to see it?" He says it as though he's buying ice cream.

"Nope."

"It's filled with local art and sculptures. You might want to check out the artists." He smiles, it's slight, but I don't miss it.

I push off the edge and kick with my feet, floating on my back. "Nice try."

"I'm not trying. Stating a fact." He slides into the pool and glides through the water, catching me in seconds. "When you come to my room, it will be because you want to."

I keep kicking until I'm backed up on the opposite side. Darcy steps in front, blocks a clear pass.

"This is me trying. This is me doing what I've wanted to do for over a year." Dipping his head our gaze locks as his mouth lowers to meet mine.

I close my eyes. Not to shut him out but to let him in. It's just a kiss. It doesn't change anything. I can't keep denying myself emotional pleasure. I want to enjoy moist lips on mine. Feel my insides quiver with anticipation. It's a natural reaction, gratifying for the body. And has nothing to do with my feelings for Darcy. Simple pleasure in the moment.

Tongues entwine beyond our lips, the only part of us touching. As I start to relax into the kiss, he pulls back, glaring.

"As I said, you decide." He swims away from me. Steps out of the pool, grabs his towel, and heads to the gate without a single glance back.

I'm out of breath from one kiss. My stomach in knots. I want to call out and refrain from doing so. Clarity compromised in a moment. I'm not going to react after one kiss. When it comes to Darcy, decisions can't be rushed.

What I do know is how my body reacts to him, even after all this time. It's something I can't ignore.

DARCY

My phone buzzes on the Caesar stone basin. I jump out of the shower hoping its Alli, curse when it's not.

Idiot.

Wrapping a towel around my waist, I take the call from my manager.

"Baz. What can I do for you?"

"You're in Cairns," he says it incredulously.

"I am. Off season means we're entitled to take holidays." There's no hiding my sarcasm. I have bled for this man.

"Maa-te." He stretches out the word. "I'm supposed to know where you are unless you've forgotten we're still in negotiation with the club over your contract."

"You're in negotiation. That's why I pay you a ridiculous amount of money. When they agree, let me know. But I'm standing by the salary I'm asking. This will be the last time I sign a contract. We both know it. I want it to be with the Thunder, but it won't be if they don't play to my terms."

"The meeting is tomorrow. Hoped you'd be there."

"Nope. Something come up, and I had to follow it up. You don't need me. This is your arena."

"You've always managed to sway the big dogs on the day. You should've been a lawyer with your negotiating skills."

I laugh. Another skill I inherited from my father. And yet, one person is immune. And *she's* why I'm here. "Lay it on the line. When it comes to the crunch, they'll agree because *I will* go elsewhere."

It's bullshit they need to believe.

"Call me after the meeting. I'm only here a few more days. I can sign the contract *you've* successfully bargained when I get home."

I end the call and walk out onto the balcony. I lean on the railing and look down to the pool. Under diminishing light, I make out her shadowed profile lying on the bed, a light reflecting from her face as though she's reading on a device. I watch her a while before her silhouette changes. I sense her staring. Imagine those eyes staring into mine when she's lying beneath me. Hell, it's been too long. Recognition rises beneath the towel sitting low on my hips. I retreat inside and slide the door closed.

Lock it.

I need to eat. Distract myself from wanting to get Alli in my bed. I change into chinos and a button-up shirt and head down the stairs, pass the pool, double track back, and stride over to her.

"Pool closes in an hour. You can't stay here all night." She's looking at me in a way she wants me to take her right now.

Fuck this game.

"You going out?" She sounds disappointed.

"To get something to eat."

"You're dressed well to get food."

I glance down to assess my choice of fashion. Chinos and a white shirt. Standard casuals.

"You could wear boardies here. Are you getting take-out or meeting someone?"

"I'd like to be meeting a certain someone," I say without hiding frustration.

"Then maybe you should have asked that someone *out* and not only back to your room."

I study her expression a moment, ascertaining I heard her right. "Would you like to come out to dinner with me?"

"I'm in my bikini and not showered." She rolls her eyes.

"Works for me. I can wait. Have nowhere else I need to be." I smile at her and offer my hand to help her up.

"It's okay, you go. I have dinner arranged in my room. Thanks for asking."

I stare at her. "Serious?"

"Yes. A word of advice. If you ask someone on a date, you need to give them time to prepare."

I look away and realise what she's telling me. How do I constantly mess up around her? "Would you like to go out to dinner with me tomorrow night?"

"Like a date?" She tilts her head.

"Is this a trick question?" I rub the back of my neck. "Do you want it to be?"

"Do you?" she asks softly.

I'm searching her face for clues. My intention is obvious. I'll go the extra mile. Do what it takes to win her back. "I'm in Cairns because you're here. I thought I made it clear.

"If you're screwing with my emotions again, then the answer is no."

I nod slowly. She's more confident than a year ago. She acts like her life is under control. Yet, I see the cracks. Sense something is missing and damn well hope it's me.

"Then it's a date. Enjoy your night." I'm gone before she changes her mind and wait until the gate closes behind me before I send a text.

> **Me:** *Keep the next two nights free for me because I want to date you.*

CHAPTER 27

DARCY

The following morning I head to the pool.

Not a smart move. It's happy hour for the kids. The screams of play are deafening. Reckless splashing. Bumps to my thigh as boys chase, pushing to get past. Across the pool I locate a spare sunbed, passing mothers reading fashion magazines and dads entertaining the sprouts in the water.

It doesn't take long for phones to point in my direction. I'm not blind. Selfies with me in the background are not inconspicuous.

Agreeing to be in some photos, I sit down on the edge of my sunbed to fit the size of the screen since some kids are mid-thigh. One by one I filter through the children—and some fathers— the questions nonstop.

Have you re-signed with the Thunder?

Why didn't the Thunder make the Grand Final this year?

Any new recruits next year?

Then finally some youngster asks, "Why are you staying here?"

He wasn't talking about my upcoming contract negotiations.

Expressions alter, comprehending.

This is a family resort and not ideal for couples or singles in school holidays. Timing didn't come into consideration when I booked this holiday on impulse.

"I'm with a friend… of the family," I add after hearing ah-ha's to the first part of my response. The last thing I want is for Alli to be dragged into a media circus.

"Would you like me to take a pic of all the kids on your phone?"

I spin to find Alli smiling. "Thanks, I—"

"Good promo for the club." She holds her hand out, and I retrieve my phone and unlock it. "Sit over on the steps and the children can surround you. I'll take one from here." She points to the other side.

Dads, mums, and kids all join in for the poolside gathering. I'm smiling because frankly, she surprises me.

ALLI

After a dozen snapshots, there are several images Darcy could use to promote himself with fans. Something his club will be pleased about.

The guy standing on the opposite side of the pool somehow found his way into my dreams last night, hence my spritely mood. Maybe it's why I'm feeling *playful* and decide to send a text to myself on behalf of Darcy for the brilliant idea of being his social media photographer.

I open messages and type my name. I accidentally swipe the screen and it scrolls back to a message to *Kelsey*, the ghost who had shared my number and clearly still affects him. I start to read, unintentionally, and freeze at the way he begs her not to leave.

Two lines.

It's all it takes for my heart to race.

Do I really know him?

"Alli?"

I close it and hand the phone to Darcy. "They turned out great." I look up and force a smile. "You should share it now."

His brows draw together. "Yeah, thanks."

"So, I'm the family friend?" I smile, changing the subject.

"No," he says low and deep. "You're coincidently holidaying here."

I arch a brow. "Your next pick-up?"

"I am going to pick you up." He tosses his phone on the chair before throwing me over his shoulder.

"I'm dressed," I wail.

My cries fall on deaf ears as moments later I'm in the pool, wet and being dunked. Screams of joy echo even under the water. I surface inelegantly and swipe my face and hair before shooting him a glare. "Not a good role model to break pool rules."

He's laughing, along with everyone else. My white Boho dress is drenched.

I smile thinking how I appear. "I'll remember this," I say to Darcy before climbing out.

Dragging the wet dress over my head I drop it to the tiles to dry, and I spread out on the sunbed. Darcy's sunbed because all the others are taken. Minutes later, he's standing beside me.

"Care to share?"

"Not a chance." I don't even bother to open my eyes.

When I sense him move, I peek out of the corner of my eye. He lowers to sit on his towel spread on the tiles beside me.

Legs bent, elbows resting on his knees. He's watching the kids and chuckling. By my side. As though he belongs next to me.

By the time I dry out, I'm hot and ready to jump back in. Before I do, Darcy moves.

"I'm heading up to grab some lunch," he says quietly. "Want to join me?"

I swipe a trickle of moisture from my brow. "I'm considering getting back in the pool."

He nods. "Do you want me to grab something for you?"

"No thanks, I'm fine. Thanks for asking." I smile at him. "Don't you have a date tonight?"

He eyes me carefully. "I do."

"Then you should start getting ready. After today's prank, you'll need to make a bigger impression." I roll over on my stomach, turning away from him before he sees my grin.

"Is that right?" he squats beside me. "Like a fancy seafood restaurant?"

I shake my head.

"Pizza?"

I snort.

"Slow dancing... somewhere."

"You are getting colder." I push up and look him in the eye. "What do you think someone like me would enjoy? That's your challenge," I say softly so the guy beside Darcy doesn't hear.

"I'm in room 801. Be there by four." His voice is low and firm.

"Four?" I say but he's already walking away.

The heat behind those few words plays on my mind. My insides coil remembering what it's like to be around Darcy when his intentions are clear.

I need to distract myself and not worry about tonight. With a few hours to kill, I head to the markets where I can lose my thoughts to the creativity and talent of the locals.

Trinkets, gemstones, and paintings of the local rainforests capture my attention. Positive quotes on signs, I've seen them all before. There's one stand that fascinates me. A dark-skinned lady rises from her chair when our gazes lock, and I swear there's a connection like she's reading my mind. Instead of walking by like I would usually do, I go to her like a magnet drawing me closer.

"Dear child," she says. "My beautiful girl. Whose guidance do you seek?"

I smile and glance down to an array of art, drawings of goddesses each surrounded by a different element—water, the forest, the sun. I stop and return to a woman surrounded by nature, her body covered by leaves, and hummingbirds nearby.

"Aja," the woman smiles. "She calls you."

Deities, myths, how much of it I believe depends on my mood. This lady's voice serenades my mind. Her gentle eyes, her warming smile, an invitation to my heart. And the name sounds like mine. Aaliyah.

"You have someone that rode the great wind on their final journey and is now at peace."

Words leave me.

"You are searching for your own peace with Aja. With the forest and nature." She passes me a bottle of essential oil and wafts her hand for me to smell.

Logic tells me it's not possible for her to know any personal details about my life. Yet, it hangs in the air, the raw emotion of losing Gran. A complete stranger showing empathy pulls at my heartstrings, and my eyes burn with tears because I miss her.

I turn the lid and inhale. Wow. The scent is calming and fresh. "What is it?"

"Siberian Fir." She shakes her head. "For you."

"No, I can pay."

She shakes her head again. Points to my temples and rubs.

Turning my attention back to the art, there's no denying this goddess captivates me. I need to know more. "I'll buy a poster and a small card."

She rolls the poster and places it in a cylinder. The card I pop in behind money notes in my bag where I can easily access it. It's a picture you could stare at and get lost in your own thoughts.

"Thank you." I smile, and she nods as though her mission is complete. I'm not sure whether it was her words of insight that she knew a family member had passed, or if we connected. Regardless, I'm a little spooked even with the warmth surrounding her.

I hurry off because as much as I want to stay and browse, *tonight* is on my mind.

Two hours later, I've showered, painted my toenails, and deciding on a dress when I receive his text.

Darcy: *Champagne or white wine?*

Me: *I drink both. I'm looking forward to tonight.*

I reflect back to this morning and seeing the old texts to *Kelsey*.

A name. I know nothing more.

Some days I regret deleting the texts on my phone then I remind myself the messages were not intended for me. It was a knee-jerk reaction on the morning I left his apartment. Reading those texts did more damage to us than not telling him I was receiving them. So, by making them disappear, somehow it helped to forgive myself. But today... it reminded me of the raw emotion he felt for her. Part of the last message indicated he was starting over, with me. I didn't read the rest before deleting because on that day, it felt like a lie.

It's been over a year.

We have both had time to think.

Heal.

So what's next? What is it we both want out of trying to do *us* again?

I ask myself the same questions. *Is this what I want? Do I want to make the same mistakes? What have I learned?*

My brain is telling me to call and cancel. My heart is telling me to change into something more comfortable. Hell, I can't deny the curiosity of what he has planned.

My phone beeps with a message.

Darcy: *Change of plan. I have arranged for a driver to pick you up.*

CHAPTER 28

DARCY

Port Douglas is only an hour north along the highway, and the beaches are more intimate. Changing the plan gave me a chance to ensure everything is set up on the beach.

Passers-by stop to take photos. Admittedly, it's like a magazine article for a lover's getaway. Tea light candles line the beach creating a small path to a table where a glowing pillar candle provides enough ambient light for when the sun sets in another hour.

Along the shoreline, the rainforest casts long shadows across the sand. Parked nearby is a refrigerated van catering for our seafood dinner. I walk past the van to the path and sit on a log bench and wait.

In the distance, I watch her step out of the car. She's wearing a strapless, knee-length white dress that flows in the breeze. Blonde wisps of hair cover her face. I thump my chest once. Alli damn well scares me to the point I don't want to fuck up and lose her again.

"Hey. You look beautiful." I pull her to the side of the path so people can pass.

She smiles. Lowers her gaze.

I kick off my flip-flops and carry them. Alli does the same with her flat sandals. I take her hand and lead her to the edge where the sand meets the vegetation.

Her eyes twinkle when her gaze meets mine. "The view is stunning."

"It is." We reach the candle path, and I stop. I lift her hand to my lips. "And we'll be eating fresh seafood."

I sidestep to reveal the tea lights dotted in the sand leading to a table with a white cloth and two wooden seats at the water's edge. My chest tightens watching her eyes round, her soft lips part.

"Darcy." The surprise in her voice gives me a kick.

I lead her along the sandy path and nod at Tim, our waiter.

"Good evening, Darcy and Alli. Please take a seat."

"Thank you." Alli smiles at Tim and then at me.

And it's a smile I've been waiting for. Taking her slides, I place our flip-flops on the sand. I help Alli into her chair before taking mine. Remembering the little gentries my father fostered from a young age. There is an Esky on the beach filled with ice and wine. Tim pours us a glass and hands Alli her glass first.

"To us," I say and ding our glasses.

"To us," she repeats quietly, her gaze unwavering.

A hand-scrawled menu is placed on the table. "Our choices." I smile hoping I've guessed right. "Coral trout, marinated octopus, prawns, oysters, and lobster."

"No crab?"

"You want crab?"

Her eyes flicker with laughter. "No."

"And there's a side of Mediterranean salad because I thought you'd want salad."

Alli's shoulders rise and fall. She tilts her head to the side. "This is perfect," she whispers.

Out the corner of my eye I notice lurkers taking photos, not so much of me but what we're doing. Some stop and stare while others take a quick snap and keep walking. Tim manages to wave them on and let us be.

An hour later, the tide creeps closer. Tiny waves roll in. Tim works around us, cleaning away shells and topping our drinks, and taking photos on Alli's phone. Crystal glasses remain. Over the next ten minutes we quietly sip wine, sneak glances at one another, and watch the golden orb disappear behind palms creating orange streaks above us.

"Thank you, Tim." I stand and offer Alli my hand.

"Do you need a hand to pack up?"

Tim shakes his head. "I hope you enjoyed your dinner."

"We did. Thanks again, mate." I down the last of my drink and place the glass on the table. My phone buzzes in my pocket. I intend to reject the call until I see it's Clare.

"Hey. Twice in two days has to be some sort of record."

"You have your own hashtag."

"What?"

"You have your own hashtag. I used it on Insta."

"You spend too much time on social media." I walk over to Alli and mouth "Sorry."

"You're with a girl and it's not a question. There are photos of the two of you by a pool."

"And you saw it because I have a hashtag?"

"Yeah. They're saying you're not worried about re-signing as your interests are elsewhere."

"It's bullshit," I moan.

"When are we going to meet her?"

"Clare," I warn.

"Are you bringing her to dad's sixtieth bash?"

Being distracted with trying to win Alli back I'd temporarily forgotten Dad's big one in a month. "I'm gonna go, kiddo."

"Darcyyyy—"

"Bye, Clare."

I stuff my phone in my pocket. "Sorry. My kid sister. She's sixteen and suddenly interested in social media trends and what I do."

Alli is gaping at me. She holds up her phone. "Maybe she has a point. When you said hashtag I did a search. There are photos of us, and some claiming I'm a distraction."

Dropping my flip-flops into the sand, I take her face in my hands. "The best kind." I lean down and kiss her lips. "You're going to have to ignore all the crap. Tonight I don't want to hear about anything because *I am* completely distracted by you." I take her hand and lead her to the pathway where a chauffeured vehicle awaits.

CHAPTER 29

ALLI

Darcy opens the door of the black sedan.

I slide across the seat and wait for him to sit beside me after he gives directions to the driver.

"We could have stayed here the night," he says as we pass luxurious holiday resorts. "I didn't want you to assume anything."

One glance, and I grasp it's beyond my budget. I don't want him paying for me. It's not what I want. Linking my fingers through his, I whisper, "What you did tonight was enough."

"Enough?" He looks a little surprised.

"I don't need to stay somewhere like this…" I point to the next lavish resort we pass, "… for you to impress me." What he organised told me he cares.

Darcy's fingers squeeze around mine. "I want you to know how far I'd go—"

"I want it to come from your heart not your wallet," I say it in a softer tone.

Darcy lifts my hand to his lips, kissing it in a slow action. "Do you feel like doing anything in particular now?"

"I need to relax and wait for the delicious meal you organised to settle." I know he's hoping for more. Right now I want to hold onto the bliss floating within me. I lean toward him and rest my back and shoulders against his chest while angling myself to the window and stare at the ocean view in twilight as we travel along the road back to Cairns. Soft music plays from the speakers. We're both sitting back happy just to be in one another's company. Darcy plants another kiss in my hair. In the moment, I'm content, but I'm not blindsided to know it will change when we return to Adelaide.

The poolside bar is open when we arrive at the resort.

I lead him to a seat at the bar, order us both mojitos and ask for it to be put on my room tab. Darcy raises a brow then smiles approvingly. The waiter serves our drinks, and when he moves to the other side, Darcy swivels on the stool and leans closer.

"I have so much I want to say to you only I don't know where to begin." His expression his earnest. Eyes wide and searching.

"Regarding...?"

"Your Gran. How sorry I am I wasn't there for you."

I lower my gaze. "We've been over this. It's okay." I'm thankful to have the cocktail, and I take a long sip through the straw.

"No, it's not. I want to make it up to you." He takes my hand, makes little circles with his thumb.

"You are." I smile. "I'm enjoying being with you."

His lips turn up in a smile. "So, how is your Pop?"

"He's doing better than I imagined. The first six months were tough, but then something twigged, and he said we had to move on and live the way Gran would want us to." The pride comes through in my voice.

"I'd like to have a beer with him sometime." He peers at me through long lashes.

"He'd like that, too." Darcy grins. "You don't have to wait for an invite from me to go visit him."

He shrugs. "I didn't know if I'd be welcome. You're a close family and—"

"He would like you to visit." I give his hand a gentle squeeze.

Darcy takes a sip of his drink. "My dad and I are on much better terms."

It's my turn to smile. "That's good news." I look down into the ice in my glass, and when I suck, it makes that awkward air sound.

"You want another?"

I hesitate. "No. I'm ready to go up. To yours."

It takes a second for acknowledgement to pull his brow together. Darcy stands, leads me around the tables, past the pool sun lounges, through the gate to the lift. His gaze darts to mine, then he looks away. He does this several times while we wait for the lift.

"I want to tell you about Kelsey," he says when we're inside.

"Not tonight." I place my hand on his chest. "I don't want to talk anymore. From here we move forward."

It takes a moment for him to register what I'm saying. "Forward it is." He pulls me into his arms and kisses me.

Darcy holds the door open, and I head straight to a sculpture on a table near the lounge. "You weren't lying about the artwork in your apartment."

"No."

I turn. His voice has changed. One word, and he says it with meaning. He strides over to me. Takes my face in his hands and kisses me in a way I remember. In a way that curls my toes and warms my heart.

"I've missed you," I croak.

I'm swept up into his arms and carried to his bedroom. "You're not wasting any time."

"We've wasted enough time," he rasps out. "Over a year to be exact."

After placing me on the bed, I scramble to the centre and watch Darcy undo the buttons to his white shirt. I enjoy every second, each movement revealing a little more tanned, muscled skin. Darcy peels his shirt over his shoulders and tosses it aside watching me watching him. I push up on my knees when his fingers move to his zip. My dress is over my head and thrown to the end of the bed all before his pants are lowered. There's nothing sexier than watching him lower his pants, ready and wanting.

He moves like a lion, eyes fixed on mine, filled with desire.

I'm dotted with kisses as my underwear is removed, a graceful act, and it surprises me. In my head I imagined us ripping each other's clothes off.

My hands take his face, guide his lips to mine, so he's hovering over me, a hand tantalising my opening. The butterflies in my stomach are on cocaine, and I don't want to waste another minute with foreplay. I open my legs wider and lift my hips.

A gentle, slow action fills me, and yet I gasp. Simultaneously, he closes his eyes. He withdraws and repeats the action in the same slow speed.

"It's okay," I whisper. "I won't break."

"But I might," he says low and deep. He opens his eyes and watches me as he pushes into me again and again, slow, steady, and lovingly.

"Good morning."

I open my eyes to the words whispered in my ear.

Stretching my arms overhead, I offer Darcy a sleepy smile. My eyes catch up and wander down his naked body on top of the covers beside me. "It is," I say staring at his thick erection.

He pulls me over to lie on top of him. "I slept the best I have in months." He kisses my nose.

"So did I." I lace my fingers under my chin so I can stare at his beautiful face.

"Are you hungry?"

I shake my head.

"So, we don't have to jump up for breakfast?" His hands slide along my thighs edging them apart.

"Nope."

"Do you have plans for the day?"

"I do." I sit up and straddle him. "I intend to stay here with you. All. Day. Long."

His lips turn into a cocky grin. "Exactly what I had planned."

Strong hands grip my waist and my hips rise, find his cock, and lower. Like last night, his action is slow at first. We find our rhythm and instinct takes over. An orgasm ripples through me, and then another like waves rolling in. I call out his name, slump onto his chest just as he finds his own release.

Large hands stroke my hair until our breaths slow and my mind comes out of the haze.

"Do you plan on doing this all day?" I murmur.

"That's the plan."

"Then I will need breakfast."

"I need fresh air and a swim to loosen up."

His eyes darken. "You want help loosening up?" He laughs when I ignore him. "I'll take care of dinner while you're gone."

Slipping on my white dress, I head to my room before I change my mind and we go for round… hell, I've lost count. Besides all the sex, we've watched movies and snacked on whatever was in his refrigerator.

My bed looks appealing. I flop onto my back and process. With space between us, I clear my thoughts and admit I don't want our time to end. Unfortunately, the real world awaits. He's in the public eye, and it still unnerves me.

I change into a swimsuit, check my phone. A message from Paige. Walking through the foyer, I make the call.

"Let me guess. You've seen Twitter, and there's a photo of Darcy and me."

"That's not all. There are a heap of photos of him kissing you. Fans are blaming you for him not re-signing."

"It's absurd." More so because there was only one time he kissed me at the pool and barely anyone was around. This is what spooks me. It only takes one person to share something and with his damn hashtag, and a kazillion social media followers, his personal life becomes public.

"I know. I wanted to warn you. Looks like you're having a great time, though."

"I am." I smile. "He's been… perfect."

"Well, I'm glad he's got his shit together."

"He has," I add quickly as though I need to defend him to Paige.

"Enjoy your last night. Call me when you get back."

"I will. Bye, Paige."

I notice a text from Carli.

Carli: *Hey hope everything is okay. Give me a call if you need to chat. x*

I haven't spoken to Carli in over a month.

Me: *All good. Guess you've seen social media. I'm fine. Ignore the gossip. x*

I toss my phone and towel on the lounge and jump into the pool to escape all thought. Only my brain keeps ticking over... my friends are checking on me. I don't want to worry about what's being publicised about me in Adelaide.

After a few laps, I surface to find Darcy sitting on the edge. His expression dark.

"Have you cooked dinner already?"

Darcy shakes his head. "I have to fly back. Tonight." He doesn't look at me when he says it.

I wipe water from my face ensuring I can read his expression. "I understand."

He glances at me. It's brief. A moment later he's staring beyond the palm leaves. "Do you?"

"I'm not sure what's going on, but I know it impacts you more than me."

"Fans are blaming you," he says hoarsely. "The club has contacted me and set up an eight o'clock meeting tomorrow morning." He glances at his watch as though it's a ticking time bomb. "I tried to make it later, so I could catch the red-eye, only they want me on a plane in less than an hour because of bloody airline curfews in Adelaide."

"They're treating you like you're the one at fault," I whisper.

"I have to own it. Should've been there to negotiate my contract because my manager has royally fucked it up. I need to fix this shit." He leans on his knees to be closer then touches my lips. "You will see me in a couple of days. Say hi to your Pop for me."

"Darcy, we can't—"

The look in his eyes silences me.

My heart is heavy knowing everything will change when we're home. He has devoted his life to chasing a dream. To a game and people who have him on a pedestal, too high for him to jump free.

"I'll call you." He stands, and then he's gone.

CHAPTER 30

ALLI

Standing portside, I wait for Pop to come ashore.

I check my phone for a message. Again.

Nothing.

I have no idea how his meeting went and if he re-signed.

Surprised?

No.

I wave at Pop as he walks along the ship's connecting bridge in trousers and a polo. I go to him and throw my arms around him. Thin arms hug me back.

"It's good to be on land again."

"Did you get sick?" I take his bag as he juggles the smaller one.

"A little. Just feel a bit wobbly. Like I'm rockin'."

I laugh. "This is new." I nod at his striped navy polo.

"Yeah. Bought it on the ship. The weather got a bit sticky for my button-up shirt when we were far north."

"So, the weather was good?"

"Everything was good. The food, too."

I smile sharing his happiness. Relief easing some of the tension in my neck. "So, it was worth the money."

"Yeah. Made some friends who go at least twice a year." He says it as though it's a hint.

"Really?"

"Another gentleman was like me. Lost his wife a couple of years ago. He was there with her sister and his sister. They took me in. The women played a mean game of poker."

I laugh. "I'm looking forward to hearing all about it."

"Right after you tell me about your holiday. What have you been doing?"

Now is not the time to fill Pop in on Darcy.

"Not much. Relaxing and getting some sun like I planned."

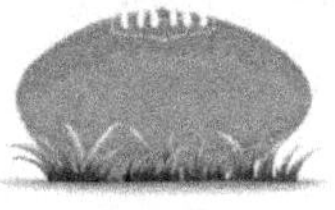

DARCY

"It's good to see you on board." Cooper thumps my back as we walk into the weights room. "All that legal shit is a pain in the arse."

I make a face agreeing with him. I've been stuck in the boardroom all day, negotiations swinging back and forth until we came to an understanding. It will more than likely be my last contract with a club I dedicated loyalty to the past ten years. I have stepped down as captain, my team unaware. Coach will break the news after our strength and conditioning session, and from there a new leadership group will be addressed.

"Always my intention. The club needed to come to the party," I say to Coops before heading straight to the bike station. Pre-season is about serious preparation and becoming stronger, faster, better than the last. Every year I'm determined to give what it takes to be one step closer to bringing home the Premiership Cup. The hysteria shadowed because the year we made it happen is the year I lost Alli. Last season we came close to repeating triumph, and yet, I thought about Alli more. This upcoming season I'm determined to change my ways. Set a different path because if I'm captain, *everyone* relies on me to lead them to their own personal glory. In my mind, the steps clear I need to climb. The first ones are behind me with a new contract in hand, and my leadership resignation about to be announced to the players.

After training, I'm heading to Alli's.

I can't plan anything more until I talk to her.

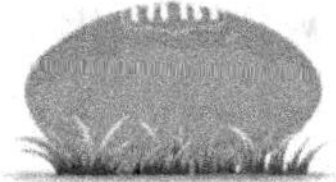

I kill the engine.

Stare at the house in darkness. Close my eyes and remember.

A security light flicks on the moment I step into the driveway. Even in dim light, I can tell her lawn needs mowing. I take in the little changes since I was here last. Collections of artsy coloured pots line the front of the house.

I knock. Listen.

No lights flicker beyond the glass.

The drapes move, she's there.

"I only want to talk," I say quietly.

The door creaks open enough for me to see her face, and acknowledge she got out of bed to answer the door.

"We have unfinished business."

Her shoulders rise and fall.

"I only want to talk, Al."

She opens the door and leaves me to lock up. A dim table lamp lights the living room enough for us to see the other. "I couldn't sleep anyway."

"Really? Your hair tells another story."

She pats her head. "I wasn't expecting visitors, Rayne."

I chuckle. Love that she's fiery when half asleep.

Alli folds her arms. "So, what's so important it couldn't wait for tomorrow or send a text?"

I take a seat on her couch. She remains standing.

"I want everything to continue like we were in Cairns."

"We were on holiday. We're back to reality now and already you're in a noose."

I shake my head. I know she partly blames my commitment to not being there for her when she needed me most. It wasn't football or the club's fault. It was me, and an unhealthy obsession to prove myself. "Things will be different. I'm different. I've renounced my captaincy."

"I know." She shrugs like it's nothing. "Saw it on the news."

I'm gaping. Not only am I shocked it's already out in the open, but for her to believe it was an easy thing for me to do. "I did it so I can focus more on us. On you. Because I can't if I have to put everyone else first."

She nods slowly. "So, it's not because you blame yourself for not getting to the Grand Final, and some of the younger guys are showing more promise."

"Is that what the media is surmising?"

She nods.

"Bastards." I rub my hands through my hair. "I only decided on it two days ago." I lean back on the couch, close my eyes for a moment and push out the anger. When I open my eyes, she's standing in front of me, and I'm hit with a déjà vu moment. Leaning forward, I take her hips and bring her forward, so I can plant a kiss on the strip of exposed skin below her navel. Her hands are in my hair. Talk, I promised her. I sigh and lean my cheek on her skin.

"I had to explain to my Pop why the newspapers had a photo of us at the pool. Explain I wasn't trying to ruin your image. Not to mention my own."

I lift my gaze. Her sad expression rocks me. "I'm sorry. I don't read the papers and should have warned you."

She nods as though there's some understanding. Her hands cup my face, and she bends to kiss me.

I kiss her back, hard.

Before it progresses further, she pulls away. "I'm exhausted. You can come to bed, and we can talk in the morning, or go, and we can catch up tomorrow."

I stand and follow her to the bedroom without further consideration.

CHAPTER 31

ALLI

Darcy's car is parked out front when I arrive home from work.

He knows where I hide my spare key.

It's one of the few things we discussed this morning while we communicated in other ways.

Walking along the path, I notice my lawns are freshly mowed. My breath hitches at the thought of Darcy doing it for me.

When I open the door, Darcy is sitting on the couch watching television as though it's a natural thing for him to do. He stands and comes to me. A wall of muscle, a protector, and with every passing moment, a piece of me chips away exposing vulnerability.

Darcy's smile fades. "Were you busy? You look tired."

"We were. Are. Tonight will be busier." Tonight because it's already after midnight. "There's this street thing I forgot about. City to the Sea Wine and Food Festival, and the council is closing the streets. I'm working from midday to midnight. Oliver even has friends coming to help out by collecting glasses and plates to ease our load."

Leaning into an embrace, he kisses me. It's loving, consoling. "If your boss needs extra hands, I could come after training."

I shake my head. Not what I meant. "I need to shower and get some sleep."

The cool water helps clear my head. When I emerge from the shower, I expect to see Darcy still on the couch.

Everything is in darkness.

I tighten my towel and walk to the bedroom. He's there. The white sheet draped over his hips, exposing a tanned, sculpted chest.

It's a hell of a sight to have Darcy Rayne in my bed.

I let go of the towel and slide in next to him. Our eyes meet when I notice he's ready for me. There are no words.

An understanding.

A silent language the two of us share.

I'm what he needs, and he's my antidote. We are Yin and Yang and together we fit. I swing my leg over his torso, and he takes my hips guiding me. Large hands mould over my breasts, and I tip my head and moan with the pleasure of Darcy loving me.

"So, you and Darcy are a thing?"

I stop wiping the wooden, heart-shaped table and glance up at Cleo—Oliver and Ava's friend. I've met her on several occasions when she's visited the restaurant. "We kind of are—"

"It's okay. I work at the club."

Of course. Oliver mentioned she's a physiotherapist. I continue wiping the table. "You know Darcy well?"

Cleo laughs. "Know how dedicated he is to the game. Know he'll take a bullet for his teammates because he was *that* good as captain."

I feel my cheeks heat because I'm part of the reason he no longer holds the position. Moving to the next table, I keep my head bowed as I clean.

"Darcy needs to focus on his future," she continues as she works. "He's played football for so long, it's all he knows. He doesn't let anyone inside his bubble. Not even family."

I stop cleaning and glance up at her, surprised by her insight. She's holding several wine glasses waiting for me to finish wiping. Black curls frame her dark skin. Brown, gentle eyes give me a knowing look.

I know little about his family. He doesn't talk about them. For now, we are focusing on *us* and everything else is in the background until we get us right.

"Elite athletes are not your normal guys," she says, casually placing more glasses on the table. "Relationships are hard. I see girls come and go at the club all the time. Darcy allows no one to get close. There are whispers why, but he shut them down and said a premiership is his main focus. In a matter of days, he has re-signed and determined not to be captain after photos of the two of you circulated. I'm guessing this kind of relationship is *not* new."

My gaze remains on the cloth serviette as I fold it in half. "It started a while ago. Ended after last year's premiership."

"Makes more sense."

"What's happening between us now is new."

"So, he has committed to you." Her expression shows surprise and understanding.

"Not in as many words…"

Oliver carries a long table past us and onto the road since we have been granted an extended area to spread tables and chairs with the road being closed. People are already lining the streets ready for the event to begin. When it comes to wine, most wine connoisseurs can celebrate no matter how early in the day.

"Can you cut some cheese for sampling?" Oliver asks. "Tessa will be here later to help after her PT class."

"Sure." Oliver's fiancée reminds me of the old me. She is OCD about exercising.

"She's still a friggin' princess," Cleo quips when Oliver is out of earshot. "Does all her hard work in the gym and too tired to pull her weight around here. I wish Ava were here. She'd pull her into line."

I've never heard anyone bad mouth Tessa. Then again Cleo is not staff and has known Oliver since school. "Ava's away another week, right?"

Cleo nods.

I'm grateful for the conversation shift.

"Have you heard how their holiday's going?"

"Great until Louis got sick. She loved India but is looking forward to coming home."

"I'd love to visit for many reasons. The yoga practises, the art, the culture."

"So, why don't you?" Cleo places the last glass down.

"Uni and I struggle to save."

"You know Ava designed these, right?"

"These tables?" My gaze sweeps over the collection of heart-shaped, wooden tables designed for couples in an array of stains and colours specifically for our footpath dining area.

"Oliver is open to all sorts of opportunities. Ask him to house your pottery pieces here as décor, and display a price, so diners have the opportunity to buy your pieces?"

I shrug.

"Your face, now. It's why I didn't take you to be Darcy's type. Seriously, this is a business opportunity for you both. Hell, I'm in the wrong line of work," she adds dramatically. "Rubbing athletes' muscled, naked bodies isn't all it's cracked up to be."

We both laugh and stop when Oliver walks past lugging a larger table. I drop my cloth to go help. Cleo signals with her eyes to mention it to Oliver.

I take the edge and clam up. It's never easy with the boss even though Oliver is more like a friend. "Can we have a chat tomorrow before I start work?"

Oliver lowers the table and wipes his moist brow. "Please tell me you're not quitting?"

I chuckle because I'm hit with nerves. "Just a chat. Tomorrow. It's nothing like that."

He nods, then heads back inside to grab another table.

Cleo smiles. "Not so hard. Anyway, I better go help him out. We'll continue our chat later."

We didn't get to finish our chat since we barely came up for air over the next four hours. Cleo had a quick break, and I'm taking the last table order outside before my fifteen-minute break when Aubree strolls by with Hunter. I almost didn't recognise her with her long dark hair now cut above her shoulders.

She walks over and hugs me. "You look great, Al," she says warmly.

"Thanks. I feel… happier." I smile, and she reciprocates.

She tucks stray strands behind her ears. Her expression changes as though she needs to speak. "I'm no longer working at Blue Skies. Thought you should know."

I lower my gaze when my thoughts momentarily shift to days spent with Gran. "We have more of Gran's belongings to donate. Pop wanted to hold onto them a little longer," I explain.

She touches my arm. "Of course. I know these things take time." She turns and fans herself as though she's looking for someone. Only now I note her cheeks are flushed.

"Can I get you something? A drink? Do you need to sit?"

Aubree chuckles. "You sound like Hunter. I'm tired more so this time." She pats her stomach, and I notice the roundness. "It's a girl," she whispers.

I lean in and hug her. "Congratulations. Such wonderful news. Hell, you'll be busy. No wonder you stopped working."

"My boys keep me on my toes, but I have a feeling this little girl is going to be trouble. I'm already awake most of the night. It's like she's grooming me for what's to come."

We both laugh. "Girls, eh."

I freeze at the sound of his voice. Not in fear. My whole body shuts down and restarts as though it's on high alert. He's several metres away talking with Hunter. I take a moment to enjoy the sight of him in a white button-up shirt and denim jeans. Hell, I could stare at him all day.

"So, you're giving him another chance," Aubree whispers, dragging me back.

"Yeah. There was always something about him."

"It won't be easy," she warns. "But then again, nothing is with footballers." She places a hand on my arm. "Hunter says he's a different man. I believe him." We both avert our gazes in the direction of Darcy. "Call me if you ever need to chat." She digs into her purse and pulls out a business card.

"Children's tutor?"

Aubree smiles. "I'm a teacher. Resigned after a year and went back part-time to the nursing home. Looking after my own kids then teaching didn't feel like I was getting a break. And my Mum is a cook at Blue Skies, so I also got to see her." She smiles. "Hunter doesn't want me to work long hours. Besides not needing the money, he wants someone to be with our kids especially with him starting a new job as a sports journo on television. And I have less energy this time around. But tutoring I can do."

I place the card in my trouser pocket. "Thanks. I may take you up on the offer. I better go inside and check what Oliver wants me to do next." I walk with her to join Darcy and Hunter.

Darcy places an arm around my waist and kisses the top of my head as though it's a natural thing for him to do. "I have to go inside and see Oliver. I have a small break now or a dinner break around seven. Wait, how are you here? I thought you had training."

All three of us are staring at Darcy.

"It's pre-season. I went to the club after lunch to work out and did a one-on-one ruck training session. So, I didn't need to stay for the team training. Occasionally, there are perks for us senior players."

Hunter laughs and pats Darcy's back. "And we use them because the young lads can run all day."

"I hear congratulations are in order," Darcy says to Aubree. He leans down and kisses her cheek. His sincerity warms my heart, but it's also a cue for me to leave.

"Enjoy the festival, guys." I pat Darcy's back hoping I'll see him later.

When I walk inside, Oliver is instructing Molly to take a break.

"Sorry. I didn't mean to talk so long."

"All good. Next time encourage them to come in." He winks at me, then continues to pour wine into glasses and sets them on a tray. "Two savs, and this one is the pinot. One shiraz." He hands me the tray. "Table six."

I take the tray and deliver the wine, and then my legs are carrying me outside again. "Hey," I say to Darcy. "We'll book out quickly, so if you wanted to eat in at Lombardi's, best to secure a table soon. Ask your friends." I nod at Hunter before heading back inside surprising myself with the frankness. Maybe I did listen to Cleo.

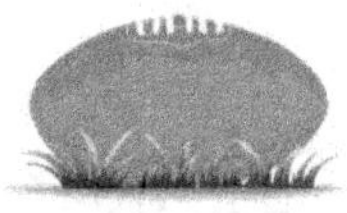

DARCY

For thirty minutes I indulge myself.

Sitting at an outside table drinking cab sav and enjoying the view.

People stroll by tasting wines and food from the restaurants and pop-up stalls. The road unrecognisable filled with tables and chairs and lights stringed above. The best view is looking into Lombardi's restaurant and watching my girl in tight black trousers. She's not the same girl I met on a plane. Reserved, and only spoke when obliged to be polite.

My gut flips hearing her laugh with the customers. It's filled with joy, and it gives me a sense of peace knowing she's happy, and I hope I'm part of the reason behind her happiness.

My phone vibrates in my pocket. I yank it out to silence it. *Clare.*

Unbelievable. I shake my head, yet I'm smiling.

"We only spoke a couple of days ago, kiddo."

"So, you shouldn't have forgotten not to call me that."

I chuckle because she sounds indignant. "What's up?"

"You haven't RSVP'd to Dad's birthday."

My hand goes to the back of my neck. "What do you mean? I promised Mum I'd come home. I'll be there."

"Your *plus one*?" she says incredibly.

My gaze hones in on Alli, aware of the alluring power she has over me.

"Darcy—"

"There'll be a plus one. Happy?"

"Yep. Bye."

Before I put my phone away, there's a slap on my back. "Hey, man."

Rhett takes the chair beside me. Going by his facial hair, it looks like he hasn't groomed himself in months. Blond hair sits lower than his collar. "Heard you re-signed. Got to admit it took a load off my shoulders."

He's concerned about his kid brother, and with good reason, but Dustin is focused and maturing. No longer a teenager making dumb decisions. He'll make mistakes. We all do. Rhett's fuck-ups led him to Tori. So, not all are bad.

"He's doing fine. Dustin doesn't need me to watch over him."

Rhett and I both know football has set Dustin back on track. In time, the fame, fortune, and women can detract good decision-making.

Rhett scratches his beard. "Helps knowing you're there. I'm glad you're taking actions for yourself. We all need to look out for ourselves in the closing chapters."

An understanding among retiring players, and we only hope injury doesn't end our career prematurely.

"How's life on the farm? No razors?"

He laughs and strokes the fair hair on his jawline. "Another charity. It will come off in six months before we head over to South America again. Could be the last trip for a while."

"And you can't go back to South America because…"

"Zika virus. Tori hopes to be pregnant next year."

"Must be something in the water. Hunter and Aubree are expecting." Since Hunter was Rhett's captain for years, I thought he'd be interested.

"Bullshit? Are they here?" Rhett leans forward.

I nod in the direction where Hunter and Aubree are walking alongside Tori. "Your missus found them first."

Oliver interrupts the conversation. "Excuse me, gentlemen, would you like to order?"

I pick up the menu. "A little bird told me the pizza is the best in the southern hemisphere. So, four of the specials."

He chuckles and taps on his iPad. "A good choice. Any bread before?"

"Herbed," Rhett pipes up. He stands and pats Hunter on the back. Kisses Aubree on the cheek.

It's like a bloody family reunion. I stand and greet Tori. Offering the ladies a chair. "I've ordered food, so you all may as well sit."

"Hey," Cleo says upbeat and walks over holding a bottle of McLaren Vale Shiraz. "This one's on the house."

"You're working here now?"

"Nope. Helping out for tonight. I'll be back at the club after Christmas. I'm meeting up with Tori in Venezuela in a month."

I stare at Rhett's wife. "You all know each other well?"

"Cleo's friend helps with a charity, working with Pemon natives in the rainforest. Same charity Rhett's involved with," Tori informs the group.

"It's my sister's friend, Eden," Cleo clarifies. "It's about medical help and educational supplies in remote rainforest villages. I'm going because there's a festival."

I chuckle. "So, these guys are going to volunteer in remote jungles and you're there to party?"

Cleo gives me the finger. "Because working half the year with you guys is one big party." She rolls her eyes, and the girls laugh as though siding with Cleo.

Alli appears carrying a couple of pizzas. After she places them on the table, Cleo loops her arm in Alli's and gives me a knowing look. "I'm heading to South America for a Yemaya festival. It's an all-girls trip, and we feel like goddesses at the end. Want to come with us?"

Alli's face lights up. "Yemaya. Like the deity?"

"Yeah." Cleo smiles.

My gut tightens, overcome with the thought of Alli leaving me for any length of time.

"Maybe…" She smiles back at Cleo. "Right now, I have to feed this lot. Could you help me with the trays?"

"Makes our trip to a remote outback station to visit Maddy and Luke seem like a walk in the park," Aubree says to Hunter.

When Alli and Cleo head inside, I turn to Rhett. "Tell me about this charity."

CHAPTER 32

DARCY

I'm a man of habit, and waking beside Alli is my new obsession.

Hell, I need her so damn much it hurts.

Since returning from Cairns, there's been a knot stuck in my gut. It stems from my thoughts, my decision-making instinct on a level I've never had to consider until now. I don't want to put a foot wrong— holding back telling her how I feel in fear it won't end well.

Only one other girl has stolen my breath and this is worse, tenfold.

For days I've struggled on how to tackle the invite. Curse, as putting it off longer achieves nothing. For the past hour I've contemplated how to approach the subject after deciding today is the day. I wait a moment for her eyes to open, get her bearings. "Any plans for the weekend?"

She lifts her cheek from my shoulder, eyes twinkling. "Apart from spending it with you?"

I smile. "Have you arranged anything with your Pop?"

Her gaze flickers as though she's searching my face for a clue. "I'm working and seeing him on Sunday if it's what you mean. And then I could spend time on my piece. I haven't given my art much thought lately."

I feign surprise. "No fault of mine." She gives a playful nudge. "Any chance you can get out of work? I have this thing, and I'd like you to accompany me. You'll need an overnight bag."

"What sort of thing?" She sighs. "Does it involve getting dressed up because that's not *my* sort of thing."

"You can wear whatever you want. You'll still look amazing." I wrap my arms around her.

"Okay, big fella." She taps my stomach. "Compliments are not going to get you far. I have an early start." She begins to climb out of bed.

"I'm serious."

Alli sits on the edge, looks over her shoulder. Hell, I want to pull her back in my arms, hold onto her for the entire day.

Her hand reaches for mine, our fingers link. Brown eyes search my face. "I'll ask Oliver. A whole weekend to…?"

"Attend my father's sixtieth birthday bash." I swallow.

As I expect, Alli's eyes round. "In Sydney? With your entire family?"

"And probably a couple of hundred guests," I say low.

Alli goes to pull her hand from my mine only I tighten my grip and pull her into my chest. "I need you to be there with me."

"Are we at that stage?" she whispers.

"I am." I stroke her hair, hoping the action will calm us both. I want to tell her how she makes the day somehow brighter even when there isn't a cloud in the sky. Her presence lights up the room, dazzles me like Singapore at night. How my core aches for her, needs her, and I can't explain why. I can't imagine a future without Alli. And knowing what I did to her, I have to take it slow, build the trust, so she has faith in us. If I rush it, she'll panic, and I'm afraid she'll disappear like the last time.

Afraid I'm asking too much of her, my throat constricts, and I struggle to swallow with a dry tongue sealing those three words from spilling out. I haven't said those words to anyone but Kelsey. I'm scared it's a fucking omen.

She pushes up on her elbow. "Okay. If you want me there, I'll be there."

I kiss her with all the proof of how much I appreciate her.

"Who are you texting?" I ask Alli while waiting in the members lounge to board the plane. She's been quiet all week. I know it's a big step for her—for us both. I haven't taken a girl to my parents' house since...

"Carli... and Paige." She looks up at me with those big brown eyes.

"Both are messaging you?"

She nods, and I sense her friends are texting out of concern. "Carli will be on our flight home."

"It's going to be okay," I tell her and loop my arm over her shoulder. And yet my gut is tense with overthinking introductions to my family, and the guests, because I expect a certain guest to attend out of courtesy.

Closing my eyes, I force out thoughts of Kelsey. Hell, I should have addressed this before now. Alli and I haven't mentioned the messages—the monkey on our backs—or should I say ghost. I've been waiting for her to bring it up. The last time we spoke she said it was in the past and she wanted to move forward.

"Hey. This is a surprise," she says warmly when she answers a call. Her eyes twinkle. I'm curious as to who is on the other end. She glances at her watch. "It must be around eight in the morning in London." She glances up at me, and smiles before mouthing, "It's Nate."

I nod toward the bar. "I'm getting a drink, do you want anything?"

Alli shakes her head, her concentration directed to the phone call.

Deciding on a cab sav, I take my glass with a bowl of nuts and return to Alli, still in deep thought. The wine glass empty by the time the call ends.

Alli looks up at me. "Nate's struggling because Becca's depression has progressed. She wants a divorce." She blinks quickly, then wipes her nose.

"You want to go to him?"

"Yes, but I can't. Before you say anything, it's not the cost, more he needs to sort it out himself. If he needs space, he can come here. The last time he was this upset he..." she shakes her head as though expelling bad thoughts, "... he used."

"I believe it was a long time ago. He was younger. He knows better," I say to comfort her.

"I know," she whispers. "It's the pain. I remember the pain."

"Hey." Sliding closer, I tighten my arms around her. "He'll get through it. In the meantime, if any of you need any help, let me know." She nods against my chest. We both know she won't ask for financial help, so I might need to speak to Nate myself.

"Let me get you a drink. It will be a late dinner by the time we get there."

Alli shakes her head. "Not before I meet your parents."

Admiration fills me. She's stronger than me.

ALLI

Point Piper.

It's where Darcy directed the taxi driver.

Are you bloody kidding me? And it's no ordinary taxi. We are sitting in one of those luxurious black ones where you pay quadruple for the same distance travelled.

Point bloody Piper, I repeat in my head. It's up there with Mosman, Vaucluse, and those bayside elite Sydney areas. I turn my head to the window, afraid to look at him.

Wear jeans, he had said. *Whatever you wear, you'll look amazing.*

I brought a dress, in case, but hell!

"What do your parents do?" I ask casually because Darcy doesn't freely talk about them. Because "They live in a nice area and not too much traffic," is the only thing he had divulged when I asked about their house. I sensed he was nervous about something, so I let it slide. Now, I'm cursing for allowing him off the hook so easily.

He reaches across the seat and takes my hand. Squeezes it as though it will be okay. The action yells it is *not* going to be okay.

"He has his own business."

I nod. "Doing..."

"Construction. He's the owner and CEO of Rayne Construction."

I laugh and pull my hand from his to wrap both arms around my stomach. I tilt my head back and silently laugh only it's sarcastic. Previously, when I've stayed here, I noticed Rayne Constructions signs around Sydney. Huge developments.

Business and high-level apartment living. "You're loaded," I murmur.

"My parents are wealthy. I'm comfortable and doing fine on my own," he says through clenched teeth.

"You're loaded," I repeat. "And you didn't consider mentioning it before."

"Why is it a problem for *you*?" he asked it like he's wearing all the weight on his shoulders.

I shake my head. "I'm not comfortable with this. I'm unprepared..." I take in a deep breath and close my eyes, focusing on calming thoughts.

When I open them, I turn to Darcy staring out the opposite window. Both fists clenched over his thighs.

What the hell am I doing?

Tall, rustic automatic gates open to a paved circular driveway.

I'm mesmerised by the Tuscan inspired house.

A beige, rough stone exterior with glossy wood windows and doors. Wisteria has climbed the walls of the triple storey building, framed windows so perfectly it reminds me of a painting. Darcy takes both our cases from the driver and comes to stand beside me.

"This is something else."

"Yeah." He gives me a long look. "Come this way."

We don't enter the front door. Instead, I follow him around the side of the house to another brick wall and black iron gate taller than his seven feet. He punches in a code and opens the gate to a path lined with garden lights and rose bushes. "Don't stumble here," he says. "I can vouch you'll come off second best."

I follow, a step behind. "Stumble? Like drunk stumble?"

He chuckles. "We're staying in the guesthouse if it's okay with you?"

"You say it like it's a shack."

He doesn't respond, and when we turn the corner of the main residence, I struggle not to let my jaw drop. Perfectly manicured circular hedges in terracotta pots border the pool area without obstructing the glass fenced in-ground pool. Purple lights twinkle beneath blue water. A dozen sunbeds surround one side of the pool, long enough to lap it for exercise. On the far side of the water is another exposed brick residence, I presume to be the guesthouse. As with the main house, wisteria features on the pale brick walls, the deep violet flower harmonising with the colours of the pool.

Darcy unlocks double wooden doors framed with several panes of glass. They open to a large bedroom. I slip off my shoes before entering. It is gorgeous with a king-size, four-poster bed lined with a mosquito net. Terracotta tiles cool beneath my feet. A large pot sits in the corner of the room with an arrangement of fresh summer flowers, their aroma filling the room. A white leather couch and small television are in the other corner. There are three doors to our right.

As if reading my mind, Darcy interjects, "This leads to our private kitchen." He opens the door. My legs fail to move. "This is to our walk-in robe." He opens the next door and then steps to the side. "And this is to our bathroom." His gaze lands on me.

My heart thumps hard in my chest. I should be excited to be here and meet his parents. He should be excited to have me here, yet something is amiss. His attitude is scaring me. And now I'm in a strange place. A strange, beautiful, grandeur house, and I can feel myself falling apart.

He nods to the end door. "The fridge is stocked if you need anything." Darcy places our bags in the walk-in robe. He hesitates. "I'll unpack later." He walks to the bed, sits on the edge. Pats the space beside him. "Come and sit with me."

I do what he asks, only I leave a space between us as I sense he needs it.

His gaze lowers to the tiles. "I moved away around ten years ago. Only returned for short stays because it was expected. The past year was easier, but I came home alone and always stayed in my old room. Not here." He closes his eyes momentarily and I'm not sure if he's trying to recall a memory or banish it. "I've never brought a girl home to meet my parents. This room…" He shakes his head gently.

My chest hollows a little sensing his anguish. "You didn't have to bring me if it's difficult for you," I whisper.

Without looking at me, his arm reaches and pulls me into his side. "I want you here." Curling into him, I relish the warmth of his body, allowing it to soothe my own insecurities.

"Is anyone home?" I need to know because I feel like I've snuck in the back door, and it's making me nervous. I didn't want a grand entrance, followed by fake happy introductions. I only want to feel welcomed, and right now I feel like we're hiding.

"No, they're all out to dinner. They'll be back soon. I said we'd grab something here and wait."

"So let's go raid the kitchen," I say trying to sound upbeat.

Darcy's gaze remains lowered. He doesn't react.

"There's something wrong. I don't like it when you act like this. If it's not me, then tell me what?"

Darcy lifts his gaze, and his expression startles me.

"I don't have great memories here. I hope by bringing you here, you can help me make new ones."

I take his face in my hand, and he leans into it, closing his eyes. "Challenge accepted," I whisper.

He leans and kisses me. Running my fingers through his hair I kiss him back, reminding him what his touch does to me.

CHAPTER 33

ALLI

Clare smiles at me from across the red cedar table.

Only it's more like a grin. Her cheeks must be aching as her expression hasn't changed since Darcy's family walked through the door. I know this because I've sneaked peeks at her. She reminds me of myself in a way. A female clone of an older brother. Same coloured hair only longer, and straight, ending at her waist. Same eyes. Only Clare's hazel eyes lack the intensity in Darcy's.

His mother smiled when we were introduced. She's a blonde with long hair falling past her shoulders. Unlike Clare, her attention to me is minimal. Her gaze continually flicks between Darcy and her husband, and I sense concern in her beautiful blue eyes. Eyes bordered by extremely long lashes, and I realise where Darcy inherits his. Only on Darcy it softens his serious appearance.

His father unsettles me.

He has looked twice my way. I've counted the seconds each time. His poker face unapologetic. I meet his gaze for a couple of seconds before looking away, unable to maintain the embarrassment of heat creeping up my neck knowing you're being visually examined. I'm easy to read, and not sure why he's looking deep to find whatever it is I'm hiding.

The dining room is filled with valuable artefacts that snare my attention to which I'm thankful. When his parents arrived home, we were waiting in the expansive living room. His father directed us to the dining room consisting of black leather chairs, all fourteen of them. And it feels more like a boardroom by the way I'm being scrutinised.

Darcy's arm lifts and settles along the back of my chair. His fingertips touch the skin of my bare shoulder. It's subtle, yet reassuring.

"And what is it you do again?" Daniel Rayne asks me. His brow pinches together as though he's trying to fathom how Darcy and I are together.

"I work in hospitality, and study arts at university, part-time." At this stage, he doesn't need to know anything further.

"But you met when you were a flight attendant working the same flight when Darcy was flying to Melbourne," Clare says in a tone like she's discovered a hidden secret.

"I can't believe you remembered that," Darcy says, and rubs the side of his jaw. He shakes his head at his younger sister.

I tilt my head at Darcy. "Have I missed something?"

"It was two years ago, and Darcy was playing in Melbourne. We met for dinner. It was during my first year, and I was lonely. Told him he needed a girlfriend because he's been alone like forever. He said he wasn't lonely. I harped at him because I didn't want to be old like him and not have a boyfriend." I laugh and so does Darcy. Him, more so embarrassed. His parents' gaze unwavering on Clare, waiting. "He said there was this hostie, and he was too shy to ask her out. He described her to shut me up, but now I know it was you. I imagined what she would look like. And it was you."

Darcy groans. His large hand wipes over his unimpressed face. "I *was* trying to shut you up."

"Was it me?"

Darcy looks around the room to waiting eyes. I watch his Adam's apple bob with a swallow. "Yeah," he murmurs.

"Shy? You were arrogant..." I stop myself remembering where I am.

"Why did you quit your job?" Daniel sets his gaze on me. Not at all interested in the love story only the story behind me as though he's investigating my character.

"A tale for another time," Darcy interjects. "Thanks for the scotch. Alli and I are tired. We'll see you all in the morning." He turns his attention to his mother with no further regard to his father. "Let me know if you need me to do any last-minute errands for the party." He stands, pulls out my chair. Takes my hand and leads me out of the room.

It takes skill to ignore the intense gaze of his father. One I haven't even began to acquire. "Good night," I say over my shoulder and smiling at all three. Sending a gentle message I'm not here to go to war despite whatever has passed before.

Daniel Rayne holds my gaze before I'm through the dining room door.

Darcy's grip remains tight until he opens the door of the guesthouse. He turns and kisses me. Slowly our lips separate, the hint of scotch on his breath tantalising my senses.

His forehead rests on mine. "Thank you," he murmurs.

"For what?"

"Being here. Supporting me. Suffering."

"I'm not suffering." I laugh once in a mocking sound. "Challenged by your father but not suffering."

"He's met his match." There's a hint of pride in his voice, and it surprises me.

I lean away so I can see his face. "I have you. I don't need anything more. You're my armour."

He presses his forehead to mine, and closes his eyes, as though he's allowing my words to absorb.

DARCY

My body awakens momentarily at four hours past midnight. A time of night—or morning depending on which way you look at it.

If I were sleeping, and for some reason I'd check the time, it would be four.

When I was sixteen, pool parties ended around four. I'd bc taking some chick to the guesthouse or leading her out to go home. Until I met Kelsey, at seventeen. Then it was only ever Kels. Since my sexual partners were not allowed in the house, the guesthouse became about Kelsey's and my time together while I lived in Sydney.

My father had asked me to consider Clare and their values.

I didn't want Alli out here. She deserves to be in the main residence as she stands for more. Something my parents fail to comprehend.

Especially when memories of Kelsey flooded my mind when I opened the damn guesthouse doors.

Good memories and guilt. Guilt of not caring as much as I should for someone I loved. Hell, I've gone over it a million times. I loved her, yet I'm not sure it was enough, or whether I was capable of loving to the degree a man should.

She died because I didn't care enough. I promised her father I would look out for her if she moved to Adelaide with me.

What I didn't tell him was football would always come first. Even before his daughter.

I was a rookie with the world at my feet. I didn't know my commitment to football would push her away. I trained hard, it was expected. Long hours were dedicated to the field and in the gym. I partied hard—but never cheated. Not once. I flirted because hell, I liked the attention, bathed in the fans devotion with the rest of my teammates. It wasn't until after her death I followed the same path as the forever-single players. Played the 'fame game' and drank excessively to forget.

An hour ago I woke, ironically at four to a nightmare reliving the night Kelsey died. Recalling the moments in time leading up to her death. Like other nights, the outcome ended the same, and even by changing certain events in my dream, I couldn't prevent it even knowing her fate.

Alli is sleeping peacefully beside me. The moonlight shining through the glass doors and onto her face, to the one person keeping me sane. Beyond the doors, the pool lights flicker, calling me.

I creep out of the guesthouse and wade in the cool water until I'm fully immersed. The water covers my body. A membrane. Not like a blanket. A barrier preserving emotion. With every step, deeper thoughts of the fatal night unfold, playing out like a movie before my eyes. I sink to my knees, immersing, hoping to block it all out. The scenes play out even louder with water in my ears to exacerbate the sound, trapping the memory in a freeze frame. The opaque liquid blurs my vision until all I visualise is Kelsey's smiling face and then the car rolling and rolling until it lands upturned on its roof. Both occupants bleeding and unconscious. They died before help arrived, their injuries fatal. Nothing and no one could have saved them. That, I understood. But I could have stopped her from getting in the damn car. Put up a bigger fight if my ego wasn't so bruised.

My memory reverts to our argument. It's been eight years, and it feels like yesterday. Bubbles flow from my mouth, and I spring out of the water gasping for air. Paddling to the side, I rest my head on my arms and allow the water to take the weight of my lower body. My chest hurts. My head thumps uncomfortably. I'm puffing like I've just run ten k's. To hell with positive affirmations. I need to get my shit together.

I should swim laps to tire myself out and not think. Then I notice Alli out the corner of my eye. She's watching through the glass of the door. I don't move or acknowledge her. She's giving me space. How she knows what I need is beyond me. Yet, she does. And does it with a rare kindness that makes me want to be a better man.

One thing is clear. I will, for her.

"I was wondering where you were?" I say to Alli.

She's sitting on the king single bed in my sister's room.

Clare pops up after sliding something under her bed. "Hey, Darcy. I'm showing Alli photos of when we were kids."

I take a swig of my beer. "I'm not sure what's worse, suffering through family memories or being downstairs surrounded by stuffy guests?"

"We had fun as kids," Clare admonishes.

"I moved away when you were five. I wasn't a kid with you."

Both girls stare up at me.

"The memories I have were happy ones." Clare bows her head. "When you came home, you spoiled me. I remember being excited to see you."

I remember those times as well. I did spoil her. She was the one thing that made me want to come home. "Why don't you show Alli photos of your dance recitals?" I shift the attention to Clare. "She is brilliant," I say to Alli. "It's why she moved to Melbourne at fourteen." And it made coming home less appealing, and then I stopped coming home altogether.

"Every photo is the same," Clare quips. "I'd rather find dorky ones of you."

Alli tries to smother a laugh.

"When *you're done,* I'd like you to return my girlfriend to me. There are people I'd like her to meet."

More so, I need Alli by my side.

"I'll join you in a minute." Alli smiles. I nod and go to walk away and freeze when Clare's tone of voice changes.

"I'm coming home because I'm too tall to be a dancer now. I mean, I know why Mum emphasised I should finish junior high because it's taught me to be light on my feet. Graceful, really at my height? Who am I kidding? Have you ever seen a ballet dancer the same height as a football player because my last orthodontic x-ray indicates it's how tall I'll be."

"If you love it, you should keep doing it. Your height shouldn't matter," Alli says in her gentle voice.

I close my eyes and thank the universe for Alli. I keep walking knowing I can trust in Alli to work her magic with my sister.

When I take the last bend of the circular staircase, I see *him,* standing below, in the kitchen foyer chatting with other men. *The person* whom I feel I've failed.

Failed myself.

My family.

His daughter.

On instinct, I hesitate wanting to turn and ascend the stairs to Alli—my safety net.

Merrick senses me and looks up. Our eyes lock, and I feel the tension strike between us. I was unsure if he'd be invited, and I didn't want to ask my father. Expected he would be since there are some business connections. Be it, Kelsey's accident strained those relationships, yet I understand why he remained on the guest list.

Willing my feet to move, I descend the final steps until I've entered the same space as him. He turns away as he speaks, refusing to meet my gaze because it would mean looking up. "Darcy. Hope you're well." There's no affection in his tone, only animosity.

A number of suits gather behind him, already spilling out of the triple doors to the pool area twinkling with lights.

"Mr Reynolds. Likewise."

Hearing my mother's voice, I migrate closer. "Anything I can do to help, Mum?"

"Darcy," she sounds relieved to see me. "Can you check outside to see if everything's in order?"

"Sure." I head out past Merrick Reynolds on a mission and unsure of what is expected of me. The standard dress code appears to be a black suit because everyone looks like extras on the set of *Men in Black*. Then I notice the ladies in long gowns seated at tables arranged in the western section under the marquee, erected only today between the main residence and the guesthouse. One of Mum's last-minute decisions. Time means nothing to Mrs Daniel Rayne. My mother can snap her fingers, and it happens.

Weaving around circles of associates, I receive courteous nods. One of the gentlemen comments, "Well done, Darcy, on your premiership win last year."

Impressive.

The guests have crystal in their hands. The caterers are weaving with hors d'oeuvres on silver platters. The band is playing orchestral music, and the ladies… it's where I draw the line. An invisible 'do not pass' line at the entrance of the marquee. I've experienced the touching, the quiet propositions, eyelash batting all before. My mother's fiftieth was only five years ago, and I refuse to repeat past mistakes. I wonder if Mrs Drescott still offers blowjobs? Then I remember Dad saying her husband was transferred to Perth, and I quietly thank the universe for something going my way.

Hell, I thanked the universe, again.

It was Kelsey's thing.

On instinct, I pull out my phone and read the last message I sent her—sent Alli.

The one where I told Kels about Alli and thanked her for having the universe on my side. I know Alli didn't read it before she deleted all the messages. It's time she knew what was in the message because tonight might not end well. I find the message, copy it, and resend it.

> **Me:** *I need to share a secret with you since we told each other everything.*
> *There is this girl. She gets me like really gets me.*
> *It's taken me years to let anyone in, but she's different.*
> *Kind, beautiful, sexy, and smart.*
> *Perfect.*
> *I know what you're thinking… I'm batting above my average… and I probably am. Our secret.*
> *You once told me you know when you've met your soul mate. We thought it was us only we really weren't soul mates. More soul friends who loved each*

other, and were physically attracted to the other for a while. With Alli... I believe she's the one. You never told me how we know. I believe it comes down to trust.
I trust her with my heart.
Just thought you should know.
So, if you did something from heaven and aligned the stars with the universe, I want to thank you.
Thank you, for Alli.

Then I head into the guesthouse and locate her phone. The partial text on the screen. I pop it into my pants pocket and walk out the door to an incoming glare from Merrick Reynolds. *Did he follow me?*

Fuck! I have to walk past him, there's no other path. Double-checking, I look over the crowd to Alli standing near the doorway of the main residence. Our gaze meets, she smiles, before zigzagging through the crowd.

My heart thumps uncomfortably in my chest at the thought of Merrick meeting her. Merrick follows the direction of my gaze. I wait for his expression to change, to soften. It doesn't. I'm watching him, watching Alli make her way toward us. There's no avoiding it, so I stand behind him, and she stops and smiles up at us both, assuming we're friends.

"Sorry. There was no deviating Clare away from the family history of photos." Her gaze flicks to Merrick, then to mine, her smile fading.

"Alli, this is Merrick Reynolds. Merrick, I'd like to introduce you to my girlfriend, Alli Bradley." Alli takes my hand and squeezes it.

"How long have you known Darcy?" he says directly to Alli.

"A couple of years. We met on a flight and were friends first," she says. I know she's tensing up by the way her voice cracks.

"You have a message." I retrieve her phone and hand it to her. "You should read it." Alli starts to read the message, pauses to look at me. My eyes remain fixed on Merrick. "It's been a long time." He can take it twofold.

"Time means nothing when you've lost everything."

"I understand," Alli says looking up from the screen to me. She then turns to Merrick. "I lost my parents when I was ten. Thought my world was going to end, but we keep going. We find the strength to take each day as it comes.

He stares at her a few seconds too long. I sense the anger building in him.

"Mr Reynolds," I say, a clear warning in my tone.

"I hope he does the right thing by *you*." Merrick gives me a long look. I don't say anything. I let him be. So, I nod, and it's enough for him to walk away and join another group of suits.

Only when he starts a conversation with one of Dad's employees, do I take my eyes off him. "I think he wanted to say more. Probably would have if you didn't show up."

"What happened?" she whispers.

A waiter walks by. I swipe a beer from the tray and take a few gulps before leading Alli to the far corner opposite the pool, away from the crowd. "Take a seat." I point to the white, wrought iron chair. I sit on the other. Taking her hand in mine I cover it with both my hands, stare at it as the memory unfolds.

"I dated his daughter, Kelsey, for a year before moving to Adelaide. She wanted to come with me. We were in love, so I agreed despite everyone saying we were too young to understand the meaning and responsibility of a relationship at eighteen, especially alone in a strange city. We made it work for a couple of years, but Kels hated being second to footy. To cut a long story short she started hanging out with new friends. People I didn't agree with. This guy, Stoner, a nickname for obvious reasons, took a liking to her and paid her attention, well more than I did. The timing sucked because the senior ruck got injured that year, and I was thrown in the deep end to take his spot at nineteen. I had to train harder and spend more time in the gym to build myself up, so it left little time at home with Kels.

"She went out with her new friends, and on weekends I went out with my teammates. She saw me out one night getting a lot of attention from fans, but I never cheated on her. The following weekend we fought. Next minute I knew he was out front in his car waiting. She threw some stuff in a small case and said she'd be back for the rest later. I tried to stop her." I look up into Alli's eyes, round like the full moon above us.

"I begged her not to go. Promised her things would get better. She only laughed." I shake my head at the memory. "Said she knew me better, and I wouldn't stop until I proved to everyone I was the best." I bow my head because I'm still doing it. "Then she told me this druggo, Stoner, was a far better person than I could ever be because he shows her how much he cares." I stare up at the stars. "Said the universe was no longer aligned for us, and she didn't love me anymore. She cried at that moment, so I knew she was lying. She was hurt and reacting to get my attention. She waited for me to say something, but I didn't. I let her go." My throat burns with the memory. "Let her walk out the door and get in the car with a guy who was over the limit. Minutes later I realised my mistake. Tried to call her. Sent numerous texts. Dickhead must have known because he was speeding, took a corner too fast and rolled the car. Killed them both." For the first time in years tears spill onto my cheeks. "All I remember is I tried to fight for her until it came to her attacking my ego. Then I gave up. If I'd stopped her…"

"Darcy." Alli's soft hand rests on my cheek. She guides my face to hers and kisses my lips. "It's no one's fault. The timing. Fate. We have no control over these things."

"She was my responsibility."

"No. We are responsible for our own lives. I don't expect you to protect me and stop me from making mistakes because I wouldn't be living." She kisses me again. "Life is about taking risks. I realise it now."

"I keep telling myself that, yet I blame myself."

"Then it's time you stop. Time to change. You know my grandmother told me you can't change the past but you can the future."

The microphone screeches a little as it's switched on. Lifting her hand, I press a kiss onto delicate knuckles. "Will you stand beside me when I make my father's speech?"

"Of course."

"I want to introduce you to all the guests. Make it known one day I intend to make you part of this family."

This time when Alli smiles, it reaches her eyes.

EPILOGUE

ALLI

Nine months later...

"There's a cup of green tea beside you."

Warm lips kiss my cheek. Heavy lids flutter before opening to Darcy leaning over me in a sweater.

"Good morning," I whisper. "What time is it?"

"Almost eight. Go back to sleep. I'm heading out for a bit. See you when I get back."

I sigh and curl into a ball in the warmth of his bed. Then I remember it's Saturday. Game day.

A man of habit, Darcy doesn't leave his apartment this early.

Friday nights are busy at Lombardi's, so come morning I'm wrecked. Our Saturday routine is Darcy beside me, spooning and then we make out.

He doesn't break routine on game day. Unless something needs shaking up. I pad to the shower, thoughts whirling.

He has won the last four games.

He is more relaxed... maybe too relaxed. Is he complacent? Comfortable and therefore vulnerable?

Over time I have taught myself to let go of insecure thoughts.

I trust him. He would tell me if something was wrong.

I zip up my jeans, pull on a sweater, and reach for my phone to call him.

"Hey. Awake already?"

"Yeah." I unlock the glass door. Step onto the balcony and look to the ocean. "Is everything okay?" An icy breeze hits my bare face. A cold day for football.

"Yeah. I'm sitting here having breakfast with your Pop."

"You're with Pop?" I head back into his heated apartment and lock the door.

"Yeah. He made pancakes for me."

I spin, searching for my keys. "What? He cooked? This is not routine."

He chuckles. "Did you get my note?"

"No—" I turn and spot a yellow sticky note stuck to the espresso machine.

If you read this before I'm home, call me.
I'll be at your Pop's.
<3

"Got it. You thought I'd make a latte first. I like the way your brain works."

"And I like the way you—"

Pop's voice sounds in the background.

I laugh quietly. "Why are you there?"

"I had to drop something off. Are you coming or am I eating your share?"

"He's never cooked *me* pancakes. "I'll be there!"

Spying keys on the lounge, I grab the set and head out the door.

A short time later I pull into the driveway, my gut tightening at the sight of both my favourite men sitting on the prided outdoor setting. A new patio gas heater burning between them.

"Morning." I lean and kiss Pop on the cheek. "This is new." I nod at the heater before pulling out my chair. We all have a favourite spot.

"Darcy dropped it off this morning." He pats my shoulder. "I'll get your pancakes. A cuppa with it, love?" Pop rises, and I sense his eagerness to leave Darcy and me alone.

"What's going on?" I whisper. "I missed you this morning."

Darcy smiles, yet there's a glint of uneasiness behind his eyes.

"You don't do this on game day."

"No." He picks up his china cup and sips tea. His gaze lowering. "I didn't want to wake you. I ran an errand, was in the area so stopped by to see your Pop."

My brain tells me not to panic. The way my stomach tightens tells me otherwise.

"An errand to buy him a heater?"

He glances to the road and nods.

I turn, follow his line of sight to a red sedan parking out front. "Is that Carli?"

Carli steps out, then the passenger door opens, and I recognise the blonde hair pulled into a ponytail. Paige.

"Okay, mister... what's going on?"

He stands and says nothing, only heads to his new Mercedes truck and returns with a chair to match the outdoor setting. "I made a dash to Bunnings before coming here."

"You planned this?"

"Hey, Mr B," Paige calls out. "Hope you left some pancakes for me." She hugs me before moving to Darcy. "Does she have any idea?"

"No, I don't." I hug her, then Carli. "You also knew about the pancakes?"

"Afraid so. Although, I've already eaten."

They all chuckle.

I lower to my chair. "Someone please explain."

Darcy places another chair at the corner for Carli and turns up the heat level on the heater. "When the footy season is over, I want to take you to Fiji for a holiday with family and friends. We need to plan it now. Book somewhere nice."

"When we get dates, I'll book flights." Carli smiles at me. "I still get the perks."

"And I've narrowed it to three options." Paige places her iPad on the table with resort images on the screen.

My arms wrap around my middle. Lost for words.

Darcy sits beside me. He leans to look at the screen in the centre of the table. "We get the final say." He smiles, then it fades. "Don't you want to go?"

I nod quickly. "Of course. I'm just taken aback." I place my hand on his. "Surprised. I'm not good with—"

"Surprises. We know. This is different, Al," Paige reassures.

Darcy squeezes my hand, holds my gaze. His expression is unreadable.

"Here we go." Pop places pancakes covered in strawberries and syrup on the table. "I mentioned to Darcy about getting a passport and cruising to Fiji. He thought it a good idea to meet me there."

My chest expands with pride at how far Pop's come. For a few months, I worried about him slumping into darkness, refusing to eat, and visiting Gran's grave daily. One day a priest from Gran's church was at the cemetery and spoke to Pop. Over the next few weeks, he showed signs of being positive about life. Made a bucket list of things he'd do with Gran if she were alive, and well, now he tells her about those adventures when he visits her on a fortnightly basis. Knows she'd have wanted him to keep living.

I'm thankful we have all gained wings to lead us to new chapters in our life.

"If it's what you want, love?"

I blink and acknowledge Pop's voice bringing me back to the present.

To the table.

All eyes on me.

"Alli."

My attention turns to the voice that warms my soul.

Darcy slides to one knee. His gaze locks with mine. Eyes that have the potential to be stormy like the sea are calm summer oceans of blue. He reaches into his pocket and pulls out a silver band. The diamond sparkles between his fingers.

"I love you and want to spend the rest of my life with you. I thought we could celebrate in Fiji with your Pop, my family, and closest friends. It's why they're here."

My throat burns.

I force myself to blink through the happy tears welling in my eyes.

I'm vaguely aware of anticipation hanging in the air.

I'm fully aware of the nervous energy now radiating off Darcy. I glance down to trembling fingers.

"I had a note. Wrote down what I wanted to say. Left it in the damn car. You'll hear it later when it's only the two of us." Darcy's eyes search my face. "I love you. Trust you. Hate every minute I'm not with you. The list of reasons why I love you will grow with every year we're together. I want it to be a never-ending list. Alli, will you marry me?"

My heart swells with so much love despite the shock catapulting through my body.

Where do I start?

I also have a list of why this man makes my life complete. He'll also hear it, later. "Fiji is a great idea." I meet his gaze, smile, lift my shaky left hand and place it over his. "I'd already planned to spend the rest of my life with you." I wink. "Glad you can keep up."

Darcy grins. "You want to challenge me? Now?" Long lashes frame adoring eyes. "Is that a yes? I'd like to hear you say it, Al."

"Yes," I whisper. "Yes. I want to spend the rest of my life with you."

His smile broadens showing perfect white teeth. One hand reaches for my cheek, guides my face to his and kisses me, gentle yet full of promise.

Cheers and applause come from around the table.

"I'll get the champagne for the girls," Pop announces. "Might have a glass myself."

"Wait. You organised a champagne breakfast?"

Pop tilts his head to the man sliding a ring on my finger. "This good man arranged it all. Have to say I hesitated after the last time he wanted to surprise you."

A short laugh bursts from me. I pause to admire the sparkling white diamond on my finger and look up into eyes gleaming with equal sparkle.

"She knows I'll never stop trying," Darcy says to Pop.

And then he's kissing me again.

Playing for Time

The Bay Series

Winning the Player
Charming the Outback
Jardine
Caught Out
Winning the Game
Playing for Time

ACKNOWLEDGEMENTS

First and foremost to my husband, Lynden. Thank you for your encouragement, love and support of my writing journey. You are my rock.

To my four beautiful daughters, Jamie-Lee, Shauni, Ashleigh, and Demi, who helped with character names, plot, and provided constant inspiration. Also to Cameron, Charlie and Cruise, who answered my questions on sport.

To my wonderful parents, Pam and Vic, and my sister Vickie and her family for believing in me and helping in any way possible.

A big shout-out to my friends, and biggest fans: Mum, Deanne and Helen, Dayna, and Alison for believing in me from the day I decided to give authoring a shot.

To Marilyn, Shelly, and Frances for reading my book in its raw form. And to Kim, Anastasia, and Tarsh for the back and forth messages and the feedback, while tolerating my insecurities while I rewrote this book a thousand times. I'm so grateful to you all for believing in me! I thank you from the bottom of my heart, as your words of praise mean so much.

To Kim Sutton at *Blogging for the Love of Authors*, I am so lucky to have found you! I couldn't have done this without you. Thank you for your encouragement, words of wisdom and late night chats despite the time difference between our countries. And for helping me choose the right cover. Thank you for loving my book!

So much love and appreciation to my Facebook reader group, Leesa's Lovelies, and all the blogging community for helping to get my book out to the world. You all make the book world a much better place. Especially *Blogging for the Love of Authors and Their Books*, *Be My Book Boyfriend*, and *Give Me Books*.

To my author friends: Jennifer Ann, Maggie Mundy, K E Osborn, Nina Levine, Sasha Cottman, Louise Reynolds, Emma James, Carla Caruso, Lilllana Rose, Kendall Talbot, and Tania Joyce, I can't express enough gratitude for all your advice and inspiration. To all the authors whom I've met at signings and at social gatherings in Adelaide, Sydney and Brisbane, you are my writing family and I love you all.

To Kaylene Osborn at *Swish Design and Editing*. Thank you for all your expertise, answering endless questions, and making my book beautiful. Most of all for calming me when I message or call in a state of panic. You are my rock and I love you!

To Najla at *Najla Qamber Designs*, thank you for my beautiful cover. Your brilliance amazes me with every new cover, and I look forward to working with you on future books.

My appreciation extends to Kelsi for answering my questions on cabin crew.

A special thank you to my son-in-law Charlie Spurling for the football photograph on the front cover. The perfect shot of you playing and inspiration for my ruckman character.

Most of all I want to thank my dear friend Mark Daniel whom I miss with all my heart. Writing Playing for Time has spanned four years and during that time Mark and I attended many football games to watch the Crows play. We loved those Showdown games against the Power. He gave me much advice on a ruckman's role while he sat proudly in the stands watching his son-in-law, Sam play for the Crows. I miss you very much. This book is for you!

Check these links for more books from Author LEESA BOW.

NEWSLETTER

Want to see what's next?
Sign up for my Newsletter.
https://landing.mailerlite.com/webforms/landing/t7i9x8

GOODREADS

Add my books to your TBR list on my Goodreads profile.

AMAZON

Click to buy my books from my Amazon profile.

WEBSITE

https://www.leesabow.com/

TWITTER

https://twitter.com/LeesaBow

Leesa Bow

INSTAGRAM
@leesabowauthor

EMAIL
leesa.j.bow@gmail.com

FACEBOOK
https://www.facebook.com/Leesabowromance

ABOUT THE AUTHOR

LEESA BOW

Leesa Bow loves to read and write spicy romance. She spends her spare time with her family, catching up with girlfriends in cafes, or taking long walks along the beautiful, southern beaches of Adelaide, Australia.

Leesa's love of sport has inspired her to write stories about hot Aussie heroes and the strong women they fall in love with.